The Breaking Of Day

G. Wayne Jackson, Jr.

ALSO BY G. WAYNE JACKSON, Jr.

Forced Out of the Darkness

G. Wayne Jackson, Jr.

The Breaking of Day

---

a novel by

G. Wayne Jackson, Jr

foreword by

Joseph S. Boynton, Jr.

G. Wayne Jackson, Jr. Publishing

G. Wayne Jackson, Jr.

DEDICATION

There are so many people who have played a part in my life. *The Breaking of Day,* for me, is about Family. Not necessarily to those who are related by blood, but those who have shown their love to you and are there for you. Mom, I love you always. To the best example of a father I have seen…my brother Darris. To my son…Justice. To my Godmother who was/is always there for me…Darlene. To Marcus and Joey…words can't express the love I have for you two. To Shermaine & Crystal…my bestest friends in the world. To Dale & Jerald…amazing men with incredibly large hearts. To Jacqueline it is hard to put into words how much I love you. Thank you for being a rainbow on some of my cloudy days!

In Loving Memory
Carol I Thomas
Eddie Walker
Anthony Matthews
Rayshawn Gardner

ACKNOWLEDGMENTS

I'd like to acknowledge those who have paved the way for people like me to do what I enjoy doing. To the late E. Lynn Harris, Ricc Rollins, Kevin E. Taylor, James Earl Hardy, Lee Hayes, Mike Warren, Stanley Bennett Clay, James Baldwin. These are pioneers and giants in my eyes. Thank you for sharing your gifts for the world and for letting me find pieces of myself within the pages of your works. You each have given me a voice when I couldn't find it within.

I'd also like to acknowledge the affirming churches and pastors for providing safe havens for LGBTQ people to find the loving Spirit of God. My hat is off to you all for believing in a Loving God who embraces all his people.

To my readers…thank you from the bottom of my heart for taking time out of your life to check out what was going on in my life. Byron, Dale, Crystal, Jerel, and Jaylawn. Y'all mean the world to me.

I would like to acknowledge those in my corner that helped me get this project off the ground. To my Lord & Savior Jesus Christ for life and freedom. Thank you for showing me you loved me and called me Just as I was. To my love and my right hand…Walter, for putting up with me and for encouraging me to do this. You help me find passion. To Mommie…your undying love, support and encouragement means the world to me. When I was concerned about the content of my writing you let me know it was okay. You mean the world to me. To Jasmine Harris…words can't describe how you have inspired me, encouraged me and held me up. I love you. To my buddy Roderick…we share so many things in common. I am blessed to have you in my life.

A special acknowledgement and thank you to Joseph 'Joey' Boynton, Jr. I love you so much and am deeply honored that you would provide your wisdom to the pages of my work. You are a brightly lit star!

Lastly, I would be remiss if I didn't acknowledge you…yes the one reading this right now. You have supported me by purchasing this work. I owe you a debt of gratitude if I didn't tell you Thank you. From the bottom of my heart…Thank you, Thank you, Thank you. Please continue to support and give me feedback. Love you all!!!

WHAT READERS ARE SAYING ABOUT THE BREAKING OF DAY

"What a great sophomore project…immersed in characterization, engaging twists, unfolding drama, everything a readers needs to completely become a part of each character. I turned each page with gusto never wanting to put the book down. I judge a book by four criteria…can't put down, want to skip to the end, will read it because I started it, and stopping after the prologue…this was definitely one I couldn't put down! Great read."

Byron T.

"Just got done reading The Breaking of Day by G. Wayne Jackson, Jr…One of the best books I have read in a long time. A page turner for real. Funny and the story keeps you wanting more…I loved it."
Jaylawn A.

"G.Wayne Jackson truly pays homage to E.Lynn Harris in his second novel. Each of his main characters has a chapter to follow, allowing the reader to engage in their lives. He writes a story that truly honors gay men and their real friendships with women breaking stereotypes that are often portrayed in the media as fag hags and flaming queens."

Dale Guy Madison
author of "Dreamboy: My Life as a QVC Host and Other Greatest Hits"

Table of Contents

Foreword

When first approached to provide this for my good friend, I have to confess though exceedingly honored, I was also extremely terrified. How do I begin to introduce you the reader to such an important work by someone who has become so much more than family to me?

This man came into my life in a very loud and aggressive manner and initially gave me much, as we often say. As I got to know him, his intelligence and creativity began to shine through and we found ourselves connecting on a great many levels. Though we started as frat brothers, we have become friends and confidantes and have been a part of important events in one another's lives.

In our many discussions we have agreed on some things and agreed to disagree on others, but in all things, G Wayne has been a genuine individual always intent on keeping it real. If you readers have anyone like that in your life, hang on tight. Trust and believe, these folks are a rare breed. Know that he inspires me as much as he says I inspire him. Only my husband has inspired me more. As the author has stated, no one walks alone on the journey of life. I am glad all our roads have intersected and merged.

When he told me about his first book, I was intrigued, but not surprised. This man has stuff in his head he wants to get out and stories to tell. It was simply a matter of time and how to get it out. As someone who loves to read, especially being supportive of same-gender loving men who are writers, I looked forward to *Forced Out of the Darkness.*

To say I enjoyed it would be negligent. I devoured it. It easily gave me as much enjoyment as anything I have sat down and dove into by E Lynn Harris or James Earl Hardy. See, I love stories about Black Gay Men and their struggles to find love told in a way that isn't idealized. The story told comes to my mind from a real circumstance. These men have *issues* that make it coming together a challenge. Seeing them begin to face those challenges was exciting for me as a reader and though I ended my initial journey into these lives just a little angrily (that cliffhanger ending was something right out of Dynasty, lol), my palate was now wet for more. This is good storytelling in my humble opinion.

So if you haven't read the first book, go back and get into the beginnings of Monti and Cameron's love story as well. If you have, then let's dive into their next chapter. To paraphrase one of my favorite TV belles, I find G Wayne Jackson to be a lover of all kinds of words. When he works to string those words together between two book covers, you know it's going to be a rip-roarin', firecrackin', shady roller-coaster of a ride and we'll all be better for having bought a ticket. It's gonna be good, trust and believe!!

Joseph S. Boynton, Jr.
Co-Host of the Papi Chulo Internet Radio Show
Reali-TEA

Regrettably, love can't overcome everything. It doesn't matter how strong love is; fate can meddle in love's business. Poor choices and ignorance can put love on life support. Other times, life happens with tragic results or other forces oppose love. This unsettling fact is seen through the lives of many. Countless relationships cease to exist where love once existed; however the night is the darkest just before

The Breaking of Day.

G. Wayne Jackson, Jr.

The Breaking Of Day

G. Wayne Jackson, Jr.

CHAPTER ONE-MONTI

Monti approached Mr. Williams's door and heard him on the phone so he waited outside the door. Monti stood there with his khakis and polo shirt on, heavily pressed from the cleaners... Once Mr. Williams was off the phone, Monti knocked on the door.

"Come in." Mr. Williams said. Monti entered the office and Mr. Williams said, "Have a seat, Mr. Burroughs."

Monti sat down in front of the director and watched him write something down on a note pad.

"Um humm." Mr. Williams said as he jotted down more notes. "Is that so?" He asked. "Well, that puts this in more perspective."

Monti could hear someone was talking on the other end of the phone but he couldn't decipher what the caller was saying or even whom the caller was.

"Okay well thank you for that information. I have Mr. Burroughs sitting here in front of me now. I will talk to him about this. Thank you very much." Mr. Williams hung up the phone.

"Mr. Burroughs, I'm sure you know the reason I'm calling you into my office, correct?" Mr. Williams asked.

"No, Sir. I'm not sure why you called me in. I know you have been out of the office for two weeks. I have complied with your directive of wearing more comfortable and casual clothes and I have been working in the trenches with the staff." Monti said as he wiped the sweat from his forehead.

Mr. Williams pulled open a drawer and pulled out a manila envelope and Monti's heart sunk. "When I returned from vacation, I found this envelope was under my door. Not only did I find this envelope but also I received emails and voicemails from other people in this hospital. In addition, I found myself in front of the Director of the hospital having to answer questions regarding the contents of this envelope. So, again do you have an idea of why I'm calling you into my office?"

"Yes Sir, I do. I don't know how I can possibly explain the contents of the envelope." Monti said. Monti was in fight or flight mode and had to think fast. He remembered the sermon the Pastor preached two weeks ago when his world came crumbling down. On that day, Monti lost the secrets he fought with all his being to keep within. He was exposed to the members of his church, his mother and his partner, Cameron.

"Well, go ahead try, I'm listening."

"About three weeks ago, I received an envelope similar to the one you are holding in your hand. It was given to one of my employees to give to me. I opened it up and there was a note that told me I had a certain amount of time to call this person back or else I would live my worst nightmare."

Mr. Williams was confused at what Monti was saying. He

raised his eyebrows and listened as Monti continued to tell his story.

"At the time, I didn't know who this guy was. When I finally figured out who he was, I couldn't call him because I had lost his number. So after work, I went to the parking lot and found another envelope on my truck. It had another note on it where the same person began to threaten me and my relationship."

Mr. Williams stirred in his seats as he was hearing what Monti was saying.

"Then this guy met my friend and had a conversation about me and asked my friend to ask me some questions. Later that night, he followed my friend and me to a restaurant and took photos of us. He said I would pay for all the things I had done."

"What did this guy have to hang over your head?"

Monti dropped his head as the shame of reliving the many nights in the park and other places hit him. He wiped the tear that had formed in his eye. "He had some incriminating information about me, of which he was threatening me with." He said.

"Wow that's quite the story you shared with me. I would have never thought you would get yourself so caught up in such a situation. You seem to be such an upstanding guy. Honestly, what is in this envelope is your resume because the company is considering you for a promotion."

Monti's stomach turned, realizing the Director didn't know anything about what had happened two weeks ago. When Calvin called, he asked Monti about calling the Director. Monti thought Calvin had actually fulfilled his threat, but he was hoodwinked and now he just told the Director what was going on.

"In the light of such poor judgment, on your part, I can't in good conscious recommend you for a promotion at this time. In fact, your actions outside of work have the potential to bring undesired attention to this facility and this company. We can't afford to jeopardize our contract with the hospital because you can't keep your personal life outside of work. You are supposed to set an example for the employees to follow."

"I'm so sorry, Mr. Williams. I never meant for this to happen like this."

"If memory serves me correctly, didn't you write up two employees not too long ago for having sex in a cleaning closet?"

"Yes, Sir I did."

"Now you have a lapse in judgment, which I have to address."

"Mr. Williams, I can guarantee you something like this will never happen again."

"How can you make such guarantees? You can't control someone you don't know. What other detrimental information do they have about you? How did they know you worked here?"

"Sir, I don't know and I don't know any other information they may have." Monti held his head in shame.

"I need some time to think this over. I have to consult Human Resources to see how they advise me to handle this. It is about lunchtime right now. Please report back to my office prior to you leaving today. That will be all, Mr. Burroughs."

Monti got up and left Mr. Williams' office. He was angry with himself for buying into the preacher's message about paying the price. He was angry because he didn't want to pay the complete price by possibly losing his job. He was angry with himself for falling into the trap. He was angry because one night in the park was costing him this much. He was angry because after two weeks, Cameron still wasn't talking to him. He was angry when Cameron packed up his things and involuntarily moved Monti out of the house. "That piece of ass was good but not that good." He thought as he walked back to his office.

Monti sat in his office for about thirty minutes trying to absorb what had happened. The past two weeks had been some of the worst in his life. He knew he was at rock bottom and he could only move up from this place. Emotionally, he was on a roller coaster. Physically he hadn't even gone to the gym since that fateful Sunday when Calvin did as he promised. Mentally, he didn't know how he was holding it all together. He just put on the best face he could for each passing day. He decided to make his rounds and check on the employees.

* * * * *

Once he completed his rounds, he came back to his office. He checked his email and found most of the messages were company-wide correspondence. He deleted them and was about to pick up the phone to call Cameron again, when someone knocked on his door. "Come in." He responded.

"Hi, Ms. Thomas. How are you doing today?"

"I'm well Mr. Burroughs. I'm doing well."

"That's great to hear. How can I help you?"

"Mr. Burroughs, I wanted to thank you for talking to my son for me last week. Since his dad left us, he has been acting out and I was at my wits end. He seemed to listen to what you said and hasn't been giving me much trouble since. I can't thank you enough, Mr.

Burroughs?"

"Oh, it isn't a problem. I don't mind helping when I can."

"I have to ask you this because you have done so much to help me up to this point. Have you ever thought about being a Mentor?"

"No, Ms. Thomas, I haven't thought about that before."

"You do great work with the children. I know of an organization that's looking for Mentors for young at risk youth in the city. I think you would be a great asset to this organization. You should look them up. It is called M.E.N. It means Men Empowering the Neighborhood. Here is one of their cards. You should give them a call."

"Thank you Ms. Thomas. I will do that. I need something positive in my life right now."

"Oh Mr. Burroughs, that will be wonderful. Thank you so much."

"You are welcome."

"Okay, I'm about to head home now. I hope you have a very nice day. I will see you tomorrow."

"You do the same."

Monti smiled to himself. "See, I'm not all that bad." He told himself. His day wasn't completely a wreck. He sat down at his desk and worked on his reports to turn in to his counter. Once he completed his report, he looked at his watch and saw it was already 2:00 pm. He had to make his way back to see Mr. Williams before he left for the day.

Monti walked down the hallway to Mr. Williams' office. Once in front of his door, he took a deep breath and knocked. "Come on in." Mr. Williams said. Monti walked into the office.

"Mr. Burroughs. Please come in and have a seat." He said, looking over the rim of his glasses.

Monti sat down. "You told me to come back prior to the end of my shift, so here I'm." Monti tried to make light of the situation.

"I've had the opportunity to speak with our Human Resources about the situation. With the new information provided by you, I've made the decision to place you on probation for a 6-month period of time. During which time you are expected to do your job with no other incidences."

"Thank you, Mr. Williams." Monti said.

"Don't thank me yet, Mr. Burroughs. In addition to the probation, you are being transferred to our Southfield facility."

"I have to transfer?"

"Yes, you have brought your personal life into the work place and your actions could jeopardize our contracts. We aren't willing to take that risk. If you have an issue with the transfer, I'm prepared to accept your resignation immediately. The choice is yours."

"I guess I don't have any choice. I need my job so when am I supposed to start at the new location?"

"Effective Monday. They are expecting you there at your same work time."

"What about my staff?" Monti asked.

"Don't worry about them. I will brief them Monday morning.

You will report to Ken Taylor. Please go clear out your desk and bring me your keys."

"Thank you for giving me another chance."

"Mr. Burroughs, please don't make me regret this decision."

Monti went to back to his office, got a box and packed his items. Before he went to give his keys to Mr. Williams, Monti picked up his phone and called Cameron. Again, just as the numerous times before, he was immediately sent to voicemail. He returned his keys to Mr. Williams and went to his truck. He didn't leave right away. He sat there in the truck in the middle of September contemplating his day…contemplating his life. He realized he might have hit rock bottom. He had to salvage whatever he could of his life. That day when he was at church he wanted to be free of his demons but he didn't know what a price he would have to pay to get that freedom.

CHAPTER TWO-CAMERON

Hey Cameron. I know you are still angry with me. I know I messed up. I let the best thing that has ever come in my life walk away because I wasn't man enough to face my past. I created the past and then allowed it to control me to the point of being so paralyzed when having to face it. I know this is a long shot but I would like you to just give me a chance to talk to you. I'm not asking you to get back with me, right now; I'm just asking you to let me talk to you. Let me see you. Please.

Cameron had gone into the employee break room at his new office just off of Woodward in the Campus Martius area to listen to the message. Every time he saw Monti's name come across his caller ID, a flood of emotions came over him. He felt hurt because Monti couldn't trust him enough to tell him what he was carrying. He was angry because Monti had the nerve to question his every move; but at the same time, Monti betrayed the relationship while Cameron was at work. He felt inadequate because he wasn't enough to satisfy his partner sexually. He felt embarrassed when the world knew his partner was whorish and he didn't have the slightest clue. He felt stupid because he ignored all the signs telling him to beware. Yet, he stood there sad, empty and alone.

Cameron didn't know what emotion would take predominance in his psyche because he was all over the place emotionally. A part of him loved Monti; yet another part hated him. Part of him wanted to make it all better, though another part wanted him to stew in his filth. A part of him wanted to hate the ones who uncovered him, but another part wanted to thank them for not allowing him to be ignorant to the truth. Cameron had to find his way out of this dark place he found himself in. He was searching to identify his responsibility in this situation.

He thought back to the letter he received two weeks ago. He didn't know who the messenger was and he didn't know the person who signed the letter. He thought about what he read. The letter told him of his partner's extracurricular activities he was engaged in without regard to his relationship status. It told of Monti being given a choice to tell Cameron the truth. The thing which confused Cameron the most was the last two sentences. *You deserve better. I hope you do what is right.* What was the right thing to do? How was I to do better?

"After work today, I'm going to finally make some steps to getting things in order." Cameron said to himself. He looked at himself in the bathroom mirror and gave the man in the mirror a pep talk. "You can do this. You can make it through this. You have to take control of the situation and make it work for you. Sort through your thoughts, your feelings, and snap out of this rut you are in. We are depending on you to do the right thing." Cameron wiped his face and hoped his customers wouldn't notice the tear induced redness which surrounded his dimmed hazel eyes.

Cameron walked back towards his desk. "Are you okay?" Kim asked.

"I'm good. I just had a situation that I needed to take care of." Cameron replied.

Kim was the nice lady who answered the phone when Cameron called Mr. Welsh to set up his interview. She seemed to be a cool lady about the same age as Cameron. She did some time in the U.S. Navy. Both Kim and Cameron had similar work ethic, which helped them connect as friends and also helped them compete for business. They had a good working relationship. Kim was involved in some management training program designed to help her on the path of becoming a manager. The program was a selective one which didn't allow just anybody; they only accepted the top-producing candidates. Cameron felt honored to work alongside Kim. He listened to how she handled business so he could hopefully follow suit. This industry was completely foreign to Cameron…it was the beginning of a new chapter in his life.

"Ok, I'm just checking on you. You seem to be absent from work the last few days."

"Thanks Kim, I appreciate your concern. I just have some stuff going on and I have to find my way through it."

"I know we have only known each other for two weeks but I'm here to help you and if you need someone to talk to…I got your back just like the Navy always supports the Marines."

"Oh you got jokes today I see." Cameron said as he perked up. He knew the Navy thought they were better than the Marines because they transported them where they needed to go, also that the agency name on every Marine's paycheck was "The Department of the Navy." The comment worked. Cameron knew he and Kim would be good friends.

She continued to work with him though the rest of the day. Towards the end of the day, Kim looked at Cameron and said, "Make sure you have your heart follow your head. When you do it the other way around you will set yourself up to be hurt. Logically think about whatever situation you are in and make sure it makes sense before you jump into something. Take this job for instance, you thought about the pros and cons of taking this position. I know being a flight attendant is a fun job, but logically, you knew you had to get something different because you were missing something. Take that same logic into whatever you are dealing with. I guarantee you won't be upset with yourself later."

"Wow, thanks Kim. I needed that. I have to get my head together. My heart is saying one thing but I have so many thoughts and emotions going on right now; I can't figure it out. I'm here in a new job trying to learn all I can learn but my world is in such disarray. Today is the day I start picking up the pieces and putting my life back in order."

"Are you guys ready to get out of here?" Mr. Welsh asked.

"I'm ready." Kim said enthusiastically.

"Me too." Cameron added.

Within a few minutes they had powered down their computers and had grabbed their belongings. They headed out the door while Mr. Welsh set the alarm. Cameron got into his car and headed home. Once he got on the expressway his phone rang. He looked at the caller ID and a smile came across his face. "Hello?"

"Hey Papi, How are you doing?"

Cameron knew that heavy Puerto Rican accent. "Hey Manny, how are you?"

"I'm good Papi. I heard something and I couldn't believe it so I had to call you. You quit flying?"

"Yes, I did. I was tired and wanted some advancement

opportunities. I was stuck in the flight attendant world so I decided to make a change."

"But you didn't tell anybody."

"I know I didn't want to jinx myself. So I kept it quiet until the last day."

"*Dios mio*. I'm sorry to hear you left. I'm going to miss working with you and I'm going to miss our down time too."

Cameron couldn't help but remember their night in Amsterdam. They had a great time and if it wasn't for his relationship with Monti, Cameron would have considered pursuing a relationship with Manny. Things were slightly different now, and Cameron was fortunate to have the friendship. "I know me too."

"So what are you doing tonight, Papi?"

"I don't have any plans. I was going to hang around the house. Why?"

"I'm flying in today. I will be there by 7:00 pm. I want to see you. Can you make time for me today? I'm going to Amsterdam tomorrow afternoon."

"Ok, that's cool. I need something positive in my life right now. Maybe we can have some drinks somewhere. That's sure to make for a good time. Plus, it will give us time to catch up."

"Great Papi, that sounds good to me. I will call you when we land and we can go from there."

"Manny?"

"Yes, Pa."

"Thank you." Cameron said.

"For what Papi?"

"For being a friend."

"You know it. We are aces."

"Ok, I will see you soon."

"Good-bye."

"Bye."

Cameron smiled at the idea of him seeing Manny today. They had so much to catch up on. Tonight Cameron would jumpstart his life again. He has been on life support for far too long. Manny was that boost. He knew Manny would give him a new perspective in life allowing Cameron to get his heart back to its normal self. Cameron looked at his watch as he pulled into his garage. It was 6:00 pm on the dot. He was getting used to the grind of the 9-5. It was a considerably different working environment than he was used to, but after two weeks on the new job he was settling in well.

CHAPTER THREE-YOLANDA

"Corey?"

"Yes Mom?"

"I need you to come here and show me how to use this computer."

"Ok, Mom. I will be there in a few minutes. I'm finishing up my homework."

"Ok, just let me know when you are done."

Yolanda needed to move on with her life. She had been at a standstill since her divorce with Monti. She was tired of sleeping alone. She was tired of being angry. She felt she needed to get out of the house and see the world. She had two children and didn't have confidence that any man would want her with the kids. Monti left her with the kids when he ran off to be with men. She realized her life was her own and she needed to make the best of it. She made decent money and felt she would make a good mate. The thought of Monti being exposed to his whole church and his family was the funniest thing Yolanda had heard of in a long time. She felt karma came around and added one in her win column.

"Yes Mom. What do you need to know about the computer?"

"I want to know how to use the internet."

"Mom, that's easy. You see the 'e' button on the bottom of the screen?" He said.

"Yes."

"Click on that." Corey said.

"Okay, so how do I find a website?" Yolanda asked.

Yolanda was determined to learn how to use the Internet. She had seen the commercials for online dating sites and she wanted to try her hand at one. Corey took an hour to show Yolanda how to use the computer. She listened to him intently, taking copious notes as he showed her the ropes of websites and passwords. With his help, she created an email account and created a profile on a dating site. She even had Corey take some photos of her so she could post them on the site. She was serious about moving on and finding companionship.

"Thank you, Son."

"No problem Mom. Can I say something?" Corey asked.

"Sure Corey. What is going on?"

"Mom, I was thinking the last few days. I want to apologize to you about wanting to go live with Dad. I like it here with you and I know you do a lot for us. I'm the oldest so I know I have to take responsibility and do what is right."

"I'm so glad you said that. I know I may put a lot on you. I'm going to do better and make sure you aren't burdened down with a lot of the house stuff. I'm sure your brother can do his share more."

"Thanks Mom." Corey said as he prepared to leave the room. He got to the door and stopped.

"Is everything okay?" Yolanda asked.

He ran back to Yolanda and gave her a hug and kiss. "I love you, Mom."

"I love you too, honey."

Yolanda felt good because Corey saw what she did trying to keep the house together. It was difficult for her after her Monti left. Becoming a single mother with two kids was rough. She cherished her ongoing relationship with Mrs. Burroughs. Yes, she was a pistol at times and could make you feel down right little, but she did love her grandkids and always stepped in when Yolanda needed help. It took all that was in Yolanda not to tell Mrs. Burroughs the real reason why she and Monti were getting a divorcing. Today, was the day she started on the right course to regain her identity and her life.

"This is a reason for celebration." Yolanda said to herself. She went to the kitchen to get a glass of red wine. After pouring her glass, she went back to the computer room. "…To a new beginning." She said as she raised her glass toasting to herself. She heard the computer make a sound indicating she had an email. She opened the email and found she had been matched with four potential matches. "Maybe I needed to do this a year ago." She said as she clicked on the first guy.

Chris was looking for a good time. He wanted to meet someone who enjoyed traveling and wanted to settle down. He wanted a woman who didn't mind having children because he wanted a large family. Yolanda passed him by because she was beyond having children. Her child birthing days are a thing of the past and she wanted to keep them there.

Damion was looking for someone who wanted to spend time getting to know someone at the skating rink. He liked to ride motorcycles and wanted his potential match to like bikes also. He enjoyed going out and painting the town red. He described himself as a kid at heart and wanted to find someone who wanted to grow up with him. Yolanda didn't want another kid in her life. She wanted a grown bonafide man.

Alfonzo described himself as a mature man of a certain age. He wanted a lady who was refined and enjoyed the finer things in life. He wanted to take care of his lady and wanted her to maintain the house. He loved cigars and black tie affairs. Yolanda didn't want to be a young widow nor was she a fan of cigar smoke. She decided to pass this one by also.

She was feeling discouraged at the start of her quest for companionship. She initially was going to just log out but something told her to check this last one.

Roderick was handsome man around her age. He had one child and wanted a lady with children. His idea of a perfect night was taking his lady out for a nice dinner and finishing the evening with drinks and music at his home. He said he was stable and had a career. He appreciated if his lady had a career. He said he wanted to know his lady's heart. Yolanda was impressed at his posting. She also loved the photos of Roderick. He looked like he was no stranger to the gym. He was far from where Monti was but he looked as if he could grace the cover of a GQ magazine. He was the one Yolanda wanted to meet. She decided to send him a message.

Roderick,

How are you doing? I hope you are doing well. I just came across your profile on the dating site. I think we would hit it off well. I would love it if you review my profile and let me know if you would like to chat some more.

Looking forward to it.

Yolanda

She was excited for the possibility to get to know this guy. If the photos were really him, she knew she would be pleased with the physical attributes of Roderick. She hoped this would be a possibility for her.

CHAPTER FOUR-SHAINE

"I'm not able to come to the phone right now, but if you leave me a message, I will return your call as soon as possible." Beep...

"Hey Honey-Bunny, I'm just checking in on you. I know it has been some time since Monti's exposure and you are probably still hurting from it but it is time to get out of this funk you have been in. I think we need to have a bestie date. Let me know something. If I don't hear from you soon, I'm coming over and I'm going to make you get up and get out that house. I love you very much. See you soon."

Shaine was worried about her best friend. It has been almost two weeks since he discovered the facts surrounding Monti's lies and cheating. Cameron was in such shock he got depressed. She was concerned when she received the call to help coordinate Monti's involuntary move out of Cameron's townhouse. Her concern was more about her friend surviving this heartache and being health and happy again. Her phone began to ring.

"Hello?" She answered.

"Hey honey, how are you?" Cameron said on the other line.

"Cameron, honey I've been worried about you. I was going to come over to your house until you either came home or you came out.

"I'm ok. I've been out for many years. What are you talking about?" Cameron joked.

"You know what I mean. What have you been up to?"

"I have been picking up the pieces of my life. I can't believe I didn't see the handwriting on the wall. He had been cheating on me from day one. I should have known better. My mom didn't raise no fools Shaine. It hurts that I allowed myself to fall in love with Monti. I allowed him to move into my home and he brought this craziness to my peaceful home."

"I know you are feeling bad right now but look at the bright side. You found out. Now you know better and I'm sure you will do better this time."

"Yes, that sounds good on paper *Dear Abby*, but it doesn't do thing for my shattered life right now.

"It is easier said than done, I know. I just want you to be okay. I'm worried about you. How is your new job?"

"I'm going to be fine. I'm going to get back up and into the saddle. The job is okay. I'm learning a lot of new things and new skills, so that's a good thing."

"Back up in the saddle? Cameron, are you dating again already?"

"I wouldn't say I'm dating but my buddy Manny is in town today and we are going to work it out tonight."

"Well you know the saying…the way to get over someone is

. Wayne Jackson, Jr.

to get on top of someone else. Well you be safe. We need to hang out soon. I'm going to get ready to go to a fall charity fundraiser. You know I have to ensure I'm doing my share of giving back to the community. There will be plenty of executives there. I plan on doing some networking. You never know who may be in the room."

"Oh that sounds nice. I hope you have a good time. I agree; we need to schedule a time to hang out soon. You are right I'm going to have a great time with Manny tonight. We will talk soon. Love you very much, Shaine. And Shaine?"

"Yes Love."

"Thank you for being my friend."

"You got it honey. Anytime and anything for you."

"Bye."

Shaine hung up the phone and continued to get ready. She had her short tresses laid earlier at Derrick's hair salon. She went into her closet and pulled out a long flowing strapless black gown. She knew she would be a shining star at this event. She went into her bathroom to put a little make-up on. Shaine normally didn't wear make-up but for special affairs, she would add some light make-up to give her a light evening look. She was a fan of the smoky eye for black tie events.

Shaine pulled her diamond-encrusted watch, which she inherited from her late grandmother, out of its case. She also located a pair of diamond earrings she received from a man who was head over heels for her. She was very into him, however the thing which stood in the way of their potential relationship was his wife and grown children. Shaine refused to be a home-wrecker because she wanted her relationship to be blessed from the beginning. She tried to return the earrings, but he insisted that she keep them. She put on

22 | P a g e

her jewelry and knew she was stunningly beautiful.

"God, when you send me my husband, I'm ready. I have one little request though God. Please don't wait too long to send him because a sista's got an itch that needs scratching."

She stepped into her gown, which accentuated her womanly figure. She wasn't an anorexic looking woman, she had curves in all the right places, her breasts sat up and made men pay attention, and her smooth radiant skin glowed. She looked in the mirror, as she made sure every detail was addressed. She dabbed on some Chanel No.5 for an added touch as her cell phone rang.

"Hello?"

"Ms. Holloway, this is your car service letting you know your driver, Jamal, has arrived at your home."

"Thank you very much. Please let him know I'm on my way out right now."

"My pleasure, Ma'am. You have a great evening."

"You do the same."

Shaine was ready for this evening. She descended the winding staircase of her home, grabbed the light grey cashmere pashmina shawl that Cameron had brought her back from his trip to India and headed out into the late September weather. She saw the silver stretched limousine waiting with the driver holding the door for her to get in. She walked poised and confident to the vehicle and was soon on her way to the charity fundraising event.

CHAPTER FIVE-MONTI

"Hello?"

"Hey Stephanie. This is Monti, how are you doing?"

"Wow, look what the cat drug in. I haven't heard from you in a few months. I thought you didn't like a sista anymore. What is going on with you?"

"No, it isn't like that at all."

"What is going on?"

"I wanted to talk to you about something. I'm really nervous about talking to most people but I need to have people that know who I really am and since you and I have been cool since we started our undergrad, I thought I would start with you."

"Oh shit. Hold on a second. Let me sit my ass down for this one. I feel you are about to drop something deep on me." She said as she walked over to her bed. "Ok, first let me ask you something."

"Ok, go ahead."

"You ain't killed nobody have you?"

Monti started laughing because he knew how much fun Stephanie was. They had several classes together in undergrad, but since Cameron started helping Monti with his schoolwork, Monti and Stephanie had spent less and less time together. "No. I haven't killed anyone."

"Okay, because I can't get involved with no illegal stuff. You know I don't pay for cable. My neighbors been giving it to me for free for years. That's how we do it on the East side."

"You are crazy Stephanie. Okay, stop playing. I need to tell you something that's serious."

"Damn, a sista can't be herself with you bourgeois uppity dudes. Go ahead."

"I know I haven't been around much these past few months." Monti started. "I met someone and was trying to cultivate that relationship."

"So when do I get to meet her? What is this girl's name? Is she some chickenhead?"

"That's what I wanted to talk to you about." Monti cautiously proceeded. "I really hope me revealing this won't change our friendship. I've been seeing this guy named Cameron."

"Named who?"

"Cameron…I met this guy, as in a male, a dude, named Cameron."

"Oh shit, you are gay?"

Monti stopped to ponder how to answer this question. He had never really believed he was gay. He thought of himself as an open-minded guy who liked to have sex. In the dark, it really doesn't make a difference. "Yes, Stephanie. I'm sexually attracted to women and men."

"You waited all this time to tell me that?"

"Yeah. It took a lot for me to tell you."

"So why did it take you this long? You thought I wasn't going to fool with you?"

"To be honest, I didn't know what to expect."

"Monti, you are my friend. You have been there for me and my kids and you have been the shoulder for me to cry on. I don't care whether you are gay, straight, bisexual, blue or purple. I just care about you as my friend."

"Wow, thank you. You don't know how much that means to me."

"I can't believe you thought I wouldn't accept you. I've got so much stuff in my closet that I can't judge nobody. You can talk to me about anything you need to talk to me about. I will be a listening ear for you. That's what friends are for. I don't know if I will understand all of it, but I will be open. So, tell me about this Cameron guy? And if you are so into this guy, why you sounding all down and depressed?"

"We met back in April and we were having such a great time getting to know each other. We didn't' even have sex on the first date. You remember these stories, right?"

"So all those stories you been telling me this past six months was about him? You just made 'him' a 'her'?"

"Well, you can say that." Monti said putting his head down.

"I'm cool with that. You don't have to hide behind twisted pronouns for me. We are friends and we have both been there for each other. It is ok. So when can I meet this Cameron."

"That's the problem. I was blackmailed by some guy who I had messed around with while Cameron and I were together."

"You cheated on Cameron?"

"Yeah, I did. I didn't mean to do it. I was just…well, it doesn't matter. This guy blackmailed me and when I didn't bend to his demands, he put my business all out in the street. He sent photographs of me with him to the people of my church, my mom, and Cameron. I thought he sent it to my job but that's another completely different story."

"What does a photo have to do with anything? You have been around guys before and have taken pictures with other guys before."

"Yes, I know but these pictures were of me in a sexual act with this guy." Monti's voice lowered as he felt the weight of the shame on him again.

"He sent X-rated pictures of you to the people of your church, your mom, and to Cameron?"

"Yes. I was at church and had a good time. That Sunday, I found my strength to finally be transparent with Cameron and to tell him what was going on about the things of my past. I was going to tell him at Sunday dinner. Unfortunately, this guy beat me to the punch. He had made fliers with the photos on them and put them on the church member's cars. They even hit those cars parked on the street. I don't know how far he went."

"Why didn't you tell me about this before? Did this just

happen or was this something that came over time?"

"It happened over a few days. I panicked and didn't know what to do. He gave me his number the night we hooked up but I don't know what I did with it. I don't even know why he wanted to do this. I don't know what his motive was. I just know I haven't talked to Cameron since that Sunday."

"Monti, you are just going to have to chill out and not stress too much about this. If you both had anything substantial, he will take time to get his head together and then you all will work this situation out. But there is a possibility he won't want that. Cheating is a hard pill to swallow."

"Are you sure about that? Just getting his head together may not be enough. I have to tell you something else."

"There's more?"

"Yeah there is more. He had his friends come over to his place and they all packed my stuff. Then, he rented a moving truck. He had my stuff put in the truck. He put my stuff in a storage unit and gave me thirty days to get it. He changed the locks on the doors of his place too."

"Oh hell no! You were living with him and you was acting a fool too?"

"I know I messed up badly."

"You need to be horsewhipped. Monti, you need to go see a therapist and work through your stuff, if you want any hope of getting back with Cameron. You were really happy these past months. Here, I thought some girl was fucking your brains out but you was boo'd up with a guy. You ended up falling in love and messing it up."

"You are right. I'm going to find a therapist tomorrow. I have a lot of work to do on myself." Monti said. He couldn't argue with anything Stephanie was saying. He had a good guy and he messed it up. Monti showed growth because he wholly accepted his part of the demise of the relationship. Monti didn't know if he would be able to get Cameron back; however he was willing to do what he had to do to show Cameron he was working on the situation. "I'll talk to you tomorrow. How about we do dinner or something this weekend?"

"That sounds good. Monti, keep your head up. You will be ok with this. Don't rush anything; just take the time to work on you. It will benefit you in the end tremendously."

"I appreciate that. I will do what I have to do…for me."

"Sounds good. Talk to you later this week."

"Thanks again for not judging me. Bye."

CHAPTER SIX-CAMERON

Cameron pulled up to the arrivals terminal at the Wayne County Metropolitan Airport as Manny was walking out of the airport. Manny had a swagger about him which Cameron liked. They had connected on a deeper level a few months ago when they worked together. Both of them knew there was a connection but they never acted on it after that. Cameron was becoming involved with Monti at the time and Manny was playing the field. Now the tides have changed and Cameron was single. He needed to get his life together and back on track.

"Hey Papi." Manny said as he approached Cameron.

"How are you doing, Sexy?"

"I'm glad to be off that plane. Those New York flights are always packed, but I'm really excited to be here with you tonight." Manny said.

"I'm happy you are here with me too. I've missed you."

"We got so much to catch up on Papi. Let's get out of here."

"I agree, come on."

The two of them got into Cameron's car and they left the airport.

"What time do you have to be at work tomorrow?" Cameron asked.

"I'm on the early flight so I have to be at work by 10:00 am."

"Okay. Are you hungry?"

"Sure. How about we pick up something to eat and head back to your place?" Manny suggested.

"Sounds like a plan." Cameron agreed. "How about pizza?"

"I'm okay with that."

The two old acquaintances called to order a pizza. They stopped at the liquor store to get some beer and headed home. They made small talk while they were making their stops. Once back at Cameron's place, they sat in the living room and ate their BBQ chicken pizza and drank Coronas while they continued to catch up with each other.

"So Cameron, tell me what's been happening to you." Manny asked.

Cameron thought about how much he wanted to share. He figured it was best if he kept the conversation light.

"A lot has happened but it doesn't change the fact that we are here together. I'm very glad you called. You helped brighten my day."

"I'm glad you answered my phone call. I've been thinking about our last trip together and I haven't been able to get it out of my mind."

"I remember it very well also. I had a nice time and that trip opened me up to some new experiences. I've thought about it many times since our trip."

"You have got to be one of the sexiest guys I know, Cameron,"

"Manny, you live in New York City; there are plenty of sexy guys there."

"You don't realize I see them every day. They are a dime a dozen. You are unique, down to earth and not arrogant. I've wanted to get to know you for some time. I hoped we would one day fly together and hook up. You can only imagine my surprise when I looked at the crew manifest and saw Cameron McNeil. I was happy as hell, Papi."

"You are so kind, Manny. All the years we have been flying and you never said anything, nor did you leave me any signs."

"Cameron, you don't know what it is you do to me. I used to get so nervous when we would see each other. I just didn't know what to say. Then when we flew together, I intentionally worked with you so we could connect even if it was on a co-worker basis."

"Wow, Manny. I'm flattered you would think of me like that. I'm a good person and would have talked to you in a heartbeat. You are sexy as hell."

"I'm glad the feeling is mutual." Manny got up, walked over to where Cameron was seated and kissed him. "I miss you, Cameron. I'm hoping even though you don't work for the airline anymore, you would still come and visit me in New York or allow me to see you on my off time."

"Manny, I would like that. It is no secret that I'm attracted to you. I need to explore more. I have been sexually restrained for many years but I need to liberate myself and explore more."

"Thanks, Papi. Let's experiment together."

"I'm down with that, Manny." Cameron said.

"I definitely want a replay from our night in Amsterdam. I have jacked off many times reminiscing on our night together. Starting at the bar then back at your room."

"I've thought about that night many times as well. Maybe tonight we can make a new memory."

"Let's start making them now." Manny said.

It had been a few weeks since Cameron had sexual relations. Cameron was well overdue and he knew Manny had just what he needed to help get him back on track and back to living. He needed something to take his mind off the lies and secrets Monti played him with. Tonight was the start of Cameron's re-emergence into the world; he decided he would put the lies and deception of Monti behind him.

Manny straddled Cameron and kissed him as if he had been in a desert and Cameron was his drink of water. He yearned to feel Cameron inside him again. He fantasized about how he would take advantage of another night with Cameron and he wasn't going to let it go to waste.

Manny slowly unbuttoned Cameron's shirt, exposing his chest lightly covered with sandy brown hair. The cool air in the room caused Cameron's nipples to become erect. Manny paid them immediate attention as he traced the outside of Cameron's nipples with his tongue. Cameron's manhood began to stiffen as his nipples received attention. Manny sucked Cameron's now fully erect nipple.

When Manny released one of Cameron's nipples from his mouth, he immediately began sucking the other. Cameron relaxed and yielded to Manny's attention.

After Manny worked Cameron's nipples over, he moved up and looked Cameron in his eyes, "Damn Papi, just like I remembered." Leaning into Cameron, he closed his eyes and kissed him. Again, Cameron yielded to Manny's oral skills as he probed Cameron's lips with his skilled tongue. Cameron enjoyed the feeling of Manny's tongue wrestling with his. He wrapped his arms around Manny's waist, letting his hand grope his round ass cheeks. Manny broke their tongue war long enough to seductively unbutton his shirt. Cameron enjoyed the visual show Manny was providing.

Cameron was beyond aroused as he felt the wet spot from the pre-cum touch his skin. Cameron remembered how beautifully masculine and sexy Manny's body was…it reminded him of a Puerto Rican version of Michelangelo's David but more defined and sculpted. As lust took over Cameron, he pulled Manny back onto his reclined body. It was something about the feeling of Manny's weight on Cameron, it made him feel some kinda wonderful. He loved the smell of masculinity. He loved the image of masculinity. He yearned for the feel of masculine passion. Cameron wanted to inhale the masculinity of Manny's scent. It wasn't an offensive musty scent but a masculine musky scent given off from Manny's body.

All Cameron wanted to do was satisfy Manny's body and Manny wanted to reciprocate the favor. With one swift move, Manny was again invading Cameron's mouth with his tongue. Cameron felt Manny's hands slowly unbuttoning his pants while continuing to kiss him. The heat between the two of them caused moisture to form on Cameron's bare chest, despite the coolness of the room. The light moustache and goatee on Manny's face caused goose bumps to form on Cameron's arms as Manny worked his way down Cameron's chest and torso. With Cameron's jeans open, Manny buried his face in Cameron's crotch. He inhaled deeply, taking in Cameron's scent. "You smell just right." He said as Cameron's natural manly scent invaded his nostrils.

Cameron's breathing became shallow as Manny took his time kissing up and down his manhood. Instinctively, Cameron's legs spread slightly to allow Manny more room to explore his sex. Cameron kept his groin area neatly groomed. His reddish brown hair was short and stubbly; which didn't stop Manny from enveloping Cameron's jewels into his mouth. Cameron's eyes closed as he enjoyed the attention given to his sex. Occasionally, he would reach down and run his fingers through Manny's short black hair. He was enjoying the moment but wanted to share the pleasure with Manny.

Cameron sat up and took his shirt completely off, while Manny worked Cameron's pants and underwear down to his ankles. "Stand up, Manny." Cameron said.

Manny obliged Cameron's request. Cameron unbuttoned Manny's jeans and in one swift motion pulled them down exposing Manny's fully erect stiffness. The fine straight black hair that framed his sex was too much for Cameron to resist. He took Manny's stiffness into his warm salivating mouth as Manny let out something in Spanish that was inaudible to Cameron. Manny braced his body by holding onto Cameron's defined shoulders. Cameron cupped Manny's ass as he was working his stiffness. Passion ensued. Cameron hadn't had any ass lately, so he wanted to feel Manny from the inside.

As Cameron worked Manny's stiffness, he slid his hand in the crack of Manny's hairy ass. For a Latino, Manny wasn't very hairy on his body but his ass was different. Cameron loved this difference. As he continued to swallow Manny's stiffness, he blindly found his way to Manny's asshole. After getting hot and bothered, Cameron brought his hands to his nose and inhaled the sweetness of Manny's ass. "I want you now." Cameron said with pure lust in his eyes.

"Te quiero ahora tambien, Papi." Manny responded.

Cameron knew then he was going back to the place he had thought about so many nights after he got back from Amsterdam.

"Get up on the couch and face the kitchen." Cameron instructed.

Manny did so without hesitation. Cameron came behind him and got on his knees. He grabbed Manny's ass cheeks and spread them as he buried his face in between them. Manny started speaking Spanish as Cameron took him to a place of pleasure with a combination of his tongue and his stiff sex. They fucked all over Cameron's living room. They came over and over again until both of them couldn't give any more of themselves. They held each other in front of the now lit fireplace. Cameron loved the feeling of Manny lying on his chest breathing softly with a smile of satisfaction on his face. They didn't move from this place of comfort and acceptance all night.

CHAPTER SEVEN-YOLANDA

Yolanda woke up feeling good knowing she started the process of moving forward. She felt her life was turning around. She took last night to reflect on how she let bitterness and anger overwhelm her. She didn't down herself because she realized that was where she was at that moment in time. She had been betrayed by the man that she gave her heart to. Betrayed by the man she gave her body to. She was hurt beyond measure and at the time she felt it was irreparable. She gave her virginity to Monti and she felt slighted and tainted at the same time.

She realized she had to take responsibility for herself and she couldn't gain her self-worth from a man who didn't love her. She knew she had to shed this anger and betrayal because she had let it paralyze her. Anger left her treading water in a cesspool of bitterness with fresh open emotional wounds. She didn't want to be that bitter woman any longer. She had a heart to heart talk to the woman looking back at her in the mirror and last night she made a promise that today was a new day and she would no longer tread water. She consciously decided to do a full-out freestyle away from the bitterness and hurt. She didn't want to remain a statistic of her broken husband. She wanted to be a whole woman for her intended mate. It was the breaking of a brand new day for Yolanda.

Yolanda got out of her bed and walked into the bathroom. She looked at herself in the mirror, naked and exposed. "You are beautiful. You are lovely. You are love and you will attract that which you are. I reject brokenness and broken people. I call out wholeness to match the wholeness within me" She spoke her affirmation to her reflection. Today was different because she spoke with conviction and passion. She was completely ready to move forward and reclaim her life. She wrapped her arms around herself and gave herself a good morning hug.

After she finished in the bathroom, Yolanda returned to her room. She was impressed at how neat and organized she was today. Last night, after making a pact with herself, she cleaned up her room from top to bottom. There wasn't a thing out of place. Her closet was organized and tidy, her purse was cleaned out. She needed to have her surroundings in order so the outside reflected the changes being made on the inside.

She went and got her laptop and logged into the dating website she signed up to last night with the help of her oldest son. Once she put her username and password in, she was surprised to see an email with another batch of potential matches. She knew the sun shining through her bedroom window was a sign of brighter days coming. As she scanned through the emails, the last one caught her attention.

Yolanda,

Thank you for writing me. I'm doing well. I won't complain. Life has been very good to me lately. I'm just in need of someone to share the goodness with. I don't come with a list of rules and expectations. I just want someone who's honest, loving and desires to be in a committed relationship. I looked at your profile and I'm very impressed with what you have shared. If it isn't to forward, I would like to say you are a beautiful woman. I'm honored you would reach out to me and no, I wouldn't like to chat with you…I would LOVE to chat with you and get to know you better. I'm generally off on the weekends. If it is ok with you, I would like to exchange phone numbers so we can chat off of this site.

Looking forward to hearing from you.

Roderick

Yolanda sat in her bed as a tear ran down her cheek. This wasn't a tear of sadness but it was the last tear that she would shed from her failed marriage. She also allowed one more to drop from her brown eyes that symbolized a clean new beginning.

Roderick,

I'm very open to speaking with you. I look forward to it. My number is…I'm available all day on the weekends. I look forward to speaking with you real soon.

Regards,

Yolanda

She got up from the bed and looked in her closet to find something that was bright and full of life to match how she felt inside. She decided to take a brisk shower and head to the Eastern market to get something to brighten her day even more. She went into the bathroom and turned on the shower. Within minutes, the steam permeated the bathroom and Yolanda disappeared into the steam. As she allowed the hot water to cascade down her caramel colored skin, she felt relaxed. The water purified her as if she was freshly baptized in the river Jordan. As she was basking in the warmth of her shower, she heard her cell phone ring.

Her first thought was to let it go to voice mail and she could answer it later. The phone stopped ringing. So she put it as an afterthought. Within less than a minute, she heard her phone ringing again. She didn't know who would be calling her this early in the morning but decided to go answer it. She got out of the shower and wrapped her oversized towel around her size two body and walked to the nightstand. When she picked up the phone she saw "Fuck up" on the caller ID.

"Good morning, Monti." She answered.

"Hi, Yolanda."

"What can I help you with?" Yolanda asked.

"I was just calling to see if you were doing something with the boys this weekend."

"No, I didn't have any plans. Did you want to come pick them up?"

"Yes, I'm at my mom's now and she wanted to see them." Monti said.

"You got up early to go visit your mom."

"No, I'm up at my regular time. I ended up moving back home for a moment." Monti said.

The old Yolanda would have used this time to lay into her estranged husband but today she let this opportunity slide.

"Sorry to hear that you are living back at your mother's. But to answer your question, what time do you want to come get them?"

"Can I come by in about an hour? I will bring them back tomorrow by 8:00 pm so they can be ready for school."

Yolanda was about to respond to Monti's request when she heard her phone beep. "Can you hold on for a second? I have another call coming through."

"Sure no problem."

"Hello?" Yolanda answered to the other caller.

"Hi Yolanda. This is Roderick. You sent me an email on the dating site."

"Wow. How are you, Roderick?"

"I'm doing well now that I can hear your sweet voice. I must say you sound better than I could have imagined."

"That's sweet of you, and you sound good yourself." Yolanda said. Listening to him talk made her even more excited to meet him. His voice was deep and manly. She felt his presence come through the phone from just his voice. She wanted to know more about Roderick.

"I know this may sound premature, but I would like to meet you. Do you happen to have any plans today?

Yolanda took a moment to gather her thoughts. "Actually, no I don't have any plans today."

"Would you mind meeting me out for coffee or something this afternoon?"

"Roderick, I would love to meet you. What time would you like to meet and where?"

"I have no plans today and if I did, I would drop them for the opportunity to meet you. What about Starbucks at The Somerset Collection?" Roderick suggested.

"Okay, I'm familiar with that. What time?"

"What about noon?"

"That's great. I can't wait to see you."

"Likewise, I'm looking forward to it. I will talk to you then."

"Okay, good bye." Yolanda said.

"Bye."

Yolanda almost hung up the phone and then remembered Monti was still on the other line. "Hello?"

"Hey, what took you so long?" Monti asked.

"I had to take care of some business. I apologize. Now, where were we?"

"I was asking if I could be by in about an hour to pick up the boys?"

"Yes, that's perfect timing." She replied.

"Why are you so happy Yolanda? You are different; you haven't given me a nasty comment or anything today. Are you ok?"

"Yes, I'm different. Today is a new day and I've decided to live my life. I'm no longer going to be bitter because I married a confused, gay man."

"Oh, well I'm glad you decided to do something healthy for you. I have told you that for a long while."

"Monti, please don't flatter yourself to think you are more than you really are." Yolanda said.

"See, the bitterness comes out."

"Fortunately for you, it isn't coming out. I'm good and am moving on. Did you have anything else you wanted to talk to me about?"

"No, that was it." Monti replied.

"Okay, you take care."

"You too."

"Oh…and Monti?" Yolanda asked.

"Yes, Yolanda."

"Nice photos." Yolanda said as she hung up the phone.

Yolanda was feeling good and wasn't letting miserable ex to ruin her day.

CHAPTER EIGHT-SHAINE

"So tell me about your night last night." Cameron said as he and Shaine waited for their lunch to be prepared.

"Cameron, I had a fabulous time at the fundraising event."

"I need something more than '*a fabulous time*'." Cameron responded.

"Well first of all, I looked stunningly beautiful in my black strapless gown and my diamonds. You know I was feeling good."

"What you broke out the diamonds?"

"You know how I do it. I got to the event and there were about two hundred or more people there to raise money for this charity. Well, you know I went there single so I had to mingle and network. So after dinner, the band began to play and everyone was dancing and having a great time.

"Okay, we all know people have great times at these events." Cameron said.

"Don't be so impatient. I was sitting in my seat enjoying my martini when a handsome gentleman came up to me and asked if he could have the next dance."

"Very nice…tell me more."

"Yes. He asked me if my date would mind. And you know what I told him, right?"

"You told him I was in the bathroom and would be coming back soon." Cameron joked.

"You are so silly. No, I told him I came by myself tonight and he could have the next dance."

"What did he look like?"

"He was tall. I'd say about six feet and he was slender. He was wearing his tuxedo and I could tell he was fit. His tuxedo looked like it was specifically tailored for him."

"Sounds interesting."

"He wore your favorite cologne." Shaine said.

"Marc Jacob?"

"You know it. And when I tell you he wore it, I mean that thing."

"You are a mess. Get on with your story girl."

"We danced and talked. Talked and laughed. I asked him where his date was. He told me he came there by himself."

"Okay, that sounds promising."

"For the rest of the night, we both became each other's dates for the evening. Cameron, he is an executive for one of the automotive companies."

"Oh…really?"

"Yes, he and I had a great time. He is single and has no children."

"What? You have got to be kidding me."

"I kid you not, Honey. He wanted to wait to find the right one. He didn't want a woman who was into him for the material things he could provide. He was looking for a lady who was secure in who she was and wanted to forge a strong relationship."

"Humm…this sounds like y'all may have something going on. You sound like you are happy and had a great time."

"Yes, Cameron. I can't tell you how much of a good time I had last night."

"Well, did you get his number?"

"You know I didn't let that slip. We exchanged phone numbers and we set a date for dinner tomorrow."

"Are you serious?"

"Honey, yes I'm serious."

"Wow. He must be something good that you would make time for him like that. I'm so happy for you. What is his name?" Cameron asked.

"I'm sorry. I was so excited I forgot to tell you. His name is Jonathan."

"Okay. I'll forgive you this time."

"I don't want to jump into any relationship but what I know of him…I like. And I'm open to see what the outcome of this will be."

"Don't rush into anything honey. Just take your time. You know what I went through in my last situation. I had a liar and a cheat. I don't think you want that in your life."

"Honey, I'm going into this with eyes wide opened."

"Okay. I'm going to be watching you. I need to meet him soon before you decide to do the hoochie coochie with him."

"Oh…like I meet all the pieces you mess with?"

"Okay but you know what I mean. I just want you to be happy and have a healthy relationship."

"I believe this is nice. It is something worth pursuing to see what the possibility could be."

"Well, I'm so glad you had a wonderful time."

"Okay, enough about me. What about you? You look good and you look happy." Shaine said.

"You know you can't keep a good guy down."

"I know you bounce back but I gotta keep my eye on you."

"Manny and I had a great evening. I relieved so much tension last night, so I'm okay for now."

"Okay, very nice. Just don't go rushing into anything. You are still trying to figure out what is what and get your sure footing again."

"Honey, I'm here and I'm good. That damn liar Monti keeps calling me and leaving me voicemail and text messages. I haven't answered him or even responded to the messages yet."

"Yet? You act as if you are going to respond to him soon." Shaine said.

"Time will tell."

"Cameron? Time will tell? You can't tell me you are seriously considering talking to that fool?"

"Well, I don't put it past me. I do want to hear his side of the story." Cameron defended himself.

"Hear his side? You saw all of his sides while he was doing you know what with God knows who. And let's not forget this was done while you were at work. He has no respect for you, for your relationship or for himself. If he did, he would have kept his dick in his pants."

"Wow…did you just say that?" Cameron asked.

"Yes, I did just say that. I mean that too, Cameron." Shaine said.

"You are right. You know how I'm though."

"Cameron, don't be no sucker. I can't believe my best friend is trying to punk out. For what, Cameron?"

"I got this babe. I got this. Just trust me."

"When do you plan on talking to him?"

"I'm not sure, but when I do, I will do it on my terms."

"I don't like the sounds of this, but I'm going to let you figure this out."

Cameron grabbed Shaine by her hand and he squeezed it. "Shaine, it will be alright."

Cameron and Shaine finished their lunch. Cameron had to do some thinking about the last time with Manny and he needed to address the elephant in his room, called Monti. Shaine decided to be a homebody today and was going to head home and see how little she would allow herself to do.

CHAPTER NINE-MONTI

"Hello. Dr. Carlyle's office, how can I help you?"

"Hi, my name is Monti Burroughs. I need to set up an initial consultation with Dr. Carlyle. I have some trust and insecurity issues which are negatively impacting my life."

"Okay. Dr. Carlyle sees new patients on Tuesday and Thursday evenings. He has an opening on Tuesday at 5:00 pm and on Thursday at 6:30 pm. What works best for you?"

"How about the Tuesday slot?"

"Okay, I just need to get some information from you and you will be all set."

Monti answered the questions and gave the receptionist the information she needed to schedule his appointment. He was trying to get his life back in order. He wanted to show Cameron he was serious about changing and he wanted to be able to be a better partner to him. The only problem he had was the need for Cameron to buy into the idea of giving him, yet, another chance. Monti wasn't going to give up the only man he ever fell in love with.

He was headed to Yolanda's place to pick up the boys for the weekend. He wanted to see how they were doing and spend more quality time. He figured he would try to call Cameron again. He desperately needed to connect with him. If he didn't get a hold of him soon, Monti decided he would go to Cameron's house. He had to talk to him face to face.

"You have reached the number you dialed. I can't come to the phone at the present. Please leave your name, number and a detailed message and I will return your call at my earliest convenience. Have a good day."

"Hey Cameron. I'm calling you again to see how you are doing. I think about you all the time and I wanted to just see if there was chance for me to talk to you. Can I take you out to eat? Can we meet at a mutual place? Will you just please answer the phone or return my call? I miss you and I wanted to tell you that I love you. No games, no secrets, nothing but genuine love. Please man, just call me back. Thanks."

Monti arrived at Yolanda's. He parked his mother's truck and walked to the front door. He knocked on the door. Corey answered the door.

"Hey Dad. How are you doing?"

"I'm good son. Are you almost ready?"

"Yes, hold on for a minute. Monti is almost ready." Corey said as he went back to Monti Jr.'s room to help him get ready.

"Well, hello! How are you doing, Monti?" Yolanda said emerging from her bedroom.

"I'm okay Yolanda. Why are you all dressed up?" Monti asked.

"I'm not dressed up. I just decided that I needed to look like I feel." Yolanda responded.

"Well, you look very nice."

"Thank you." Yolanda smiled. She wondered why Monti was being so nice but she decided to take it for face value.

"I didn't like your 'picture' comment that you made."

"The good thing is you don't have to like it. I'm going to continue to like the reality of you being dealt such a harsh blow. Your life is catching up with you, Monti."

"I don't want to argue with you today Yolanda."

"Don't worry about that Monti. I'm so far beyond you. I don't argue with my ex. I live a better life than he provided me. That's the best way to get back at him. I appreciate you wanted to see your kids today. I have a date and I'm going to have a great time without having to worry about them."

"Oh you are dating now?" Monti asked.

"Aren't you? I mean you being single and all." Yolanda was taking every opportunity to hit Monti with verbal daggers. Though she was genuinely happy, she liked being able to give him back a little shade, even though she didn't know it was called shade.

"That's none of your business."

"Well, it wasn't my business to see you in the park either, but the world saw that. That was a long awaited day." Yes, Yolanda was turning over a new leaf in life but sometimes old habits die hard.

"You are still so hateful."

"No Monti. I'm not hateful. I'm enjoying life now. I'm living. I'm spreading my wings. Someone is interested in me and unlike you, he likes pussy."

"Whatever Yolanda."

"You have never apologized for your infidelities. You have never apologized for lying to me our whole relationship. You didn't even think anything about me or how I felt or if I would survive the heartache you caused me."

"Is that what you want? An apology?" Monti said.

"No, you would probably be lying about that too. Anyway, hope your little boyfriend is doing ok. I feel for him. We share one thing in common…well maybe two. We were involved with a man that's incapable of being honest, and we both witnessed him get caught with his pants down. Maybe one day I will be able to meet him. The boys said Mr. Cameron is a nice man. Isn't it time for you to be going?" Yolanda said.

Monti couldn't come back from what Yolanda told him. He felt it would be best if he just get the boys and got away from this situation with some amount of dignity left.

"Boys?" Monti called.

"Here we come Dad." They came running from their room.

"I love you, Mom." Corey said as he hugged Yolanda.

"I love you more than Corey does." Monti Jr said as he gave his mom a hug and a kiss.

"I love you both. Be good and mind your manners. I will see you tomorrow."

"Bye!" They said in unison.

Monti and the boys got into the Jeep and left. Once in the car, Monti said, "Boys, what we do when we are together is our business. You don't have to share everything with your mom. You know she doesn't like me."

"I'm sorry Dad." Corey said. "We had a nice time with Mr. Cameron so we told Mom how nice he was."

"You heard our conversation?" Monti asked.

"Yes. I wish you and her would get along. It makes me sad because you both hate each other." Corey said.

"Me too." Monti Jr. chimed in as he put his earphones on to listen to his iPod.

"I'm sorry boys. I will work harder at trying to get along with you mom." Monti responded.

"So…Dad. Can I ask you a question?"

"Sure Corey. Go ahead."

"Why did you and Mom split up?"

Monti took a few moments to stop and think about how he was going to answer this question. He pondered whether to tell him what really happened or deflect the question.

"Well Son, sometimes adults get together and things don't work out. Your dad had some issues with being honest and faithful. So because I choose to not tell the truth and live the truth, I caused our relationship to break up. I only wish I was strong enough to have been honest from the beginning, but because I didn't have the courage and strength, you both have to live without me at home all the time. For that, I'm sorry. I want to make this up to you two the best way I know how. I hope you both forgive me."

"We forgive you, Dad." Corey said.

"When you get older and have a family, I want you to be honest and true. Never lie and never cheat. Your family is all you have son. Make sure you treat it as the most important thing in your life after God."

Monti may be a poor man in relationships and may have infidelity and insecurity issues but being a parent and showing his children what to do, brought out the softer, tender side of Monti. No one saw this side of him but his boys. He didn't want them to have to go through anything he went through and he didn't want his grandchildren to hurt the way he allowed his actions to hurt his own children.

CHAPTER TEN-CAMERON

Cameron looked at his phone as he saw *Don't Answer* come across the screen. He thought it was probably Monti calling. He knew he would eventually have to have a conversation with him. Not for Monti's sake but for Cameron's sake. He was at a loss for words at what he should say to Monti. He didn't know what the expected outcome he wished to achieve through this conversation. He had neither spoken to nor seen Monti after he had left the church that Sunday. Cameron thought back to that Sunday after he received the envelope. He remembered the conversation when he called Monti.

* * * * *

"Monti?" Cameron said on the other line.

"Baby, let me explain what happened."

"Don't motherfucking 'Baby' me. You are a fucking lying, cheating bastard. I asked you repeatedly to be honest with me and you denied what was going on."

"I can explain."

"No, you can listen. I put up with your bullshit all this time. I took you back time and time again. I ignored the signs, which told me to leave you alone. You jumped through hoops trying to make sure I wasn't cheating or lying to you, but you were doing it all along. Calvin told me to ask you about your ex and your friends but you refused to tell me anything. It is no wonder you didn't want to talk about it. You were too busy fucking anything with a hole or anything that would give you the time of day. What…I wasn't satisfying enough for you?

"Cameron, it isn't that."

"Do you have a logical excuse for any of this?" Cameron asked.

"Well…"

"Exactly…you don't have anything that you can say to explain any of this. You went through such great lengths to try to catch your ex cheating, you played games with him. You blame your wife for ruining your marriage…"

"How can you comment about my marriage?"

"Maybe you should have commented about it. Maybe you should have been a man and addressed the issues in your marriage…that would explain why you sent your wife into the arms of your best friend. Oh yeah, he wasn't much of a best friend to you because he was FUCKING your WIFE."

"Cameron, that isn't fair. I know you are angry."

"ANGRY. Don't tell me what I'm. How else do you think I would be to find out my sick ass boyfriend is in the park fucking people while I'm at work? What am I supposed to think? How am I supposed to look at you knowing you can't keep you stubby ass dick in your pants?"

Monti stood there with tears in his eyes as he listened to Cameron. He didn't want to hear it but he knew he deserved what he was getting from Cameron. He knew he wasn't faithful. He knew he cheated several times and he knew he should have told Cameron what happened so they could go through it together. He should have placed trust in his partner's love rather than in trying to talk Calvin out of revealing his dark side.

"Oh you don't have anything to say to me, the one you said you loved. That was probably a motherfucking lie too. Do you have anything else to tell me?" Cameron continued. Cameron was so angry; nothing that Monti could have said at that moment would have made a difference.

Monti was choked up with emotion. His life had crumbled and his foundation was on the other line reading him for filth. "I'm sorry. I will make this up to you." He managed to get out.

"Make this up to me…Well at least half of you statement is correct. You are a sorry assed bastard. I don't want to see you. I don't want anything from you. Matter of fact, you better find somewhere else to stay indefinitely. I will put a week's worth of your clothes outside my front door today. I will have someone call you to make arrangements for you to get the rest of your belongings. I can't believe I was that stupid to let you in my life. I never had any of this craziness when I was with Guy. I hope you have a miserable life." Cameron hung up the phone.

Cameron let out all of his emotions on Monti. He spewed all the venom and anger into the receiver of his phone. His eyes tear-stained red. His heart broken into pieces. His world shattered because Monti refused to address his issues. Cameron stood there outside of his church completely empty. He had nothing left. He was emotionally bankrupt. He began to cry again as his legs gave out from under him. He felt foolish and shameful because he didn't listen to neither his conscious and nor his friends.

Sitting there on the curb, Cameron was in a state of destruction. Cameron had never been in this type of situation before. The tears poured out from him purging him of the situation. It wasn't until an elderly woman, who was walking down the street, interrupted him.

"Young man, is there anything I can help you with? I'm not trying to pry in your business but you look like you just found out someone just died."

"No thank you, Ma'am. I need to get up from here. Thank you for stopping and showing me that you care."

"I don't know who you are but just know everything will work out the way it is supposed to."

"It doesn't feel like that now from where I'm sitting but I know you are right."

"I will tell you this...I've been here on God's green Earth for many years. Just know life ebbs and flows. You will have happy times and you will have some times you wish you could erase. Know that there is a lesson in everything we go through. I don't know what lesson you are supposed to get from this but from the looks of you baby, you need to learn this and learn it good. I'm going to pray for you tonight in my prayers and I know God will help you with this."

"Thank you Ma'am. I appreciate that, and I appreciate your words of wisdom. I will be okay."

Cameron got up from the edge of the street and brushed himself off. He had some things he needed to do. He had to clean house. He wasn't going to sleep in his home that deceit and destruction permeated. He called the Hilton and made a reservation for the evening. He knew Shaine was supposed to be coming over tomorrow for the holiday but he would deal with that in the morning.

* * * * *

"Cameron, when are you going to deal with this?" He thought. His phone indicated there was a voice message. Cameron listened to the voice message and saved it instead of deleting it. He decided he would return the call before the weekend was over. He wanted someone to talk to so he decided to call Calvin.

"Hello, you have reached Calvin. Leave me a message and I will holla back at you soon."

"Hey Calvin. It is Cameron. I know it has been a minute since we talked but I needed some advice about Monti. So because I don't know any of his friends and you seem to know more about him, I thought I would call you. I hope you are doing well and I hope to hear from you soon.

Cameron hung up the phone hoping Calvin would call him and they could talk about this situation. Maybe he could give Cameron some tips or advice on the situation.

CHAPTER ELEVEN-YOLANDA

"You must be Roderick." Yolanda said as she walked up to a man sitting alone at a table in Starbucks.

"Wow, yes. I happen to be the lucky man named Roderick. You must be Yolanda."

"Yes, that's me." Yolanda replied nervously. "You are definitely a handsome man."

"I'm glad you agreed to meet me today. I know it was short notice and we are complete strangers but I hope you enjoy our time together."

"I'm glad I agreed to meet you. I look forward to getting to know you."

"Would you like to get something to drink?" Roderick asked.

"Sure, I would like to have a Caramel Macchiato."

"Any particular size?"

"No, whatever is fine."

"Okay, I will be right back." Roderick said as he smiled.

Yolanda was attracted to him and knew she wanted to know him more. If things didn't work out she would have to get back on the search, but if his profile was true and they hit it off, she welcomed the potential awaiting them. She was resolved to avoid the challenges she had with Monti.

Roderick was definitely pleased when he saw Yolanda. She was beautiful and her photos did her no justice. He looked forward to getting to know her more. He did want to talk to her and find out more about her. He ordered their drinks and turned around hoping to get a few moments to visually take her in. When he did look, Yolanda was looking back at him still smiling, so he did what anyone else would and waved to her. Once the drinks were ready, he made his way back to the table where they were sitting.

"Here you are." Roderick said as he handed Yolanda her drink.

"What are you having?"

"I'm having a soy Chai tea latte. It is one of my favorites." He responded.

"I will have to try that next time."

"So Yolanda, tell me why a lady like you is single?"

"I was married for several years. About a year and a half ago I filed for divorce from my husband because he preferred facial hair and muscles over a woman."

"You mean he is playing for a different team?" Roderick asked.

"You got it."

"Well, I'm not one to judge but I like what I see in front of me. How have you coped with that reality?"

"I just know he has his own issues and needs to deal with them. I let that get the best of me for a while. I know I'm a beautiful woman and deserve to have the finer things in life and to have a heterosexual man in my life that loves only this woman."

"You are right. You do deserve to have love and the finer things in life. How long have you been on the dating site?"

"I just signed up the other day. I got a few matches but I was interested in getting to know you more over any other match. Something about your post resonated with me."

"Well I hope I can live up to your expectations." He said.

"Just be yourself and be honest and we will be okay. What about you? Are you single?"

"Yes, I'm very much single. I've been single for about a year and a half. My ex and I didn't ultimately mix well and so we parted ways. I wanted to take time to evaluate myself and understand how I had changed after the break up. I didn't want to carry any negative baggage into my next relationship. So, I attended some therapy sessions and made sure I was psychologically ok and ready for a serious commitment."

"That sounds good. I should have done that myself. I just realized I had to get rid of the hurt and the pain and not allow it to make me an angry, mistrusting woman. It wasn't easy letting the hurt and pain go and I'm sure I may have some flashbacks but I don't want it to interfere with my next relationship." Yolanda said.

"That's why I sought out counseling to help me get over that hump. My therapist is Dr. Carlyle. I can give you a referral if you ever need it."

"Oh…so you think I need therapy?" Yolanda said flirtatiously.

"No, I didn't say that. I was saying if you ever needed something I could make a connection for you. I'm very interested in seeing this through. I'm liking the Yolanda I'm seeing before me. I hope you can say the same about me."

"Roderick, are you kidding me? You are quite handsome and I like your conversation. I feel good getting to know you. Give yourself some credit." Yolanda smiled.

"That's what I wanted to hear." Roderick said.

The two of them continued to get acquainted over coffee. As Yolanda shared some of the events that transpired in her marriage, Roderick couldn't understand why a gay man wanted to be involved with a woman such as Yolanda. Roderick was physically and mentally interested in getting to know Yolanda better. Something in his mind told him this was a person that would bring something good to into his life. His job as a police officer for the city of Detroit, made it difficult for him to find a substantial relationship. Many women didn't want to deal with the stress of dating a law enforcement officer yet alone marry one. There were times when he wouldn't get off work as he should and that caused women to question his fidelity to their relationship.

"So your profile said you have children." Roderick said.

"Yes, I have two boys. They are growing up fast. I'm so proud of the men they are becoming."

"That's great. I have a daughter myself. She is seven years old."

"Oh really? Do you have baby mama drama?" Yolanda asked.

"I will say we have our ups and downs. I don't get into the drama stuff much. I just want to take care of my daughter and enjoy being a dad. Our relationship is over and I've moved on."

"Ok, that's understandable." Yolanda was enjoying the interaction between her and Roderick. She felt she needed to take a step towards her complete liberation and separation from Monti. "Do you have any plans for this evening?"

"No, I'm off work this weekend. What about you?"

"I have no plans. I was wondering if you wanted to meet for dinner."

"Aren't you a forward, liberated woman?" Roderick said smiling at him.

"I just feel I need to see how this is going to turn out, and I wanted to spend more time with you to get to know you better."

"It feels great to know you are feeling the same way I'm. It is also refreshing to see you are okay with speaking your mind."

"You could say I'm outspoken."

This was a departure from the Yolanda of old. She had a voice and she realized she had to be vocal about things which affected her life. This was a new day and traditional wifely duties were not going to pre-empt her from being happy. She knew she could be a forward woman but be sexy and desirable at the same time. She refused to accept being an angry black woman and a single parent.

"I like that in you. I like a woman who sees what she wants and goes for it. It is a turn on actually."

"Then that means I'm doing what I'm supposed to be doing." Yolanda said as she ran her fingers through her hair. Yolanda has silky flowing shoulder length auburn hair. She uses her 'good hair' to her benefit. She wasn't a fan of weaves and really didn't need them.

"So what about we meet for dinner tonight? My treat." Roderick said.

"That sounds great."

"What about Italian? I like Bravo!, they have a great menu selection and great ambiance."

"Okay. That's fine with me." Yolanda said.

"They have a location in Rochester Hills."

"What time do you want to meet?"

"What about seven-thirty?"

"Great. I will see you there."

Yolanda stood up to prepare to leave.

"Can I walk you to your car?" Roderick asked.

"Definitely!" Yolanda was feeling the chivalry Roderick was extending. She didn't get this treatment when she was with Monti. To say he was a poor excuse for a husband would be an understatement.

Roderick walked with Yolanda out of the coffee shop, after opening the door for her, he reached out and held her hand. Yolanda felt safe, a feeling she hadn't had in a long while. Once they made it to her car, Roderick gave her a hug and said, "I enjoyed your company this afternoon, and am looking forward to more this evening." He kissed Yolanda on her cheek and opened her door.

"I had a wonderful time as well. I will see you tonight."

Yolanda got into her car. Roderick closed the door for her. He stood in the late September sun, as Yolanda pulled out of the parking space, watching her exit the parking lot safely.

CHAPTER TWELVE-SHAINE

Shaine arrived at Ruth's Chris Steak House where she used valet service. When she stepped out of her vehicle, she saw Jonathan waiting for her at the front door. She walked towards him as only Shaine could do. Every step she took was poised and confident. Shaine visually took Jonathan in as she made her way to the front door. She was excited to see him. They had such a pleasant evening at the fundraising dance. He was just the type of man she was attracted to visually. His chocolate frame perfectly accentuated by his dark Armani suit. He looked runway ready, yet masculine.

"My, don't you look breathtaking this evening Shaine." Jonathan said as he gave Shaine a single long stem red rose. He hugged and kissed her on the back of her hand.

"Thank you Jonathan. The rose is beautiful. You are quite the sight yourself."

"Thank you Shaine. Shall we?" Jonathan held the door for Shaine as she walked through the restaurant entryway. Jonathan walked beside Shaine as they made their way to the host stand. "Reservation for Blanchard." He said with the rich baritone of his voice.

Shaine enjoyed talking with Jonathan because he was educated and sensual at the same time. His voice marched through her eardrums beating its way to her imagination. She'd been celibate for close to a year. After the fundraiser, she imagined hearing his voice in her ear again. When they danced to a throwback Roger Zap's *I Wanna Be Your Man*, Jonathan sang to Shaine seductively as they embraced in the trails of the dance. He wasn't afraid to press upon her and pull her close to him. Shaine rested her head on his chest and was taken to places her mind wanted her body to follow with him. They were seated at their table and presented with the wine menu.

"Would you please give us a moment to look over the listings?" Jonathan said to the server.

"No problem, Sir." He replied and made his departure from the table.

"I just am mesmerized by your beauty, Shaine."

"You are too kind Jonathan. I'm glad we met. Your story is truly one of success and perseverance. It isn't often you hear someone being so open about their struggles and slow start in life to make it to the executive level of a multibillion dollar corporation."

"Oh, you have been doing some research on me, have you?"

"Well, a lady has to make sure you are a suitable suitor. I would hate to waste your time as well as mine."

"That's what I admire about you, Shaine. You aren't afraid to put in the work and research to get the information needed to make a thought out decision. When you were telling me about your job with the department store, I couldn't help but to see how methodical and calculated you were when you laid out your career goals. I do have a question for you though."

"Sure what is it?" Shaine asked.

"Do your plans have room for a relationship?"

Shaine thought about the question. She wanted to say yes immediately, but she wanted to make sure she was being honest and accurate. She knew she wanted a relationship which would lead to a marriage but she didn't factor that into her long-term goals. "I'm sure with a few adjustments, I would be open a meaningful relationship."

"That's what I want to hear. Have you been married before?"

"No. I'm waiting on the right man."

"Oh really?"

"Yes, really. I'm worth more than many women see themselves as. I'm not meaning to sound conceited or arrogant, however you hear countless relationships ending because the woman found out their husband or boyfriend was out cheating on them. It is especially important for me to have someone who is willing to commit to me every morning he wakes up, as I do the same."

"That's a strong statement. You are quite the articulate lady I see. That's very attractive to me."

"Yes, I agree it is a strong statement but it is a truthful one. I vowed to God that I would recommit to my husband on a daily basis. I want someone who values our love in the same way."

"I love your resolve to your beliefs. I happen to agree with you. Relationships and marriages are a work in progress. It involves committing yourself to your significant other every day, sometimes multiple times a day." Since they first met, Jonathan had a difficult time getting Shaine out of his head. She was everything he'd hoped to have in a wife. Though he didn't know her fully, the amount he did know about her was refreshing and he was interested in seriously dating her. He wanted to be a father and to have a family eventually but wanted to do it only once with one woman.

He didn't like going to charitable events alone. He could have taken an escort to these events but he chose to go solo each time. He chose to remain one of Detroit's most eligible bachelors because he didn't want just anyone in his life. He had dated in the past and ultimately found women who wanted him for the status and lifestyle which accompanied the relationship with him. He questioned the emotional attachments they had with him. He didn't want his wife to work, if she didn't want to but would support her goals and career dreams if she did. He knew from their conversation, that Shaine was a career-orientated independent woman. She brought her own success to the picture. His seven figure annual salary wasn't on her radar. This allowed him to be open, honest and transparent with Shaine.

"Sir, have you all decided on a beverage at this time?" The server said.

"I would like a glass of Cabernet Sauvignon."

"And for you Ma'am?"

"That sounds good for me as well."

"My pleasure." He said as he departed the table.

"So where were we, Jonathan?" Shaine asked.

"You were telling me how you agreed on going on a second date with me." Jonathan said.

"Oh is that so? I don't remember you asking me for a second date."

"So, all I have to do is just ask you for a second date?"

"I don't mind going on a second, third or fourth date with you Jonathan Blanchard."

Jonathan reached his hand out and Shaine placed her hand in his. He smiled as he held her hand in his.

"Shaine, you are truly a remarkable woman. You have made this past few days the best days I've had in a while. I look forward to more times with you. I look forward to standing behind you as you carve out your successful career. I look forward to the day you wake up in my arms, and honestly, I hope it isn't too far off."

"Thank you for your encouragement. If things work out and you are everything you have been showing me, I can't wait to wake up in those sculpted arms of yours either." Shaine smiled as she dimmed her eyes. Her mother taught her how to be a lady at all times without sacrificing her power.

"Anytime. That's what a man is supposed to do. I promise I'm everything you see and more." Jonathan said as he continued to hold Shaine's hands firmly yet delicately. She enjoyed his masculinity, even though it was in a simple act of affection. Shaine enjoyed the way the light from the flickering candle danced off his hazel eyes. She studied his chiseled facial features. She could see strength in his jaw line. She didn't seem to mind the absence of a moustache or goatee. His hair was just long enough to show Shaine he had some mix in his blood as she studied his loose curly jet black meticulously tapered hair.

"You always seem to say the right thing, Jonathan. I almost believe you when you say them." Shaine said.

"Almost…Is that so?" He asked.

"Yes, it is."

"Shaine, what can I do to make sure you believe what I'm saying? I'm sincere and true in what I'm saying. I also know I'm serious about getting to know you better. I know I'm highly attracted to you. I know I hope we fit together and work towards something serious."

"Jonathan, the only thing you have to do is keep doing what you are doing. As long as your actions line up with your words I'm sure I will believe you and we will click."

"That's the only way I know how to be. I have a lot on my plate and I don't have time for games and other added stuff. I will continue to show you who I'm and hope who I'm will ultimately win you over."

Shaine loved Jonathan's willingness to be transparent in his feelings. She knew men generally guarded their feelings. She knew in time, any façade would be broken and the true nature of Jonathan would surface. She was going to enjoy getting to know him and see how the situation evolved.

"I'm game for it." Shaine said.

The two ordered and ate their food while they enjoyed conversation. The chemistry developing between the two of them was visible to others around them. They had the potential to be one of the Motor City's most influential power couples. Automotive executive meets fashion executive. Shaine was financially solvent and didn't need a man to support her; however what she did need was the comfort of a man, to be her rock, her lover and her friend. She felt some kind of way when she looked into Jonathan's eyes. There was something about looking into a person's eyes. What Shaine saw in Jonathan's eyes was a loving, caring and compassionate man who was genuine. She didn't see deception or manipulation.

Jonathan knew his meeting Shaine wasn't by happenstance. He saw his future in her eyes. He saw the spark of destiny. He knew his only job would be to love her with all he had. To provide her with whatever she wanted. He wanted to give her the world. Being abandoned by his mother when he was a baby and being raised in a white foster home didn't taint Jonathan's views on women. He was neither bitter nor angry at his circumstances. His foster mother did all she could do for him. She sent him to school and urged him to finish college. She pushed him to be the best in everything he did. She pushed him to never give up. She taught him to persevere through adversity and to avoid being a victim at all costs. Ironically, Jonathan saw the same qualities of his foster mother in Shaine's eyes.

It saddened him when he lost his foster mother to pancreatic cancer when he was twenty-four. He still remembered her last words of wisdom to him as she was lying in her hospital bed. "Son, I love you very much. I'm going to have to leave here soon but I will be on the other side cheering you on through every phase of your life. You are somebody and I'm so proud of the man you've become. Don't settle for less than the best. Find you a good woman who loves you for you. You will know when you find the right one. I'm honored to have been blessed to have such a wonderful son. I love you."

His foster mother gave him strength and courage to face everything head on. He felt Shaine was the right one. She gave him goose bumps when they were together at the charity event. Sure, Shaine was aesthetically beautiful; but beyond her beauty, she reached his heart. Not because he fell in love with her, but because the essence of who Shaine was touched the essence of whom he is.

Jonathan paid for their dinner and walked around the table and pulled out Shaine's chair as he helped her out of her seat. He helped Shaine into her coat and offered his arm as they made their way out of the restaurant. Jonathan waited with Shaine as the valet went to bring her vehicle around. Once he arrived, Jonathan walked her around to the driver's side and tipped the valet.

"I really enjoyed your company this evening, Shaine. You are a remarkable lady."

"Thank you Jonathan. I had a wonderful time as well. You are truly a gentleman."

"Would you mind if I called you once I get home before I call it a night?" He asked.

"I would like that."

Jonathan gave Shaine another hug and kissed her on her cheek. She got into her car and he closed the door for her.

"You drive safely. I can't have you getting hurt on me."

"I will. You do the same."

"You got it. Good night Shaine." Jonathan said. "I'll call you when I get home."

Shaine pulled out of the parking lot and onto the expressway. She'd waited thirty-four years to meet Jonathan. As she was driving, she looked into the night sky and thanked God for the blessing of Jonathan. She thanked him for the potential Jonathan represented. "God, you did a great thing tonight. I'm eternally grateful for him." Shaine felt today could be God's answer to what she'd prayed for and she was going to let what will happen, happen.

CHAPTER THIRTEEN-MONTI

"Mr. Burroughs, I'm Dr. Carlyle. What brings you in to see me today?"

"I came in to see you because I need some help trying to sort out things in my life. I have trouble maintaining relationships. I have trust issues and I'm really tired of living like this. I figured you are the doctor and would help me sort through some of this."

Dr. Carlyle was writing on a notepad as Monti continued to speak. "Prior to you coming in, I reviewed your intake assessment. I find some of your answers to be interesting. So you are a thirty-seven year old gay male..."

"Doctor, I don't like to be referred to as being gay. I'm a man who is sexually interested in other men."

"If that's how you like to refer to yourself, I'm okay with it. So you are a thirty-seven year old male who is sexually interested in other men. You are coming here because you say you have trust issues and difficulty maintaining relationships. Is that correct?"

"Yes, that's correct Doctor."

"Ok, so what I would like to do is to give you an overview of the objectives of therapy, give you some information of my background in psychology and then set up some goals for our session today. In order for therapy to be beneficial to you, Mr. Burroughs, you have to be open and honest. You also need to be realistic about what our work together will be. Therapy is not a magic pill you take and all your troubles are fixed. It takes work on your part. There will be moments where you will be uncomfortable and feel like you want to quit. I want you to make an effort every time we meet to stick with the process and do the homework. You will only get out of therapy what you put into it. Also, remember I'm not here to judge you or create assessments of you personally, I'm here to help navigate you through the situations you are in currently and to help you make better choices in life through addressing your current cognitive behaviors. I'm merely the guide. If we get to a place where you aren't comfortable, let me know and we will adjust accordingly. Do you have any questions for me thus far?"

"No, I don't."

Monti spoke to Dr. Carlyle candidly about his current situation. He felt comfortable with Dr. Carlyle, and knew what he spoke about in counseling was privileged information. He wanted to seriously address the issues plaguing his personal and private life.

* * * * *

Monti turned on his phone when he got to his vehicle after his therapy session. His phone showed he had three voice messages. He got into his vehicle and dialed into his voice mail.

Monti, it is Stephanie. Just checking on you making sure things are ok. Call me when you have a minute.

Delete.

Hey Dad. It is Corey. I need to get something for school and Mom told me to call you. Can you call me back? Love you. Bye.

Delete.

Monti, it is Cameron. I got all your messages. I guess I do need to talk to you. I don't have any plans this weekend so I'm ok with meeting you out somewhere on Saturday. Preferably during the day. Just text me and let me know where you want to meet, and it needs to be in a public place.

Monti hung up the phone. He was excited Cameron agreed to meet him. He needed someone to speak with to tell the good news to. He quickly dialed Stephanie.

"Hello."

"Hey Stephanie. How are you doing? Sorry I was unable to answer when you called. I was in with the doctor."

"You had a doctor's appointment? Are you sick?"

"No, not that kind of doctor. Today was my first session with the therapist. I'm seeing Dr. Carlyle."

"Oh, ok. What I was calling you for was to see if you wanted to come over next weekend for a small get together I'm having here at my place."

"I can probably do that. I don't have any plans. What do you want me to bring?"

"I'm glad you asked. Can you bring that heart attack macaroni and cheese you make?"

"Okay. Just remind me when because you know I will forget."

"I won't forget because if you don't come, then I will have to make the macaroni and I'm going to be busy doing other things."

"I got it."

"How was your therapy session?" Stephanie asked.

"It was good. I feel comfortable with the doctor. I'm glad I went."

"That's good. Anything new with you and Brandon?"

"Brandon?"

"Yeah, you know Brandon the one you just went through all that stuff with."

"Oh, you mean Cameron." Monti corrected.

"Brandon...Cameron. You know what I meant."

"Actually, he called me while I was in therapy today."

"Did he?"

"Yes, he wants to talk about us getting back into a relationship." Monti lied. He didn't know why Cameron wanted to talk. He was just happy they were on speaking terms.

"What brought about the change? He just out of the blue wanted to get back with you?"

"I'm not sure. We are going to meet this weekend to talk about it. I'm excited I'm going to get a second chance at this."

"Well, Monti, take it slow. Don't rush into anything. Take your time and remember you are in therapy for a reason. When is your next appointment anyway?"

"Did you just change the subject on me like that? Wow. My next appointment is next Tuesday. We meet once a week. So I'm hoping I will have something good to talk about in my next therapy session."

"Just take your time. Don't just jump back into a situation when you know good and well that you aren't ready to be back in this relationship. You have to address those things which caused you to have the issues in the first place."

"I will be alright. Listen, I'm about to grab something to eat."

"Take care and we will talk soon."

Monti didn't want someone messing up his excitement. He wanted something to eat and wanted to just enjoy the day. His life was looking up. When you hit rock bottom, you have nowhere else to go but up. Monti wanted to get back up sooner than later. He decided to head to his spot…Capers.

* * * * *

Monti pulled up to the parking lot of Capers. He parked and got out of the Jeep. Looking towards the guard shack, he saw Michael. Today was different and Monti wanted to make sure things were good between Michael and him. He walked over to where Michael was.

"Hey Michael. How have you been?"

"I'm doing well, Monti. How are you?" Michael replied.

"Man, I've seen better days. I'm cool though. Things are looking better for me."

"That's good to hear. I heard about what happened with you and your ex. I'm sorry you had to go through that. It was some messed up stuff."

"Yeah, that was one of the worst days of my life. I still don't know why that dude did all that."

"Sometimes you never know what people's motives are. There are other ways to get a point across. To completely eviscerate and display one's dirty laundry like that was the marks of someone who wanted nothing but revenge against you badly."

"I know man." Monti said as he hung his head. "I wanted to come over here and apologize to you for how I acted last time I was here. I should not have said the things I did to you. I think you are a good guy. Well, you already know I'm attracted to you."

Michael's raised his eyebrow.

"No. It isn't what you are thinking. I'm not trying to hit on you or anything like that. I understand how you feel about me and I would think that if those feelings changed, you would let me know. I just wanted to sincerely apologize to you and hope you would forgive me."

"Not a problem Monti. I accept your apology. You came all the way over here to apologize to me?"

"No, I also came to have a drink. I got some good news today."

"Oh, that's great to hear. Good news is always something to celebrate. Were you meeting someone here?" Michael asked.

"No, I'm flying solo tonight."

"No new dates lately?"

"No. I'm working on me and trying to get my dude back. He

just agreed to talk to me about getting back together so I'm excited." Monti proudly said.

"Wow, that's incredible Monti. If he is even considering talking to you after what I heard happened, he must have some serious feelings for you. I hope it works out for you."

"Thanks man. I plan on it being better this time around."

"Cool man. Go ahead and get some grub. It was good talking to you." Michael said.

"It was good talking to you as well, Michael. You are a good kat. I hope you get someone good in your life soon. Whoever gets you will get a great catch."

"Aww thanks Monti. I appreciate it."

Monti went into the bar and ordered some chicken wings and a beer. He was going to enjoy happy hour and then head back to his mom's. He hoped after his next paycheck, he would be back on his feet and have his own place. Monti loved his mother but being forced to live with her after his separation with Cameron made dating and getting his freak on difficult. He couldn't come to his mother's house at different hours of the night. He had to respect Mrs. Burroughs' rules.

* * * * *

While sitting at the bar, Monti's phone rang. He looked at the caller ID but didn't' recognize the number. He decided to answer it.

"Hello?" Monti answered.

"Hey Darryl. What is up?"

"I'm good. Who is this?" Monti said ignoring the pseudonym.

"It is Allen. Remember we met a couple weeks ago. I stay in Southfield."

"Oh hey man. What is up with you?"

"Not much here. I was just seeing when we was gonna hook up again. You know you liked this good shit over here."

"Man, I'm not going to lie. I'm just trying to lay low right now. I'm not trying to be out there right now. So I'm going to have to pass right now. I'm sure you won't have any problems finding some dick."

"Aiight man, no problem. When you are ready to hit this again, just hit a brother up."

"Okay Allen. You take care and we will talk more later."

"Aiight, bet. Lock my name in your phone." Allen said.

"Okay, I will." Monti lied.

Monti was proud of himself because he was able to turn down Allen's proposition. He was working hard on his personal issues and his extracurricular activities with the help of living with Mrs. Burroughs. He didn't want a repeat of Calvin. His focus was to get Cameron back in his life. He needed to ensure nothing else could come up about him which would jeopardize his reconciliation with Cameron. Monti thought Cameron needed to see he was truly changing and the change was for the best.

Monti didn't mind telling others about Cameron wanting to talk about getting back together, because he had to think optimistically. Truth of the matter is he didn't know why Cameron wanted to talk to him at this point. He just was glad the lines of communication would be open even if it was just going to be for one more night. That was enough to give Monti some glimmer of hope.

CHAPTER FOURTEEN-CAMERON

"I don't know why Monti wanted me to meet him at this Red Lobster." Cameron said as he got out of his car. He walked into the restaurant and was greeted by an overly chipper hostess.

"Good afternoon. I'm here to meet someone." Cameron said.

"I think I know exactly who he is. Is he tall and handsome?"

"If that's how you describe him." Cameron said dryly.

"Please follow me." She said as she walked into the dining room. "How is your weekend going so far?"

"It is going well. Thanks for asking. What about yours?"

"I'm doing well here also. I'm just working my way through school."

"That's nice. What are you studying?"

"Fashion design." She said proudly.

"That's a competitive field. How much longer do you have?"

"I have about a year left."

"I'm sure you will do just fine." Cameron said as they arrived to a table in the back of the restaurant where Monti was sitting.

"Here you go, Sir."

"Thank you very much." Cameron said as he sat down across from Monti. He could tell Monti was happy to see him.

"You are very welcome. Enjoy your meal Sir." She said as she returned to her hostess stand in the front of the restaurant.

"Cameron, I'm glad you agreed to meet me here today." Monti said.

"Okay Monti. How have you been?" Cameron replied trying to be cordial.

"I've been worried about you, babe. I kept calling you hoping you would answer the phone."

"Monti, I'm a big boy. I don't need you to worry about me, and for the sake of this conversation, my name is Cameron, not babe." Cameron said brining Monti back to the reality of the situation.

"Okay Babe…I mean Cameron. It is going to be hard for me but I will try to do my best to give you that."

"Thanks. What is it you want to talk about?"

"Good afternoon gentlemen. I'm Marcus and I will be your server today. Can I start you off with something to drink or an appetizer?"

"I will have a margarita on the rocks with no salt or sugar."

Cameron ordered.

"And for you Sir?" Marcus asked Monti.

"That sounds good. I will have mine with a salted rim though." Monti replied.

"Okay, let me go put this in and I will give you some time to look over the menu. Again, my name is Marcus."

"Thanks Marcus." Monti said as Marcus made his way over to the POS terminal.

"So again Monti, what do you want to talk about? I'm ready to put this fiasco of lies and deceit behind me."

"Cameron, I just wanted to tell you I'm so sorry for all the hurt, pain and embarrassment I put you through. I know you are a good guy and you didn't deserve anything I put you through."

"I have to agree with you on that statement Monti. I didn't deserve to be lied to, cheated on or embarrassed."

"I don't know what it is I could do to make this up to you. You are my heart Cameron. I've beat myself up since that day. I've thought about the situation and replayed it time and time again to figure out I could have handled it better."

"How about being honest and truthful? Wasn't that the things you were so adamant about me being?"

"I know…I wanted to tell you Cameron. I really did. I was being blackmailed by this guy. I didn't know what he wanted. He kept…"

"Please don't go there. I don't need a play by play about what happened. You shouldn't have been in those places to have this happen. So you are ready to be honest with me, right?"

"Yes, Cameron. I'm willing to do what I have to do to make this right."

"So tell me something, how many times did you cheat on me during our six month relationship?"

"Cameron, do we really have to go there?"

"No Monti. We don't have to go there. It was so not nice seeing you again." Cameron said as he stood up to leave.

"No, Cameron wait!" Monti said trying to salvage the meeting. "If I'm going to be honest with you, I would have to say it was about four times." Monti said. "Four times."

"For the purpose of this meeting, if at any point you don't want to answer or choose not to answer any question I ask, the meeting will be over and I will leave with no hesitation." Cameron said sitting back down. "When was the first time?"

"Gentlemen, here are the drinks you ordered. Were you ready to order?" Marcus asked.

"No, we haven't looked at the menu just yet Marcus. I know you have some other tables right now so when we are ready, how about I get your attention." Cameron said smiling. He was pissed off but didn't want to take it out on the handsome server.

"You got it Sir." He replied.

"You can call me Cameron."

"No problem Mr. Cameron." He said as he walked away.

"Now back to my question Monti." Cameron said directing

his attention back to Monti.

Monti lowered his head in shame. "The night before you flew to Amsterdam."

"When we went to the movies?"

"Yes."

"Monti we weren't even in a committed relationship at that time. Don't you remember we didn't commit to a monogamous situation till around your graduation?" Cameron said as he sipped his drink.

"You did tell me you were monogamous since we first met though. Why do you feel it is necessary to lie? I was with you because I wanted to be with you, not because of your past." Cameron said.

"Babe…" Monti started. "I mean Cameron, I don't know. I wanted to tell you everything. I wanted to be honest with you but I just felt embarrassed about the whole situation."

"Was this with one guy or multiple guys?" Cameron asked.

"Multiple guys, Cameron." Monti answered.

"Do you remember when I told you there was something in your eyes that I knew you were hiding? I knew there was something there, maybe I couldn't put my finger on it, but I opened the door for you to tell me what was going on, but you refused to walk through it."

"Cameron, I was just getting to know you. I'm a private person and people didn't know my business."

"Monti, you are only private in your own head. People know who you are. People know what you do. If they didn't then how were you exposed? I should have never learned anything about you from other people. I should have gotten that from you."

"I can't argue that point. You are absolutely right. The only thing I can say is I'm sorry. I realize I made a mess of this situation. I also know I love you and your absence this past month has been hell for me. I think about you all the time. I wonder if you are with someone else. I wonder if you are smiling. I wonder if you will ever forgive me. I wonder if you will ever look at me with love in your eyes. You had love for me once before and I know love just doesn't disappear."

"Monti after you have lied so much, I don't know what to believe. I do know I'm seriously pissed at you for both living a lie and telling lies. Well, maybe you lived enough lies they became your truth. I don't know. Hell, I don't even know why I even returned your call. I don't see how this is going to fix anything." Cameron said.

Normally Cameron was one to work through a situation. He was one to show compassion and acceptance which he learned from Guy. Seeing Monti for the first time after the revelation proved to be a challenge for Cameron. He hated to be angry because he knew he held grudges, but he knew something in him made him agree to meeting Monti.

"When you called me, that Sunday, I felt like nothing. My world had just crashed. My foundation was shattered." Monti said.

"How do you think I felt?" Cameron said. "What do you want from me Montague Burroughs?"

"Cameron the only thing I want is for you to take time to think about what I'm saying. I love you. I'm in love with you. I don't want no one else but you. I realize the err of my ways and I'm taking the steps to fix those. I started seeing a therapist and I'm facing my demons. Do you remember telling me I needed to address them before they consumed our relationship? Well I'm doing that. I'm doing that for you…for us, because I have faith we will get back together."

"Well, at least one of us does."

"Cameron, don't close your heart to me. Please just stay open and let me show you how I have changed. Let me show you how I can be a better partner. Let me show you I can be the man you want to spend the rest of your life with."

"What if I cheated on you? Would you say the same thing? What if I lied to you? Would you be so forgiving?"

"I can't say what I would have done then. I know I deserve that, Cameron. I'm asking that you don't do those things though because doing them would be adding more problems to our already full plate."

"You are making the assumption that we even have a plate to add something to." Cameron said.

"Cameron, you wouldn't have come here if you were completely through with me. If you didn't have any feelings for me you would have walked away never looking back. You asked me to be honest with you, so please for the sake of your own integrity, be honest with yourself. You didn't want our relationship to end. Something happened and you unfortunately were caught in the cross fire of it. That never changed my love for you. That never changed the fact that I'm in love with you and want only you."

Cameron had an onslaught of emotions he was feeling. He wanted to be angry. He wanted to hate Monti. He wanted to hurt him, but when he looked into Monti's eyes, he knew Monti was hurting just as much as he was. Cameron pulled out of his wallet and pulled out a twenty dollar bill.

"I'm sure this will cover my portion of the bill. I have to go." Cameron said.

"Don't leave me here like this Cameron." Monti pleaded.

"I have to go." Cameron said as he turned wiping the tears that were forming in his eyes. He walked to the door, seeing the restroom he went into the bathroom. In the restroom, he washed his face and gathered his composure. He gave himself a once over in the mirror and walked out of the restroom. He saw the hostess on his way out.

"I wanted to tell you I hope you are successful in your educational pursuits."

"Thank you Sir. I appreciate that."

"Would you mind if I gave you my card. I have a friend who is involved in the fashion industry and she may be able to assist you on your way."

"Wow. No, I wouldn't mind at all." She said.

Cameron reached into his wallet and took out a business card and handed it to her. "I'm Cameron."

"Thanks Mr. Cameron. It is a pleasure to meet you. My name is Adrienne."

"Pleasure is all mine. You have a great attitude and outlook. Give me a call sometime this week and I will put you in touch with my best friend Shaine."

"Thank you so much, Mr. Cameron."

"You are welcome." Cameron shook her hand as he turned to leave the restaurant. At least someone was happy today he thought as he got in his vehicle and went home.

CHAPTER FIFTEEN-YOLANDA

"Hello?"

"Hey Sweetheart. How are you doing?"

"I'm good. I'm excited."

"Oh. Are you now?"

"Yes Roderick. You know how excited I'm to be going to the Earth Wind & Fire concert. I can't believe you got tickets. This show was sold out months ago."

"Yolanda, I told you I'm so into you. This past month, I have been so happy. I'm glad that we met." Roderick said.

"I feel the same way. I haven't felt this alive in a long time. You have restored hope in a sister."

"That's what I love about you. I love that you haven't let what happened to you keep you scared to open up to me and trust me. You make me the happiest man in Detroit."

"Aww thanks Roderick. I'm glad to know you feel that way. Let me get off here so I can be ready when you get here. How far away are you?"

"I should be there in fifteen minutes."

"Ok, I will be ready. The kids' dad should be here any minute to pick them up for the weekend, so we are all set."

"Sounds like a plan. I will see you soon, Beautiful." Roderick said.

"Good-bye."

Yolanda put the final touches on her outfit for the concert. She grabbed her overnight bag and put her toiletries in to last her through the weekend. She couldn't remember when the last time she felt appreciated. She felt loved and that feeling woke up her sex drive. Her body wanted Roderick's attention. She honestly believed Roderick was sincere in his feelings because he always put her first. His was the first voice she heard in the mornings and the last at night. They had been on several dates and he was a perfect gentleman. They shared some passionate kisses and foreplay but they had yet to cross that sexual boundary. Yolanda felt she was ready to welcome that level to the relationship.

"Boys make sure you have all your things ready. Don't keep your dad waiting."

"We are all packed, Mom." Corey said.

"Okay, that's good. Don't you boys give your dad a hard time." Yolanda instructed.

"Mom, we aren't little kids. We will be fine." Corey replied.

"I'm just reminding you." She said as the doorbell rang.

"I'll get it." Monti Jr. said.

He opened the door anticipating seeing his dad.

"Hi, Monti. How are you doing?" Roderick said.

"I'm doing fine, Mr. Roderick. How are you doing?"

"I'm doing great. It is good to see you again."

"You too." Monti replied. "Mom, Mr. Roderick is here."

"Okay. Here I come." She replied.

Roderick took a seat on the couch in the living room. He appreciated how Corey and Monti Jr. embraced him. He'd heard of stories of people not being accepted by children from a previous relationship, but Yolanda's boys were okay with him seeing their mother. He was sitting down when the front door opened.

"Who are you?" Monti said as he walked into Yolanda's apartment.

"I'm Roderick. You are Monti, I assume?"

"Yes." Monti replied.

"Hi Dad. This is Mr. Roderick, Mom's boyfriend." Monti Jr said proudly.

"Oh…" Monti was lost for words. He knew Yolanda had been nicer to him lately but he didn't know why she was being nice. Now he understood. "Are you two ready to go?" He asked the boys.

"Yes Dad. We were waiting for you." Corey said.

"Okay then, let's go." He replied. "Nice to meet you Roderick." Monti said as he went back out the door. Monti found he was jealous realizing Yolanda had really moved on. He knew the day would come eventually; however seeing it for the first time he realized her love for him had expired. The boys soon had caught up with him and were putting their bags into the Jeep. He got in the Jeep and soon they were gone.

"Hey baby. I'm ready." Yolanda said walking out of her bedroom.

"Wow. You look more stunning each and every time I see you. I keep telling you how lucky of a man I'm."

"Aren't you a charmer?" Yolanda replied.

"Here let me take that bag for you." Roderick took her overnight bag and set it on the loveseat. "Before we go…I want a kiss from my lady."

They both exchanged a passionate kiss. The chemistry between the two of them was visible to others they had been around. Yolanda felt complete when she was with Roderick. She was falling for him and falling fast.

"Are you ready to get away for the weekend?"

"Yes, I'm ready to go anywhere you want to take me."

"We will see about that." Roderick replied with a smile.

* * * * *

Roderick and Yolanda enjoyed the concert and were on cloud nine when they arrived at the Westin Hotel. Roderick wanted to spend some quality time with Yolanda this weekend away from either of their homes. He had planned spa treatments, room service and other amenities from the hotel's concierge.

They were at their suite door when he gave Yolanda the room key. She went in and was in awe of the suite, complete with Jacuzzi hot tub. The flowers and chocolate were waiting for Yolanda as she walked through the room. Roderick went over to the wet bar and opened the bottle of Champagne which was chilling on ice.

"This is so nice, Roderick." She said.

"This is just a way for me to show you just how much I care for you and want you in my life."

Yolanda walked over to him and gave him a hug. "I want to keep you in my life too."

"I'm glad." Roderick said.

"I'm going to go freshen up. I will be right back."

"I will be here waiting for you." He replied.

Yolanda went into the exquisite bathroom and undressed. She had packed some lingerie she purchased from Victoria's Secret. She was ready to give all of herself to Roderick. She brushed her teeth and sprayed a little Izzy Miyake perfume on. She looked in the bathroom mirror to make sure she looked her best. Her size two frame and flat stomach looked nice. She had some curves and she hoped Roderick was going to like what he saw when she walked back into the room. She took a deep breath and turned the bathroom door knob. When she opened the door, she noticed Roderick had dimmed the lighting in the room and lit some candles. She also heard Anita Baker's rendition of *Lead Me Into Love* playing. He'd also placed red rose petals on the bed. She looked at him wearing nothing but his black Nautica boxer briefs. His body was nice looking and Yolanda had nothing to complain about.

"Well, look what we have here." He said to her. "Bring all that sexiness over here, Baby."

Yolanda's insecurities faded immediately. She was affirmed and knew Roderick approved of what he saw. She walked over to where he was. He stood up as she got closer to him. He opened his arms and hugged her lingerie-clothed body. His hands glided over her skin resting on her lower back. He kissed her as he let his hands caress up and down her spine. As they continued to kiss, she didn't object when his hands cupped her ass.

Yolanda wrapped her arms around his neck and leaned into his bare chest. He leaned in and pressed his lips against her neck, invading her unguarded personal boundaries. He smelled her sweet fragrant skin. As he kissed her neck, she clenched his back, letting out light breathy sounds. He continued to use his lips to explore her neck and shoulders. His lips felt warm and soft causing sensual arousal as he continued to kiss her equally soft skin. His sensual and soft touch caused her to press into him. She could feel his arousal against her stomach. Her lingerie and his boxer briefs were the only thing keeping them from getting what they had waited so long to feel.

Roderick's arousal turned on Yolanda's sexual instinct. Breathing heavily, she let her hands feel Roderick's arms and shoulders. She continued down his torso and rested her hands on his firm ass. She slipped her hands in the waistband of his boxer briefs and touched his excitement. Eyes closed, she bit her lower lip thinking about how perfectly strong his manhood felt in her hands. She wrapped her hands around it feeling the girth of his now fully erectness. He let out a light deep moan as he allowed his tongue to taste her ears.

Yolanda decided to return the lip service she'd just received. On her tippy toes, her lips traversed along his jaw line and down his neck returning up over the edge of his ear. She squeezed his stiffness as she felt it pulse back. Her lips found his slightly open mouth and he kissed her again.

Roderick's hands found the back of Yolanda's bra and skillfully unhooked the fasteners. In one swift move, he raised her arms simultaneously removing her bra. He took the bra and brought it up to his nose to smell her sweetness, before dropping it to the ground. He cupped her breasts in his hands as he stepped back to admire her femininity.

"You are beautiful, baby." He said as he stepped closer to her and bent down to kiss her breasts. She exhaled feeling the warmth of his mouth on her breast. She took her hands and pulled his head into her bosom. He took time to pay attention to her dark nipples, rolling them over his tongue sucking them. The gentleness of his touch made Yolanda moist. She hadn't had sexual relations in almost two years.

Roderick stepped into Yolanda as she leaned back into the bed. He held her until she lay on the rose petals. She felt the coolness of the petals on her now hot and aroused skin. Roderick alternated between her breasts and her lips. Every time moved from her breasts to her lips, she felt his sex rub up against her clitoris.

"Tonight is your night, baby. I just want to make you feel satisfied." Roderick whispered into Yolanda's ear. He reached his fingers around her laced panties and felt the heat of her pot of goodness. He rubbed her sex and Yolanda let out some sounds of pleasure. He took his fingers and brought them to his nose and inhaled. Her scent was intoxicating to him. "You smell just right." He said as he slid her panties down her legs.

He got on his knees before her and kissed her starting from her navel making his way down to her pussy. He loved the clean taste of her moistness. She spread her legs, giving him unobstructed access. She arched her back as he slid his tongue into the depths of her tight walls. Moans of ecstasy escaped from her parted lips as she grabbed her breasts.

She felt her tension building as he licked her clitoris for what seemed like an eternity. The feel of his moustache on her shaved pussy felt good to her. As the walls of her sex began to drip, he made sure his tongue caught it. Yolanda was feeling good as she began to ride his tongue. She held his head in place as she felt a wave of pleasure travel up her spine. She had goose bumps over her entire body. Soon she felt the tension build in her stronger. She knew she was close to coming.

"Roderick?" She said between gasps of breath.

"Yes baby." He replied.

"I'm close."

"Okay Baby." He said as he slipped his fingers in her tightness while his mouth worked her clitoris. "I want your cum, Baby. I promise I won't waste a drop."

He continued to alternate between his thick fingers and his strong tongue. He was licking to the thrust of Yolanda's pelvic muscles. He felt her vaginal muscles tighten around his fingers. Soon Yolanda felt a heat building within her starting from her sex. The tension began to get stronger and stronger. Roderick kept his unrelenting oral attack on her. It was everything he imagined it would be. Soon Yolanda felt contractions coming from the tension, sending the ripple effect of her orgasm radiating through her body. She let a "Yes" come from her mouth. She came and her love juice ran down the walls her pussy and into Roderick's hungry mouth. He drank every drop Yolanda gave him.

"Perfect." He said with a smile on his face.

Still shaking, Yolanda laid in the bed with a smile on her face as Roderick climbed in the bed next to her and held her in his arms. Soon sleep found both of them. Roderick held Yolanda the entire night. He was satisfied even though he didn't cum; knowing he pleased Yolanda was enough to carry him.

CHAPTER SIXTEEN-SHAINE

"Hey honey. How are you doing?" Shaine asked as she answered the phone.

"I'm okay. Did I disturb you?"

"No Cameron, you didn't. What is going on?

"I met Monti about a month ago for lunch." Cameron started to tell Shaine.

"A month ago? And you are just now telling me?

"Well it isn't that I was trying to keep anything from you but I just had to think about some things. Getting adjusted to work and other things. I decided to take my time."

"What happened? What did he have to say about the situation?"

"First, he said he has been worried about me since the incident happened. He talked about how sorry he was for how the situation happened and said I didn't deserve what happened."

"I will agree with that statement." Shaine said.

"He said he wanted to make it up to me and said he was willing to do whatever he had to do to make it right."

"He wants to make up for what he did?"

"I asked him how many times he cheated and he told me it was four times with four different people. I tend to believe that's a lie. He probably had more. He was messing around with people even before we were serious, while telling me he was seeing only me. I wasn't happy at all.

"Honestly Cameron, why did you go to see him?"

"I guess I still have feelings for him. What happened was like sudden death. I didn't have time to grieve the loss of the relationship. I didn't have the opportunity to get closure to the relationship. I know that sounds crazy but it is how I feel about it."

"You are going to have to deal with it in the way you know how to. I know people all have their say in how you should cope with it but at the heart of the matter is your heart. You have to follow your heart in how you should deal with it. Just know at the end of the day, he is a liar and a cheater. God knows what else he has done."

"Thanks. You always know the right thing to say. Enough about me and my drama, how are things with you and Jonathan going?"

"You wouldn't believe how well things are panning out with us. We have been on a few dates and he is the perfect gentleman. He has a strong story to tell about his upbringing. Cameron, I think this is the one. Though he is well off, he is so down to earth. I think he is the man I have been praying for."

"That's good to hear. So when am I going to meet this man?"

"Hopefully soon. Maybe if you'd answered my calls, you would have met him by now." Shaine said.

"I'm good Shaine. I will do better. You know I'm cut from good cloth."

"We both are, so we will make it happen really soon."

"Great. I have to run some errands today so I'm not going to keep you." Cameron said.

"Alright. No problem. We will talk soon."

"Okay." Cameron said. "Oh yeah, one more thing Shaine."

"What's up?"

"I met this lovely young lady who is in school for Fashion. I got her information because I thought you could help her maybe by doing an internship or something like that. Her name is Adrienne. I think she will be a good fit with you."

"Oh really. Let me find out you are recruiting for me. Give me her information and we will see what is up with her." Shaine said.

Cameron gave Shaine the contact information for Adrienne and they made plans for Sunday Brunch. Shaine said she would invite Jonathan so the two of them could meet.

* * * * *

Shaine decided she should try to contact Adrienne to see if they would be able to talk about how Shaine could help her along with her career.

"Hi, is this Adrienne?"

"Yes, this is she. Who is calling?"

"This is Shaine Holloway. I got your information from Cameron McNeil."

"Oh wow. It is an honor to hear from you. I thought Mr. McNeil forgot about me."

"He has a lot on his plate. I just got your information about five to ten minutes ago. I hear you are studying fashion in school. Is that correct?"

"Yes, I'm. I'm almost finished and was looking for some guidance or some leads on how to gain some real-life experiences that would help me find a job after school. I like working with people but being a host at a restaurant isn't my ideal job."

"I understand where you are coming from. Have you thought about maybe interning with a polished fashion professional?"

"Yes, I have approached some of the major retailers but haven't had much luck."

"Well I would like to help you. I'm a divisional merchandise and planning manager for Macy's. I could pull some strings and bring you on as an intern in our merchandising department. Is that something you would be interested in?"

"I can't believe my ears. That would be great. What types of things would I be learning about?"

"You would be exposed to the management of a multi-million dollar corporate retail company, which will give you experience in the various aspects of retail. You will deal with product development, pricing, both financial and location analysis, and advertising. I can potentially give you experience in visual merchandising and even potentially have you work with some of our designers as maybe a designer assistant or assistant buyer. If there was a particular part of the industry you wanted to experience, we could potentially see if we can get you exposure to those areas as well."

"Ms. Holloway, you can't possibly understand how much this means to me. I'm very interested in this opportunity."

"Great. I like to pay it forward. I worked hard to get to where I'm and if I can help others on their journey in retail fashion, then I'm doing my industry justice. I seek perfection and will push you to be your very best. You may be mad at me many days but that's the nature of the business. Just know it is for the best of the company and your professional development."

"Thank you so much." Adrienne said.

"What I will need from you is your CV and a copy of your current transcripts. I will work with human resources to make sure I don't need anything else. I will give you a call if there is something else I need. If not, I will look forward to calling you with your start date soon. If you have any questions or concerns between now and then please let me know."

"Thank you again." Adrienne said.

Shaine gave Adrienne all the contact information she would need. Feeling as though she did her good deed for the day, Shaine decided she needed some time off and a half day at the spa would serve her well. Before she wrapped up, she wanted to call her man. Something about Jonathan's voice did something to Shaine. She enjoyed dating him. He was everything she wanted in a partner. Since they have been dating, they haven't missed their nightly calls each other before they went to bed. Shaine decided to call him.

"Hey beautiful. How are you doing?" Jonathan answered.

"Hi baby. I'm doing well. How is your day going?"

"It is going…it has been busy but I'm making it through. What about yours?"

"My day is going well. I needed to take a break so I called to set an appointment for a massage and facial."

"That sounds great. I need to look into getting a massage myself."

"You should come. I'm sure it will help you.

"Honey, I can't do it today. I have some more meetings through eight o'clock this evening. How about I have my assistant call and schedule us a Saturday pamper day. I will have her call you and you can tell her what you want and she will make it happen." Jonathan suggested.

"Okay, that sounds good. I want you to come with me for Sunday brunch. My best friend Cameron and I do that regularly and I think you should meet him."

"If that's going to make you happy, I'm happy to do that."

"Okay. Call me when you are leaving work, so I know everything is ok."

"You got it. Enjoy your afternoon. You work hard and you deserve it."

"Bye." Jonathan said.

CHAPTER SEVENTEEN-MONTI

"Hey Cameron. I know you said you needed time to think about things and you would call me soon so I wanted to give you some time."

"I know. I appreciate that you haven't been blowing my phone up. I have been thinking about what we talked about at the restaurant."

"I have been too. I hope you can find it in your heart to give me another chance…give us another chance. It has been a month since we met at the restaurant."

"Monti, I'm not sure I can do that. I don't care who was before me as long as I know there is no one during me. Unfortunately, you allowed your past to become a part of our future. You also had others during the time we were supposed to be exclusive and monogamous while at the same time you were trying to keep tabs on me. I would be the fool to allow you to run this game on me again."

"You can't be serious Cameron. We have a history and we have love for each other. The six months we were together meant nothing to you?"

"It isn't that the six months haven't meant anything. Your indiscretions showed me they didn't mean anything to you. Your true colors being showed to me and all the people who got those photos, doesn't make me comfortable."

"Cameron you have to believe I didn't intentionally do this. I didn't want this to happen like it did."

"Monti, you didn't intentionally go to the park? You didn't intentionally fuck a guy? You just fell into a piece of ass?"

"Cameron, you already know the answer to those questions." Monti responded.

"I have to be upfront and honest with you. I'm not sure what else you are capable of and because I don't feel I can trust you. I can honestly say I don't even know who you are. I can't be in a relationship with you."

"I know this is a lot to take in. I know, because I lived through it as well. I'm working on myself. I have been seeing a therapist now, because I know I need to sort through this situation and find myself. I want to have you by my side through this."

"Monti you don't need me by your side to get through this. You lived through your own lies catching up to you. You should have worked on yourself before we got serious. How could you possibly think we could have a substantial relationship built on lies?"

"Cameron, babe, listen. I'm stronger with you. I'm a better man when I'm with you. We are supposed to be together. We are supposed to grow old together. I didn't want a relationship when you and I met. You brought out that side of me. I just want to be able to show you, how good of a man I can be for you. I want to make this up to you. I'm so sorry." Monti said as his voice began to crack.

"Monti, you have painted a beautiful picture of this relationship. I'm sorry, but the picture you painted doesn't have a frame. You have given me pure lip service. You actions are what I have to go by. History can be repeated if I don't learn my lesson. The lesson I learned is if a man will lie to you, he will cheat on you. If he will cheat on you, he will steal from you. You know how the saying goes. You have lied and cheated on me already. I can't let you steal the essence of who I'm. I can't let you turn my heart cold. The problem I see with people like you is you are solely thinking about your own well-being. You never stopped to consider how your infidelities would impact my life. I take the time to think about you and how my actions affect you. This is a one way relationship and unfortunately I need it to be a two-way. You started off all wrong and I hope you take this as a lesson learned."

"You are just going to throw us away."

"No, you threw us away the first day we met, when you lied about your name. You threw us away when you were screwing those guys. You threw us away when you refused to be open and honest. You threw us away. Was there ever really an 'us'? I don't even know the answer to that question. I just as soon let the past stay in the past, where yours should have stayed. I wish you the best. I'm moving on with my life to find the guy who is right for me. You have proven you aren't him. I'm not going to waste any more of my time on this subject. I'm going to let you go."

"I'm going to get you back, Cameron. Remember this conversation. I will show you that I'm changed and am right for you."

"Monti, don't waste your time with that. Work on yourself so you don't keep making the same mistakes. Good-bye Monti."

"I'll see to you soon." Monti replied as he hung up the phone.

"How could he be so cold? I'm going to make him see he needs me." Monti said aloud as he paced the floor. "I made some mistakes but he can't just throw me out like some dirty bath water." Monti began thinking irrationally.

* * * * *

"Mr. Burroughs, have you heard of borderline personality disorder before?"

"No, Dr. Carlyle, I haven't. What is it?"

"Borderline personality disorder is a mental health condition which causes a person affected by it to have unstable moods, behaviors and relationships. Most people who suffer from this particular disorder have problems regulating their emotions and thoughts; they have impulsive and reckless behavior and generally have difficulty in relationships. Do you recall ever having high anxiety or depression?"

"I have been depressed and do have anxiety sometimes. I have even had panic attacks before." Monti replied. "So are you saying I have this personality thing?"

"I would say, based on your intake forms and our last five sessions, I'm comfortable with a borderline personality disorder diagnosis."

"So you are saying I'm crazy?"

"No, I'm not saying you are crazy Mr. Burroughs. I'm saying the reason you are having all these difficulties in life, work, and love is because you have this mental health condition. The good news is by understanding what is going on, you will be able to understand yourself better and be able to better navigate life. That's the goal. Borderline personality disorder has been known to be difficult to treat, but research shows it can be treated and you can improve over time."

Monti sat on the couch in Dr. Carlyle's office. He felt a sense of relief and anxiety at the same time. He liked that he now knew what was wrong with him but didn't like that there was something wrong with him. He had a barrage of questions for Dr. Carlyle but he didn't know where to start. "What are some symptoms of borderline disorder, or whatever it is called?"

"In your case, you describe a history of intense and stormy relationships with multiple people, your relationship with your father and brothers, your relationships with other men, as well as your wife. You have described you have problems with abandonment. In your relationship with Cameron, you didn't like him going to work because you thought he was going to leave you for someone else. This is a normal process in most people's lives, they work and sometimes their jobs take them away. You spoke of having anxiety and depression which often comes along with this disorder."

"Is that all?" Monti asked.

"One thing which really sticks out is your impulsive and dangerous sexual behaviors. You present with mood swings. Even in our sessions, I have noticed you going from mild to raging and then joyous. Typically, minor incidents cause larger reactions. Currently, you are describing your feelings of emptiness without Cameron in your life. These symptoms are classic, textbook borderline personality disorder."

"So how did I get this?"

"Research shows borderline personality disorder is strongly inherited."

"So, do I have to take crazy pills for this?"

"Not necessarily. There are many different options for treatment. Sometimes a combination of psychotropic meds and psychotherapy are used. The meds are used to help you manage certain symptoms. In your case, I would like to continue to use psychotherapy. You indicated you aren't currently seeing any other medical professional for any other issues. This makes it easier. If you do have other situations going on, I would need to know about those and who is treating you so we can coordinate care. If you ultimately need meds, I will refer you to a psychiatrist who I work closely with. Right now, it is best to stick with our psychotherapy. There will be times when you won't particularly care for me just know we are in this together working to ensure you are able to live a better quality of life."

"Okay. I think I can do this."

"I have confidence you will be able to as well. Do you have any other questions for me right now?"

"Not right now. I'm sure as I think about this, I will have more questions."

"Very well! Are we still okay for this day and time moving forward?"

"Yes, it works well for me."

"Then I will see you next week, Mr. Burroughs."

"Thanks Doc." Monti said.

CHAPTER EIGHTEEN-CAMERON

"Hello?"

"Hey Cameron. How are you doing?"

"What's going on Calvin? How have you been? Hell, where have you been? I left you messages, you left me messages and now we finally are able to connect."

"Man, I have been busy working and stuff. After I got back from Atlanta, I have been running man. What has life dealt you lately?"

"I feel you on being busy. Man, so much has happened. I wanted to talk to you about some stuff that happened with Monti and me."

"Oh really! What happened?" Calvin asked.

"The weekend you were gone to Atlanta's pride, I got an envelope after church from some guy. It had some photos of Monti in a precarious position. I can't believe he was cheating on me all this time."

"Man, I'm so sorry to hear about that. How did you handle it?"

"I broke it off with him. Calvin, you don't know how hurt I was. I had been asking him to be honest and open with me but he refused. I don't even know the full spectrum of all he was doing, but what I do know is more than I'm willing to put up with."

"Sorry you had to be in that situation Cameron. You are a good guy and you deserve more than what he could ever be able to give you."

"How do you know so much about Monti?"

"I'm going to be honest with you Cameron. I want you to know I think you are a cool guy and I want to continue to develop a friendship with you. Are you sure you are ready for this honesty?"

"Yes Calvin. I'm ready. How do you know Monti?" Cameron replied as he sat on his couch.

"Okay…Monti used to date my cousin, David. He lied to him, said he was leaving his wife to be with David. That was the furthest thing from the truth. Monti had strung him along. David broke it off with him after he saw him with his wife and kids in the mall. Monti stalked David to the point where David had to get a job out of the country to get away from him."

"Are you serious?"

"Yes. I'm serious. My cousin had to seek professional help to deal with the hurt and the betrayal. He still lives out of the state to ensure he doesn't have any run ins with Monti."

"Wow, this is a small world. I'm so sorry to hear about your cousin. I hope he is better."

"He is good man. We were close since we were kids. We happened to both be gay but I'm stronger than him in some regards. He was picked on as a kid and I stuck up for him."

"Sounds like you both are very close. So why didn't you tell me about him before now?"

"I didn't want to get in your business, seeing that you and I just met."

"You did get in my business technically. You had me ask him questions; and based on that, I was on alert. Something just didn't feel right and I couldn't put my finger on it."

"I'm glad you saw him and his secret life. You don't deserve someone who frequents parks, bookstores and bathhouses while trying to make you be faithful to him."

"What did you just say?" Cameron asked. Remembering the note inside the manila envelope he received on revelation Sunday.

"Cameron, I asked you were you ready for this honesty."

"And I said yes I was ready for it. But I have this strange feeling you are about to drop a bomb on me. I think I know but is there something else you are going to tell me?"

"Do you want to know the whole story or do you just want to know he was exposed for who he is?"

Cameron sat quietly contemplating his next question. "Calvin…tell me you didn't have anything to do with this."

"I can't tell you that."

"You can't tell me that because…"

"Because I'm not a liar and if I told you that Cameron…I'd be lying."

Cameron thought about what he had heard. Did he want to know more? Did he already know enough? Something in Cameron knew he wasn't going to stop at just a piece of the puzzle. "Okay Calvin. Just give it to me straight. I'm a big guy and can handle this. I have an inkling what you are going to say."

"I really want to get to know you better Cameron. Trust me when I say you were not specifically known of when we initially started this plan."

"What did you do?" Cameron questioned.

"The photos you received of Monti in the park…were of Monti and me."

Cameron's jaw dropped. He wanted to hang up the phone but he couldn't. He was speechless. He felt as though the wind was knocked out of his lungs. Hundreds of thoughts ran through Cameron's head.

"Cameron…Are you there?"

"Yes, I'm here. I'm sorry. You just dropped a whole lot of…something…on me just now."

"I know. I hope you will understand. Monti had to be exposed. I didn't want him to continue to lie and hurt others like he did David."

"You knew he was with me though."

"I didn't know who he was dating initially. I didn't know he was even in a relationship when I found him in the park that night. I had been going to the park periodically for a couple months hoping to find him. I was leaving the park the night he showed up. I followed him back in. He didn't see me initially. I waited in the darkness as I watched him as he leaned lean up against a fallen tree. The arrogance he had, made me know I had to fulfil the plan."

Cameron could hear the disdain in Calvin's voice. "The plan? Did you do this by yourself or did you have help?"

"I will get to that. When I saw him…I knew he had to be taught a lesson. I texted my boy who had went to the other side of the park and told him where we were. Once he texted me back saying he was in place, I walked over to Monti. He didn't even turn around to see who was touching him…almost as if he was entitled to be taken care of. Cameron, it took all that was in my power not to jump on him right there in the park. I knew I had to go through with the plan." Calvin said.

"What plan Calvin?" Cameron asked.

"The plan was I had sex with him while someone else took pictures so we could expose him. He bad mouthed my cousin and ruined his reputation at work so I had to do the same thing, even if it meant I had to sleep with him myself to get him."

"You would sleep with someone you didn't like to get photos of him to expose him?" Cameron questioned.

"Hell yeah. I told my boy to make sure I couldn't be recognized in the photos but so that he would be completely recognizable. After looking through the photos, we chose the ones I knew that he wouldn't be able to deny. If the photos were not good enough, I knew he would deny it. I made sure to keep him in front of me or have my back to the tree line so it would just be him."

"This is some crazy shit, for real." Cameron said.

"I know it sounds crazy, Cameron. I never meant to hurt you at all…I didn't know you then and I didn't know who he was dating at the time. You and I have had a couple conversations and I knew you were a cool guy. I knew you didn't need to be with the likes of Monti."

"So who came and gave me the envelope?" Cameron asked.

"My best friend Harper gave you that. He lives in Chicago but is a go to person when public figures have scandals break. He helps them do damage control and turn things out in their favor."

"Wow. This is crazy."

"So, now you know the truth. Are you mad at me?"

"Calvin, I can't say I'm mad at you. I have thought over and over whether I should be mad at the ones who did this or should I thank them. I'm not closer to an answer for the question today as I was then. I just know I needed to know the information but I'm not sure I agree with the method of how it was done."

"That's understandable. Cameron, just know I didn't do this for your benefit. It was originally to even the score for my cousin. When I met you, I knew you were a good guy and knew that fool wasn't on your level. You deserve someone who is honest and trustworthy. I hope we can continue to cultivate this friendship and you don't waste one more day dealing with this crazy muthafucker."

"We agree on that. I wouldn't go on to say he is a crazy mofo but I will say I don't need to waste another day dealing with it. I'm cool getting to know you better; you may be a good resource and a better person to have on my side than against me." Cameron joked.

"Cool. So how about we go out and have drinks this weekend?"

"Okay, just let me know where and what time. I will be there."

"Great Cameron. Let me get off this phone and head out to the gym. Gotta keep this body tight."

"Yes you do that. A tight body is always a good thing. From what I saw, your body is straight up. I will catch up with you later."

"Bet." Calvin said as he hung up the phone.

Cameron couldn't wrap his head around this. He knew Monti must have done something extreme with David to make him move out of the country to get away from him. It saddened Cameron to know that Monti, with so much potential, would be so damaged he would hurt those he was supposed to be close to.

CHAPTER NINETEEN-YOLANDA

"Boys?" Yolanda called out.

"Yes Mom." Corey answered as he and Monti Jr came into Yolanda's bedroom.

"I want you both to know I love you very much. I'm glad you have stuck by me through the tough times. This Thanksgiving, we are going to Mr. Roderick's house, so I wanted you to both think of what we should take over there."

"Oh cool." Monti Jr. said. "I like Mr. Roderick. He is nice and he makes you smile."

Yolanda reached out and hugged Monti. "He does and I haven't been this happy in a long time, but you two will always be my favorites though. Don't tell no one though. That's our secret."

"Oh Mom, you know that isn't a secret." Corey said.

Yolanda gave Corey a *don't mess it up for your brother* look.

"Is Mr. Roderick coming over this weekend?" Monti Jr. asked.

"I'm not sure. We didn't have anything planned so far. Why do you ask, honey?"

"He is fun and he likes to play Xbox with me. Dad doesn't do and he is always mad about stuff."

"Boys, your dad is going through some things right now. He has to find his way through whatever is going on with him. You are going to have to be patient with him and be sure not to give him any reason to get upset."

"We don't Mom. This last month, he has been yelling at us for nothing." Corey said.

"What do you mean for nothing, Corey?"

"Mom, sometimes it seems dad is like Dr. Jekyll and Mr. Hyde. I just try not to say much because when you don't like something he gets so mad. He always asks us a lot of questions, like he wants to see if we aren't telling the truth or something like that."

"What kind of questions is he asking you?"

"He asks if you stay over Mr. Roderick's house or if he stays here. We tell him you are always home when we are here and Mr. Roderick doesn't stay the night."

Yolanda took in the information the boys were sharing candidly. Initially, she was angered Monti was trying to keep tabs on her whereabouts and activities. She was even more disturbed by how the boys were feeling about going to visit him. She only wanted the boys to be happy and to enjoy their childhood. Yolanda had to think about how she was going to handle this situation. Her maternal instincts were kicking in.

"Okay guys. I'm going to go to the store. Do you all need me to bring anything back?"

"Oh Mom, bring me some cereal. We ate all of it." Monti Jr replied.

"I need some deodorant Mom. You know I can't smell musty for the girls." Corey said.

"I have been meaning to talk to you about that." Yolanda joked with Corey.

She knew her boys were going to grow up to be something. They were good kids. She found out just how much they loved her when Monti left her. She had to step in to be Mom and Dad. Monti spent more and more time away from the home and ultimately less and less time with the kids. She didn't want them to be hurt so she compensated and made excuses for their father's absence. Yolanda grabbed her coat out of the closet and went to the car to head to the store. She needed to take a moment away from the boys to call their father. Once in the car she dialed Monti's number.

"Hello?" Monti answered.

"Hey Monti. This is Yolanda. Do you have a minute?"

"Yes, what do you want?"

"I wanted to talk to you about the boys. I talked to them today and they told me they don't like coming with you."

"Is this some plot you are scheming up?"

"Monti, this has nothing to do with me plotting. I'm in a great relationship with a straight man who is only into me. This has everything to do with the well-being of my children…our children, so get off your high horse and tell me what is going on with you."

"Nothing is going on with me."

"The boys are telling me you are angry all the time. They say you snap at them and yell at them for no reason. So what is going on with you?"

"Nothing is going on, Yolanda. I see you still haven't learned how to listen."

"I didn't call you to argue with you. My kids are telling me they don't enjoy seeing you because you are mean and angry all the time. You get mad when they are playing the video games and things like that."

"Well they should be studying. Not playing those damn games all the time." Monti replied.

"They study during the week and their grades are A's and B's. What more do you want from them. Coming to your house isn't supposed to be punishment. They should be getting quality time with their father. I believe them when they say you are mean and angry…you were the same way when we were married, except you were nice to them and mean to me."

"Look Yolanda, I don't run your house and you aren't going to run mine. I will deal with the boys the way I deal with them. If you don't like that, then you can take it up with me through the courts."

"If that's how you want to deal with it. I can do that with no problem."

"Fine. I will come by and get them on Friday night." Monti said.

"Umm…no, they won't be coming to your place until I'm comfortable they aren't being mistreated or once I'm ordered by the courts to allow them. I'm going to suggest to the judge that their visits with you are supervised, since you are in denial about how you treat them. You do know they take the kids best interest into account."

"Oh so you are going to play like that, Yolanda?"

"I'm not playing Monti. Do I sound like I'm playing? The wellness of my boys is the most important thing to me."

"You do what you think you have to do. If you do this, you aren't going to get anything else from me other than what I'm required by the courts. Oh yes, did you get your notification? We are no longer married. I lost about one hundred pounds of dead weight from just a letter." Monti spit.

"Yes, I'm glad to have lost a poor excuse for a husband. Now, I can marry Roderick whenever we decide to set a date."

"Fuck you, whore."

"I learned from the best!" Yolanda replied back as she hung up the phone.

Yolanda knew what she was going to have to do. She hated Monti didn't want to be a husband but even more that he was neglecting the boys. She decided to call Roderick to get his take on the situation before she ultimately made her decision on the appropriate course of action with Monti. She'd grown to trust his counsel and appreciate his neutral stance at a situation.

"Hey baby. How are you doing today? I was beginning to think you didn't love me anymore."

"Why would you think that?" Yolanda replied.

"It is 11:30 am on a Saturday and I haven't heard from you

yet. I thought maybe I was replaced." Roderick joked.

"No, Honey. You are irreplaceable. I'm doing well also. I wanted to talk to you about something." She said.

"You sound serious. Did I do something?"

"No, not at all. We are perfect."

"What is happening with the boys?"

"I was talking to the boys this morning and they were saying they don't like going to their dad's because he is mad and angry all the time. I'm concerned because they are saying he yells at them for no reason."

"Some men only know how to show anger and aggression. It depends on how his parents treated him growing up. I don't know much about Monti except the things you shared with me about him. I don't talk to the boys about their dad because it isn't my place. But Sweetheart, you know I support you in all you do. Have you talked to Monti about the situation?"

"Yes, I did before I called you."

"What did he say about it?"

"He said he didn't have any issues or problems. He didn't acknowledge there was any issue."

"Well, if he is in denial, then you have to do what you have to do. I would say let the boys decide if they want to go to visit him or not. That way you keep yourself out of it as much as possible. I'm not saying for you to coax the boys in which way to go but you should allow them to choose. They are very smart kids and you should support their decision."

"That sounds good. I didn't want to go back to court with him. Oh yes…by the way…I got my final dissolution of marriage order yesterday. I'm no longer a married woman."

"How are you feeling about that?" He asked.

"I actually feel great. I'm free to move on with my life. I don't have the negative stigma of being married to a gay man. I don't have to worry about him bringing something to the table that I didn't want. It feels good. It is an end to a chapter in my life I choose not to relive. The only good I got from that chapter in my life were my two boys."

"Well sounds like we need to celebrate."

"That sounds great. How about we go somewhere tonight?" Yolanda suggested.

"I would like that. Plus, I miss seeing you."

"How was your trip? I know it wasn't a happy trip but how did it go?" Yolanda asked.

"It was well. I took care of my grandmother's estate. Everything is as she wanted it."

"Great, how are you handling her passing?"

"I'm good babe. I promise I'm ok. With a woman like you on my side, I have no other choice but to be okay." Roderick said as he smiled thinking about his time with Yolanda.

"You sure do know what to say to make a sista feel good. I'm enjoying this journey you are taking me on. You have brought fresh air to my once stuffy life."

"I'm glad. I only want to see a smile on your beautiful

face…Yolanda?"

"Yes, Honey, what's up?"

"Thank you for coming into my life. Thank you for being who you are. Thank you for exceeding my dreams of what a woman should be for me."

Yolanda was unable to respond to Roderick. She was amazed at how Roderick was able to paint a picture with his words. She was unable to stop the tear that escaped the corner of her eye. She only desired to be loved and valued. Roderick was a gift to her and she was sure she wouldn't mess this thing up. She knew in his arms was her safety as well as her happiness. Their future rested in each of their hearts.

"You don't know how good that makes me feel Roderick. I love you for being you. I can't wait to see you tonight. I'm going to show you just how much I appreciate you." She said seductively.

"I can't wait."

CHAPTER TWENTY-SHAINE

"Adrienne, how is the internship working out for you?" Shaine asked.

"It is better than I dreamed it could be. You are such a great woman. I aspire to be like you. You command attention and respect but are still down to earth and a lady. I have had my run-ins with countless women in corporate America who feel they have to belittle you because you are trying to navigate your way up. They won't help or even give you any pointers. You have been such a help to me and I appreciate you for that."

"No problem. I'm honored you would take this opportunity. I'm definitely able to use the help you've given. You are such a sharp learner. Cameron told me you had potential and you are showing me you are a valued asset in this office."

"I only hope I can be half as good as you are."

"Girl, you need to be better than I am." Shaine replied. "But only after I retire." She added jokingly.

"Excuse me, Ms. Holloway." Jacqueline interrupted.

"Yes Jacqueline. What is it?" Shaine responded. Jacqueline was Shaine's secretary who had been with her for five years.

"Mr. Blanchard is here to see you." She replied.

"Oh…send him in please." Shaine said. She turned to Adrienne. "Can you excuse me for a moment? The apple of my eye is here."

"No problem. I'm going to run to Starbucks…would you like me to bring you something back?"

"Sure, I will take my regular upside-down caramel macchiato, extra hot. Let me get my purse. My treat."

Shaine reached in her purse and grabbed her wallet. She got a twenty-dollar bill out and handed it to Adrienne. As she put her purse down, Jonathan walked in.

"Hey beautiful." Jonathan said.

Adrienne noticed his presence immediately as she turned around to walk to the door. She lost her thoughts for a moment as she took in Jonathan's physique and masculinity.

"Oh excuse me, Sir." Adrienne said timidly.

"Forgive me. Adrienne this is Jonathan Blanchard. Jonathan, allow me to introduce Adrienne." Shaine said.

Jonathan extended his hand to Adrienne. She placed hers in his hand lightly.

"Pleasure to meet you Adrienne." Jonathan said as he shook her hand.

"Likewise Sir." She replied.

"You can call me Jonathan. No need to be formal like that. I get that all day." He said.

"Oh, okay Jonathan." Adrienne said.

"Honey, Adrienne is going to go to Starbucks. I'm not sure how long you are going to be here but would you like something as well?"

"I was just dropping by to see you. I didn't plan to be here long but any excuse to spend more time with you is great on my part."

Shaine loved the way Jonathan made her feel. She knew he had eyes for only her and it empowered her to be the best woman she could be. She thanked God every day for sending Jonathan her way.

"Adrienne, could you bring me Venti peppermint mocha?" He requested as he reached into his pocket and got out his wallet. "Here…I couldn't allow either of you to pay for this. Please ask if Jacqueline would like something as well." He gave Adrienne his American Express Black card.

"Okay. I'll be right back." Adrienne said as she gave Shaine her money back and departed.

"So you were just in the area and decided to come see me? Wow, aren't I special."

"You are special in my book. There is no other like you." He responded.

"You make a sister moist in all the right places, Mr. Blanchard. So how is your day?"

"I had a slow day today. With no meetings, I signed off on

my quarterly reports and took the rest of the day off. What about you?" Jonathan said.

"Everything is going smoothly here. We are working towards our Thanksgiving sales with Black Friday coming up in two week. We had to change some of the displays because we need to make our sales targets, but we are going to be ok."

"That's great. You are one amazing woman. I'm so proud to be with you." He said as he walked over to Shaine, who was leaning on her desk. Once close enough to her, he wrapped his arms around her and kissed her on her forehead. "What are you doing Friday night?"

"Nothing that I know of. What do you have planned?"

"I just got off the phone with the governor. She invited us to an early Thanksgiving dinner at the governor's mansion in Lansing. I accepted, contingent on you agreeing to come with me."

"Of course I will. I'm sure we will have a great time."

"When I'm with you, I always have a great time." Jonathan responded.

"I'm sure I have something chic to wear."

"I don't worry about you. You are always stunning."

"What is the occasion?"

"She wants to bring more jobs back to Michigan and has a proposal for the company. The executives from the major auto manufacturers have all been invited along with our spouses."

"Wow, sounds great. So you consider me your spouse huh?"

"You may not be my spouse legally but I'm hoping you will agree to it one day."

Jonathan had a way with words. He was such a stark contrast to most CEOs. Many of them thought they were too good but he was different. He treated people with dignity and respect. He was the employee's leader and he frequently introduced incentives to the employee workforce. He believed the employees made the company great.

"You don't have to worry about that. I love you and you make loving you easy. I have no problem committing to you every day."

There was a knock on the door.

"Come in." Shaine answered.

"I'm back." Adrienne said as she entered. "Thank you so much Jonathan for the coffee."

"You are welcome." He said as he took both his and Shaine's drink from her. "I know you both are very busy. I don't want to be a distraction."

He handed Shaine her drink and gave her a quick kiss on her lips.

"I will see you later, honey?" He asked.

"Definitely." She replied.

"Okay. Again it was a pleasure to meet you Adrienne."

"Likewise." She said. "Oh wait a minute Jonathan."

"Yes, Adrienne. What's up?"

"Don't forget your card." She replied as she gave him back his charge card.

"Thank you. I totally forgot. You have a nice day. Hopefully, I'll see you again." Jonathan said.

"You have a good day as well." She said.

Adrienne was awestruck with Jonathan. She wanted to be treated well and have a good man on her side. She knew she really wanted to be where Shaine was and was willing to do what she had to do to get there.

* * * * *

Jonathan and Shaine were in the limo heading back to the Detroit metropolitan area from the Governor's dinner. After about twenty-five minutes on the road, Jonathan held Shaine's hand and asked Shaine, "Did you enjoy the night?"

"Yes. It was amazing. You are really a great presenter and you showcase your company with such passion. I can say you really fight for your purpose."

"I was always taught you should fight for what is right. I'm okay with getting incentives from the state of Michigan to give me the ability to hire more people."

"I agree. Congratulations on bringing the bacon back to Detroit."

"Thank you. I felt like the richest man in the world with you by my side."

"Aww, thank you. I'm a blessed woman. I want to make a confession, if you don't mind?" Shaine asked.

"Sure. I'm open to talking about anything you want to talk about."

Shaine took a deep breath and began to speak. "I have prayed for over a year that God would send my mate. I asked him to keep me and ensure I would be ready for him when he came. I knew I had to do some self-improvement to be ready for him. It has been a long journey but an enlightened one where I have learned about who I am, where I am in life and I learned how to love myself."

"That's a great 'confession' and I appreciate your honesty and transparency. You know my story and it took a long while for me to get to the place that I'm. I, too, have gotten myself together so I can be a good man to my wife. I do hope you are able to see a man with a pure heart and with a desire to give the best I have to offer."

"I do see that. I admire who you are and what you have become. I'm happy I went to the charity dinner and met you."

"Can you give me just a second?" Jonathan asked.

"Sure. Are you ok?"

"Yes, I'm." Jonathan said as he picked up the phone in the back of the limo.

"Yes, Mr. Blanchard. How can I help you?" The driver said.

"We are a go." Jonathan said.

"No problem Sir. We will arrive in about fifteen minutes."

"Thank you." Jonathan said as he replaced the phone on the receiver.

"What are we a go for?" Shaine asked.

"I have a surprise for you. I want to show you something."

"Okay. I have to trust you on this one." Shaine said.

"I'd never lead you wrong Shaine." Jonathan said.

Just as the driver said, they arrived at Kensington Metropark. Jonathan had made arrangements for the gate to be open that evening. He drove around to the lake. Once they had parked, the driver exited the limo and opened up the door for Jonathan and Shaine. He held Shaine's hand as she exited the limo looking slightly confused. He just smiled and said, "It will be alright." Jonathan exited after her and brought her shawl. He placed the shawl over her shoulders and took her hand.

They walked over to the edge of the lake. It was a cool evening with no clouds in the sky. The full moon provided ample light which was reflected off the smooth surface of the lake.

"Jonathan, what is going on?" Shaine asked.

"I have always loved to come here to the lake. It is a place of peace and tranquility for me. When I would be stressed after work, I came here to clear my head."

"Okay. So are you stressed tonight?" She asked.

"No, I'm not stressed. I brought you here because I wanted to share this special space with you. I wanted you to experience this beautiful place on this night."

"Okay. I agree it is tranquil and beautiful."

"Shaine, I know it has been only about two months since we met. You have been my equal. You have been the reason why I wake up in the morning. I want you to be the woman I hold at night. Shaine Holloway, I love you with my whole heart. Every fiber of my being yearns to be with you. Because I know who I'm and who you are, I would like to know if you would do me the honor of being my wife?" Jonathan got down on his knee as he pulled out a platinum three-karat channel set diamond engagement ring.

"This is so sudden, but I'm going with my heart…Yes. I will be honored to be your wife." She said as tears came into her eyes.

Jonathan placed the ring on Shaine's finger. Then he stood up and brought Shaine closer to him. He took his handkerchief out of his pocket and wiped her tears. He smiled at her and kissed her. Shaine kissed him back as they shared their intimate time together at the moonlit lake. This symbolized the start of their new life together.

CHAPTER TWENTY-ONE MONTI

"Stephanie?"

"Hey Monti. How are you doing?'

"I have had better days, but I'm making it."

"What is wrong?"

"There have been so many things going on lately. I talked to Cameron but he seems to be through with me. I know I can show him that I can be a good guy, but he isn't having it. I been sick for a couple days and can't seem to shake it."

"Are you okay? You got the flu or just being cold?"

"I think it may be the flu but I will be alright. The flu usually lasts only for a few days. So hopefully it will be clearing up in a day or so."

"Okay, Monti. Now back to the other topic you brought up. You have to realize what he went through was hard for any other person to deal with. Monti, I have to be honest with you, by not being honest with Cameron, you took away his choice to choose whether he wanted to deal with you or not. He was blindsided by the information and would probably be very hesitant to deal with you moving forward."

"I know that…I have been working on myself to make me a better man for Cameron. You just don't know how he completes me. I fucked up…I know I did. He brought out the best in me. I have to have him in my life, Stephanie."

"You are focusing on him way too much. He may never come back around to being with you. Do you know if he is dating now? Is there someone keeping his attention?"

"I don't know. He won't talk to me. I'm getting frustrated he won't talk to me. I just can't let go. He is supposed to be with me. He completes me."

"Monti, you are going to have to just wait it out, or move on with your life. You can't force someone to be in a relationship with you."

"You just don't understand."

"I know I don't know much about gay relationships, Monti. I do know about people. People don't like to be lied to. People don't like being manipulated. People don't like to get damaging information about their spouse or significant other."

"I can make him want to give me another chance. He has a big heart and he is forgiving." Monti declared.

"I don't know what to tell you about this Monti. You don't seem to want to listen to me. You know what you are going to do, so just do it. I just don't want to see nothing happen to you. You can't make someone give you another chance."

"Thanks for your concern. I'm going to figure this out."

"What else is going on? How is the therapy going for you?" Stephanie asked.

"I'm still going. The doctor says something about me having a personality disorder. He says that's why I have problems with relationships. I have to keep going to therapy to deal with it and get it under control."

"That's good you know what is going on. I'm sure it will help you focus on handling it. I have never heard about it before."

"Yes, the doctor says with therapy, I should be alright." Monti replied.

"That's great news for you then. I suggest you focus on the positive things and not deal with the Cameron things now. How is work coming along?"

"That has been okay as well. I'm still at Providence but I still got a job. I'm at my mom's place still. Hopefully I will be moving back into my own space by the beginning of December."

"See that's what I'm talking about Monti. There is so much good going on in your life and you have to know if Cameron isn't going to be back with you, someone else will be coming for you. I think you should wait for a while before you try to get into another relationship. Take some time for yourself and when the time is right, you will know it."

"Okay that's cool. I will figure it out. I'm going to head back to my moms. I'm not feeling very well."

"Just let me know if you need me. I'm here for you."

"Thanks Stephanie. I know you are there for me and I will let you know if something comes up. What are you doing for Thanksgiving?"

"You know I'm cooking here and the family will be coming by. You are welcome to come by if you like." She said.

"Sounds good to me. I'm going to my mom's house first and then I will swing by to see you. What can I bring?"

"Okay. Just bring yourself. You will have a good time and keep your mind off all the stuff going on."

Monti got up and gave Stephanie a hug. He needed to figure out what he was going to do. He hated not being in control of his life. Though he was outted, he still felt he had some control of what was going on in his life. He got in the jeep and was headed towards his mom's house when his phone rang.

"Hello?"

"Hey Tony. How are you doing?"

"I'm good man. Who is this?"

"It's Allen. You remember me? I live in Southfield near Telegraph and Franklin Road."

"Oh yeah. What is up man?"

"I'm just seeing what you are up to? When are we going to hang out again?"

"Shit man…I ain't doing nothing right now. You ready for a brother to roll through?"

"Hell yeah man. It's been a while. Since the last time we hooked up, I been thinking about the next time we would be able to have a repeat." Allen said.

"Okay, I'm on the east side right now…with traffic, it may take me about an hour to get over to you. Just make sure you are ready. Aiight?"

"You got it. See you when you get here. You remember which building and number."

"Yeah, I got it." Monti answered.

"See you soon."

* * * * *

Monti got out the elevator and walked around to Allen's door. He knew this was the building because he could smell the dank odor of the building. This particular apartment complex was known for the type of occupants that were housed here. The apartment complex catered to a deviant population. Intentional fires and shootings were a regular occurrence here. The Southfield Police were frequently on-site here.

Monti knocked on Allen's door, which was the last door of the hallway near the stairwell.

"Come in." Allen said from the inside of his apartment.

Monti walked in and closed the door behind him. The curtains were closed and the lights out.

"I'm in the bedroom." Allen said.

He didn't know exactly where the bedroom was but knew it was a one-bedroom apartment. The last time he came to Allen's house, they didn't make it to the bedroom. They found their way to the dilapidated couch that sat in front of coffee table and an old style box television. His apartment had a rundown nasty feeling about it. It was the kind of place a cheap prostitute would go…where one could get nasty and freaky without feeling guilty.

Monti walked to the direction of Allen's voice, passing the bathroom. When he got to the doorway of the room, he saw Allen lying on the bed with one leg cocked up and the other extended. He was completely naked with a pillow behind his head.

"You like what you see?" Allen asked.

"It's all good here." Monti replied. He knew Allen was thirsty and he was a mediocre fuck at that. Somehow, his tall six feet six frame didn't match up with the size of his six inch dick. If Monti was looking for someone who was a looker, Allen wasn't him. He was a darker skinned guy who was about thirty years old. He didn't get much play and was thankful for the sex he was able to get. He, too, liked the cat and mouse game. He'd seen Monti in Palmer Park many times but chose not to pursue him then.

"What are you waiting on? Are you just going to stand there looking at me?"

Monti started taking off his shirt. He wasn't really feeling Allen, but knew it was a quick nutt. He tossed his shirt off to the side, then unbuttoned his pants and allowed gravity to drop them to the floor. Allen could see the bulge forming in Monti's boxer briefs in anticipation of the incipient fuck session. Monti stepped out of his pants and leaned against the door frame.

"You still look great Monti. I see you are getting excited about fucking me."

"Yeah, you know how I do." Monti replied in a nonchalant manner.

Allen couldn't stop staring at Monti's sex that was now fully erect sex in his boxer briefs. He got excited thinking about the last time they were together. He remembered he had a hard time taking Monti's girth last time. Monti didn't have the longest dick but the girth was what many guys liked. A very limited number of guys have experienced fucking Monti; Cameron was one of those limited few.

"Yes, I remember how you do." Allen said.

"If you do, then why are you still laying back over there? Come give my shit some attention." Monti said as he slipped his boxer briefs down to the floor.

Obediently, Allen moved to the edge of the bed and knelt down in front of Monti. Hesitating slightly as he eyed Monti's now fully erect stiffness, he tried to size it up.

"Just relax. You can do it." Monti said as he took Allen by the back of the head and brought his head to meet Monti's lower head.

Allen opened his mouth to receive Monti's sex. He convinced himself he could take it. He knew he was going to love every minute of it. He savored the drops of pre-cum that quickly appeared on the tip of Monti's sex. Soon, Allen was working the head and shaft slowly taking more and more into his salivating mouth. He soon became used to the girth and was working it better and better. With his nose in Monti's crotch, Allen was able to receive Monti's scent, which intoxicated him even more. It made him want to please Monti more.

Monti was enjoying the scene as well. He readjusted his stance, widening his legs, to give Allen more access to his dick and full nut sack. Monti leaned back against the door frame not caring about anything other than the pleasure he was receiving from Allen's hungry mouth. He began to moan from the pleasure letting Allen know he approve of his head game. Monti's stiffness began to hit the back of Allen's throat as Allen was doing his best to suppress his gag reflex, which he found hard to do. Monti got an ego boost every time Allen had to reset his jaws. He knew he was too much for Allen to handle. After a few rounds of Allen struggling to keep Monti's sex in his mouth, Monti knew it was time to switch positions.

"Get up in the bed on your hands and knees." Monti ordered.

Allen obeyed. Monti stepped behind him grabbing Allen's ass. It wasn't round or fat; it was a normal size ass. Monti took the time to smack it on both sides. "Give me that lube." Monti demanded.

Allen reached over to the nightstand and gave Monti the bottle of Wet. Monti put a few drops of it on his fingers as he rubbed up and down Allen's waiting ass. Allen tried to relax, anticipating what Monti would do next. Monti had to make sure Allen was ready to take all of his manhood so he found Allen's spot and pushed two of his fingers in. Allen responded by exhaling. He received a shock of pleasure going through his body as Monti wiggled his fingers inside. With Monti's free hand, he rubbed his chest and squeezed his pecs. When Monti felt Allen was ready, he decided to tease him by barely pressing his sex on Allen's waiting deepness.

"I need to feel you inside me man." Allen said lustfully.

"Oh you do?"

"Hell yes. I have been waiting for a repeat performance. I loved how you manhandled me and took it like it was yours."

"Like this…" Monti replied as he entered Allen.

"Yeah, like that." He moaned. "Shit feels so good."

Monti grabbed Allen by his waist and pushed himself all the

way in. Once he was in, he didn't move as he felt Allen's ass muscle pulse around Monti's sex, as it was getting used to the stretch. Monti was enjoying the warmness of Allen but he knew this was just the beginning. Monti wanted to see how far he could press his sex into Allen. Pushing Allen's face into the bed, Monti mounted Allen allowing gravity and his own body weight to help pull him in.

"Ooohh. Hit that spot man." Allen said.

"I knew you was thirsty for this." Monti gloated.

Monti knew of the dangers of unprotected sex but still chose to ignore them. He was topping Allen so he felt his chances of getting together were minimized. Monti continued to long stroke Allen. He could tell Allen was enjoying it because soon Allen was throwing his ass back at him. Allen was meeting Monti stroke for stroke. Allen wasn't going to be outdone by Monti. He clenched his ass tight around Monti's sex trying to milk his shaft. The battle of each trying to outdo the other worked up a sweat, causing Monti to drip sweat onto Allen's dark chocolate skin.

"Oh fuck…that ass is getting me close." Monti said.

"Hell yeah." Allen replied.

After a couple more minutes, Monti began to get winded. "Fuck." He said feeling his imminent release. He gave three last forceful thrusts into Allen. His balls tightened up against his body. "I'm going to cum." He grunted. "Oh God…take my muthafuckin babies, Bitch."

Monti was on autopilot while his orgasm took over his body; each thrust emptying more of his sex juice into Allen. The throbbing of Monti's sex inside of Allen and the hotness of his cum, took Allen over the top. Soon his ass began to squeeze tightly around Monti's sex, as Allen's orgasm overcame him. Face down on a pillow with his arms outstretched in a surrendered position; Allen came all over his sheets without touching himself. "Fuck…fuck…fuck." Allen said as his body convulsed from the intense pleasure brought upon him by Monti.

CHAPTER TWENTY-TWO-CAMERON

Cameron parked his car at the Motor City Casino parking lot and walked towards the entrance. He and Shaine decided to meet at the casino for their seafood buffet to catch up and so he could meet Jonathan. Cameron, a fan of research, googled Jonathan's name and was impressed with the information he found about his humble background. He'd overcome life's circumstances and made a mark in the world. In the city of Detroit, he was the most eligible bachelor. Cameron had seen him on television time and time again. He knew Mr. Blanchard was eye candy and desired by many people, men and women alike.

Cameron decided to call Shaine to see how far out they were.

"Hey honey. How close are you?"

"We just pulled into the parking structure." Shaine replied.

"Okay, I'm going to get in the line. It looks like we have about a thirty minute wait."

"We will see you soon."

Cameron felt nervous meeting Jonathan for the first time. He knew Shaine liked him enough to invest time with him. It was a nervous excitement Cameron felt. In the line, Cameron decided to check his email. He noticed there was an email from an address he wasn't familiar with.

Mr. Cameron,

I wanted to send you an email to thank you for the introduction to Shaine. She has helped me tremendously in my understanding of fashion in the retail area. I hope one day, I can do something to show you how appreciative I'm for what you have done to help me. You showed me there are good people in the world that can make a connection when there was none available previously. Let me know when you have some time.

Adrienne

"That's nice of her…" Cameron thought.

"How's my bestie doing?" Cameron heard bringing him out of his thought.

"Hey Shaine. How are you?" Cameron responded as he gave Shaine a hug.

"I'm doing great, just a bit busy at work and on the home front as well. Let me introduce you to Jonathan." She said.

Jonathan smiled and extended his hand towards Cameron. "Pleasure to meet you. I have heard so much about you."

"Likewise Jonathan, I'm happy to finally meet you. You have taken my friend away from me."

"Hopefully, that isn't a bad thing." Jonathan replied.

"By the end of the evening, I will let you know." Cameron said as he looked towards Shaine, giving her a we-will-talk-about-this-later look. "Shaine, I haven't seen you in a minute. What has been happening?" He asked as he grabbed her hand. "Oh hell…what the…"

Shaine looked at Jonathan and back at Cameron. "I wanted to tell you but thought it would be better in person rather than on the phone."

"OMG…are you serious?" Cameron asked.

"Yes, I'm serious."

"Okay…we obviously have a lot to catch up on." Cameron shifted focus to Jonathan. "You didn't waste any time with this did you?"

"You know what you do when you find something that gives you reason to live? I had to do what was right."

"Well, I haven't experienced that just yet but you must be some kind of guy to sweep her off her feet. I'm happy for you both."

"Excuse me Mr. Blanchard." The restaurant manager said.

"Yes, how can I help you?" Jonathan replied.

"It is always great to see you. If you and your party would like to follow me, I would like to invite you to the VIP side. You don't have to wait in the line here." He said.

"Thank you very much." Jonathan said. "Let's go you all."

The all followed the manager to the special entrance. Cameron looked at Shaine and gave her look that she knew meant he was impressed with Jonathan's pull. Cameron was happy for his best friend but didn't like that she kept this secret from him. He wanted to know more about Jonathan. Tonight he was going to ask the pertinent question to make sure Shaine had chosen right. What true influence would Cameron have on Shaine if she made the wrong choice, when she felt it was the right choice? He knew he had to be open-minded and get to know Jonathan. Now that they were engaged, Cameron was going to be a regular fixture in their lives, instead of Jonathan being a passing moment between Cameron and Shaine's friendship.

Once at the payment kiosk, Cameron reached for his wallet. "Let me get this." Jonathan interrupted pulling is Amex Black card. "I have to make sure I make a great first impression on you."

"Visually, you have already done that." Cameron said as he looked at Shaine with raised eyebrows.

Within a few minutes, the three of them were seated in a booth towards the back of the dining room. Cameron noticed how many people in the restaurant knew who Jonathan was. He noticed many people looking their way and engaging in conversations at their table. He knew they were talking about Jonathan but based on the warm reception he received from the majority of people, Cameron assumed the conversation was positive.

They made a trip to the buffet line and once back to their table, "How does it feel to be the luckiest man in the city?" Cameron asked Jonathan.

"If you are speaking of this beautiful lady here…it is amazing I finally found my soul mate." He held Shaine's hand strongly yet with a delicacy as if hers was that of a porcelain sculpture. Cameron noticed how his eyes lit up as he described his feelings upon meeting Shaine at the charitable event. It was apparent to Cameron, within a few moments, Jonathan's world rose and set on Shaine.

"Shaine tells me you are working with National Bank now?"

"Yes, I was looking for a new opportunity. Flying was great but I was tired of it. I like a challenge and the airline wasn't challenging me mentally."

"It's great to hear you are a go-getter. That's one thing I see you and Shaine have in common."

"So how does it feel to be the CEO of a major fortune 500 company, and the former most eligible bachelor of Detroit?"

"Wow Cameron, you give me too much credit. I wasn't the most eligible bachelor; I was a man who was incomplete and waiting on the woman who was perfectly created for me. I agreed to allow the magazine to do the spread in order to bring more news coverage for my company. It was definitely not for the dating scene. I'm a true believer, when you are ready for something, God will open the door for it to happen. I just knew I needed to continue to do the work to make sure my charisma didn't take me to a level where my character couldn't keep me."

"That's a profound statement Jon. You sound like Shaine now." Cameron said as he was very comfortable and confident to give Jonathan a nickname. Jonathan didn't correct him either.

"That's right. You know my saying. I took the time to work on my inner qualities and my inner self. I didn't want to get into the sista-girl rut." Shaine chimed in. "To many times, black women want more and want better but they don't prepare themselves to receive better."

"You are absolutely right." Cameron said.

"What ends up killing me are the women look at me and get angry with me because I'm not interested in them. They automatically think I'm not into African-American women. That's so far from the truth. I just want someone who has something going for them and aren't so damaged by past relationships that they aren't able to be good for me in a relationship." Jonathan added.

"Well I'm glad I don't have that problem." Cameron joked.

"Don't do it!" Shaine said. "You know some of the guys you have dated in the past have been the same way. It isn't a gender thing but just the state of one's mindset. Too many people take on the title and burden of being a victim that they become paralyzed and a prisoner of their past. They think everyone they meet is going to be the same way or they stay with this person because they think this person will change. Often, they have a string of people that come into their lives and they can't see they are attracting the same person." Shaine said.

"Yes, that's it. They are attracting it because they didn't do the work. You attract what you are on the inside." Jonathan said. "My mom always told me to do things with purity of heart and nothing but goodness can come from that."

"Your mom sounds like she is a wise lady." Cameron said.

"Yes she was. I really miss her." Jonathan replied.

"Oh, I'm sorry. I didn't know." Cameron said. "It wasn't in your bio." He joked.

"No problem. So you did do some research on me then?" Jonathan said.

"You know I did. I had to know more about Mr. Blanchard." Cameron replied.

"Okay, was the information you got sufficient for your needs or was there more you needed to know?" He said.

"Oh lord, Jonathan. Why did you open that box up?" Shaine

said.

"It's okay Shaine. I don't have many questions. I will let the evening play out and go from there. He is already receiving an A in my book."

"Thanks. I can exhale now and be who I'm." Jonathan said.

They all erupted in laughter. Shaine was relieved Cameron was ok with Jonathan. She was elated Jonathan didn't have any issues with Cameron and he was so secure in his self that he didn't have any issue with Cameron's flirtatious nature. Cameron felt comfortable Jonathan wasn't an ax murderer and he knew Shaine would be well cared for. He could see the love that was shared between the two of them. Secretly, he wished he had that love in his life as well; but tonight was the night he enjoyed and celebrated with his best friend so he put that sentimental, emotional Cameron back in the box and continued to make small talk.

"Excuse me ma'am." Cameron said as the cocktail server passed by.

"Yes Sir. How can I help you?" She said.

"I would like a bottle of Champagne for the table." He requested handing her his credit card.

"No problem." She said noticing Jonathan. "How are you doing Mr. Blanchard? It is good to see you here again."

"Thanks Jennifer. It is good to see you as well." Jonathan replied.

"You are Mister Popular." Cameron said.

"On occasion we bring clients here. Other times, my company caters events and we use the casino along with servers."

"You really are the people's CEO." Cameron commented.

"Thank you. I'm honored to have that title. When employees appreciate and respect their leadership and know they are appreciated by management, they will do more for you and the company than if they are just collecting a pay check." Jonathan said.

"I fully believe that. That's why I treat my employees well also." Shaine said.

The three continued to have great conversation over their dinner. To others around them, they seemed to be long time acquaintances.

* * * * *

"Hello?" Cameron said answering his phone.

"Hey, Cameron. How are you?" Monti replied.

"I'm doing well, Monti. What about you?" Cameron replied trying to be cordial.

"I'm great here. The only thing that would make it better is if you would get back with me."

"Did you call me to talk about something realistic or are you still stuck in your make believe world?" Cameron replied.

"Do you have to be so bitter? I'm focusing on bettering myself so you will see I can be a good partner for you."

"Monti, be a better person for you. I have nothing to do with you being a better person. What we had is done. It was actually nothing but wasted time."

"Cameron, you know the bible tells you to forgive. I don't

want to rehash this again and again. I just want to keep the lines open for communication."

"There isn't much to communicate Monti."

"Are you seeing anyone now?"

"That isn't any of your business. Have you been in the park lately?" Cameron spit.

"Look Cameron. I'm trying my best to be nice to you to win you back, but…"

"Trying to be nice to me…I don't need you to be nice to me, Monti. I don't need you to ever remember my name, phone number, address or the fact that you wasted my time being a cheating ass liar."

"Now see, why do you have to swear at me? Being angry doesn't make you sexy. You are too sexy to be all mad."

"I'm not being sexy or trying to be anything to you. What could have been…is over. What part of that are you not able to understand. Look it is better for both of us if you and I ceased to exist in each other's lives. How about this being our last conversation?"

"Cameron you just have to know I love you and will do whatever I can to get you back."

"I think you need some meds. You aren't even thinking rationally. Good-bye Monti."

Cameron hung up the phone. He became angry because he now confirmed Monti wasn't going to move on with his life. Cameron just wanted to enjoy life solo, not life with Monti. He was determined to move on from this chapter of his life.

CHAPTER TWENTY-THREE-YOLANDA

"Roderick, I had such an amazing time with you this Thanksgiving." Yolanda said.

"Thanks. I'm glad you enjoyed yourself."

"Your family is so welcoming. Your mom is such an amazing woman. I truly admire her."

"Yes. She is the backbone of this family. I'm glad you two hit it off. It makes me happy to see we are moving closer as a couple and as a family."

"I do too."

"I can't wait to meet your family as well." Roderick said.

The two of them continued to walk down the walking path behind Roderick's house. They took time from the family to go for a walk to help their stomachs go down from the holiday meal they ate. The boys were back at the house playing with Roderick's nephews. Yolanda and Roderick wanted to spend some quality alone time.

"I guess I should make this happen." Yolanda said.

"Are you uncomfortable with our relationship?"

"No, it isn't that at all. I just don't know how my adopted mom is going to act. Nothing I do is ever good enough for her."

"Oh I understand. I'm sorry to hear you two don't have a good relationship."

"It has never been good. From the time my parents adopted me, I knew she and I wouldn't have the best relationship. My dad and I are great but my adopted mother is the antithesis of motherhood. I always felt I was just a paycheck to her."

"Aww baby…" Roderick said as he pulled Yolanda closer to him. "I know I'm not your mom and all that…I don't see you as a paycheck. I see you as my future. I can't go back to your past and fix that, but what I can do is vow to you I will work tirelessly to make our future as bright and happy as I can."

Yolanda was moved to tears as Roderick stood there as strength for her in this moment of weakness. She had never been able to lean on a man before because he husband was never there for her emotionally, yet here she stood with Roderick vulnerable and open but comfortable and peaceful because he held her in his arms. She didn't mind the emotions she was going through because she felt the strength of Roderick. This feeling is what Yolanda always wanted.

This moment made Yolanda remember listening to a psychologist on the radio about a month ago. He was giving advice to a caller who was involved in an unhappy relationship and had low self-esteem. He told the caller he needed to love himself more than he loved unhappiness. Yolanda took another step for team Yolanda and decided she was going to run towards happiness and away from those negative, hurtful feelings she bottled up and stored. She decided, there in Roderick's arms, to break the glass jars with which she'd stored her hurts.

Too many times, people bottle hurts and pains and carry the weight of abuse, neglect and self-hatred. Yolanda was one of those people. The weight of her past had kept her in a place of unforgiveness and bitterness. It only served to sabotage any chance of happiness. Roderick brought a newness…a freshness to her stale life, which allowed her to breathe again. Here on the day of Thanksgiving, Yolanda was thankful for a real man in her life. She came to know, in that moment, Roderick was her future and she embraced her dark days were behind her.

"Why are you crying, Baby?" Roderick asked.

"I'm just happy. I know I'm safe. I know I'm loved. I know my dark days are over. I'm thankful you came into my life."

"I'm honored to be in your life. In you, I have experienced a woman with great potential. I see a woman with a pure heart…one whose purity was misused because the other was unable to be honest to himself about himself. I see a woman whose choice was taken away from her. Would you have chosen to be with a gay man, had you known your ex was gay? Probably not."

"Hell no. I wouldn't have done that."

"Because of his dishonesty, you had to endure the things you had to and I'm just so sorry you had to go through that. I do believe we go through things in life to help make us better people. So, as much as it hurts, you are who you are today because of the challenges you overcame yesterday. As much as I wish I could change your past, it brought you to this point in life."

"You always say just the right things, Roderick."

"I just speak the truth and I speak from my heart."

"I enjoy knowing you are honest with me. It helps build trust and helps us continue to move in the right direction."

"I want to keep moving in the right direction with you, Yolanda. You are my soul mate. I think we were destined to be together."

"Hopefully our destiny is a beautiful one."

"If it is as beautiful as you are, then I can't wait to see it." He said.

Yolanda smiled as Roderick held her closer to him.

CHAPTER TWENTY-FOUR-SHAINE

The first snowstorm signaled the close of fall and the entrance of winter.

"Do you think it will snow all night?" Shaine asked as she sat at the edge of Jonathan's California king sized bed. Shaine was exceptionally impressed with Jonathan's choice in décor. His bedroom was balanced with Feng Shui principles, creating a space for rest and rejuvenation. The terracotta accent wall formed the backdrop for his rich tobacco hewed bed which was elevated upon a three step platform. The pillars of his bedposts seemed to grow from the floor in search of sunlight from the sky lights above. His sleeping area was the focal point of the room with opulence and majesty.

The room had an open concept flow with a distinct sitting area which was also impressive. Two armchairs upholstered in a duet of velvets-in a paisley pattern for the front and cushions, and a brown solid on the backs. A tuffed ottoman doubling as a coffee table was covered in two shades of smoky gray silk. Mounted on the wall above the marble fireplace mantel was a rectangular mirror framed in mahogany wood. An additional corner seating area featured a taupe chaise and mirror-faced armoire.

Jonathan looked out of the floor to ceiling bedroom window at the snow that had blanketed his lawn. "Looks like it probably will."

The two of them sat in silence, listening to the crackle of the fire burning in the fireplace, bringing sensuality and sizzle into the space. The smell of the cinnamon oil infused firewood brought the scent of fall into Jonathan's bedroom. Jonathan had created a romantic ambience in his room with a myriad of candles. He loved the feeling of warmth and comfort the candlelight provided. It was sensual yet subtle and just the way he planned for the evening.

"You don't have to worry about the snow though." Jonathan said.

"Oh really…why is that?" Shaine replied.

Jonathan walked over to where Shaine was sitting and grabbed her hand. "I'll keep you warm." He bent his six-foot tall frame and kissed her on the back of her hand.

"Is that so?"

"Very much so, Sweetheart."

Shaine fell silent, watching Jonathan touch and caress her hand. He traced the length of her slender fingers, sending sensations of enticement through her. He ran his smooth hands slowly over the sensitive inside of Shaine's forearm. She looked at him, his gaze intent on her arm, as chills travelled up one arm and down the other. Jonathan's eyes lifted, meeting hers as his piercing look gazed into her soul. Their hearts somehow beating in sync, she felt his heart as he felt hers.

Jonathan sat next to Shaine and turned to face her. She put her hand on Jonathan's muscular chest; even through his shirt, she could feel the definition of his physique. She enjoyed the feeling of his taught muscles in her hand. "It is so interesting… here I'm with you and I'm able to let all my guards down and still feel safe." She said.

Jonathan reached up and held Shaine's face gently in his strong, yet soft hands. "You should be…it is my job to make sure you are always safe."

She continued to rub her hand on his chest gently, focusing on the feel of it. She was exploring him and taking in every fiber of his musculature. She refused to stop and his eyes told her not too.

"You are so alluring to me." Jonathan said as he kissed her hand as it passed under his chin.

He leaned closer to Shaine. The warmth of his breath caught her cheek and neck. Shaine tilted her head as he came closer to her body. As he inhaled her scent, becoming familiar with her, a fiery longing began to grow within her. It began to own her as her body yearned to feel his lips on her. She wrapped her arms around his body and pulled him closer to her, at the same time his lips made contact to her lower ear lobe. Her body felt the current that left Jonathan's lips and travelled down her spine to her clitoris. With his lips now connected to her neck, he wrapped his arms around her. She lay back on the bed, as he followed.

The fireplace crackled loudly as Jonathan and Shaine gave into the needs they had for passion. Jonathan's hand roamed from Shaine's shoulder, down her arm and found its way to the small of her back. Their lips touched. As he kissed her, the world around them disappeared. She receptively welcomed his kisses. She sucked his full lips into her mouth. Her nipples began to harden as their tongues darted in and out of each other's mouth. She was in ecstasy as his tongue invaded her mouth with intensity, an intensity she hadn't felt before.

Jonathan broke the kiss as his sex grew. Catching his breath, he began to unbutton his shirt exposing his chiseled chest. Once free from his shirt, he resumed kissing Shaine. She ran her hands up and down his back as he slid down to her collar bone. Shaine was hot; this was the moment she waited for. Her body language told Jonathan to go ahead and he slid his hands between their two bodies, finding the bottom of her shirt. He put his hand under the shirt and followed the curves of her body until he felt the lace from her bra. His tender touch on her bra only made her body want more.

Shaine lay beneath Jonathan, enveloped amid his masculinity and his hardened manhood pressed against into her thigh. His mouth kissed intensely down along Shaine's neck to her cleavage. "Wait a moment." Shaine said.

"Are you okay?" Jonathan replied.

"Yes, I just want to take off my shirt."

Jonathan gave her space to take off her shirt. As she pulled the shirt up over her head, Jonathan was blown away at her body. The warmness of the light from both the fireplace and the many candles shown on Shaine's vanilla caramel colored skin. The red-laced underwire bra framed Shaine's full breast. With her shirt removed, Jonathan resumed his sensual oral exploration of Shaine's breast. He inhaled the scent of her femininity, furthering his sexual excitement. She embraced his body, pulling him in to her bosom.

Jonathan caressed her hair as he pressed his hardness against her legs. His wandering hands found their way to the back of her bra. Without difficulties, he unfastened her bra. In no time he had removed the only item separating her breast from his lips. His mouth found its way to an erect nipple, his tongue flicking ever so lightly over it, sending erotic sensations through Shaine's yearning body. Fighting for breath, she breathily said, "Yes." Her eyes dimmed from the pleasure stemming from Jonathan's newly confirmed skillful mouth and tongue.

Instinctively, Jonathan knew he was doing his job. Shaine's body spoke louder than her soft moans of pleasure. Her back arched, in response to his oral stimulation. He wanted to know what she tasted like all over. With her back arched, her legs parted allowing Jonathan space to work some more of his magic. He slid his hand under her panties and he could feel the heat radiating from her arousal. The heat of her arousal intrigued him. Her legs parted further allowing him more access to her.

Jonathan wanted nothing more than to please Shaine and explore her softness deeply. He slid his fingers over her labia, slightly pinching them before finding her clitoris. He felt her wetness as he slowly circled her clitoris with his now soaked finger. Shaine's arousal grew even more as Jonathan manually stimulated her with his fingers and orally with his tongue. He went from her breasts to her neck and her mouth. Shaine was taken to a sensual yet sexual place at the hands of a capable Jonathan. He had to taste Shaine. With his path charted, he pulled his finger from deep within Shaine and straight into his mouth to satisfy his inquisitive nature.

"Damn baby, you taste salty-sweet." Jonathan was hooked.

Shaine fumbled eagerly with the drawstring of Jonathan's loungewear. Jonathan noticed her having a hard time with them so he helped her loosen them and then they dropped to the floor. She rubbed up and down his back as he freed his ankles from the pants. Shaine moved her way up into the bed, while Jonathan took the liberty to get on his knees in front of her. He took both hands and spread Shaine's labia apart revealing her aroused slightly purple insides. Almost mesmerized by what he saw, he buried his face into her. He wanted to taste her sex juices. She moaned with need as he helped himself to her free flowing juices; then reached down pulling his head closer into her. The pleasure of his oral skills travelled from her turned on erotic zone up along her stomach up to her chest and throat.

He probed her entrance with his tongue; alternating kisses and sucks. He slid his muscular arms under Shaine's knees, curling them to pull her body closer to his hungry mouth without missing on beat. He moved to her clitoris, swirling his tongue around it sending jolts of sensation up Shaine's spine. She responded by clenching her legs around his head and neck. He wasn't fazed by the pressure created by her legs. He continued to please Shaine, edging her to the point of orgasm and backing down to let her come down slightly. Shaine's body responded by releasing more lubricant letting Jonathan know she wanted more. He was eager to oblige.

He rose from his knees and Shaine was able to see his fully erect manhood pointing straight out. She could even see a glimmer of his precum glistening from the light emitted from the fire place. Stepping in between her already open legs, he picked up her left leg and pushed it up close to her chest as he rubbed her right nipple with his free hand. He ran his stiff manhood gently up and down her waiting pussy, getting it wet with her dripping juices. He rocked his pelvis back and forth while he looked down at the color contrast between the two of them. Shaine's head was spinning and her insides pulsating wanting to feel Jonathan inside of her.

He slowly entered her and immediately felt the warmth of her envelop his stiffness. She gasped as he continued to fill her inside. He bent down to kiss her and reassure her all would be well. He kissed her gently and softly as he continued to consummate this relationship. Once inside, he didn't move, he just wanted to feel her muscles grip her man. Shaine was no stranger to Kegel exercises and she made sure to put them to use.

He began to rock back and forth inside of Shaine, as they

became intimately connected. He began to find his rhythm and she met his thrust. She reached down and grabbed at his hip with one hand pulling him into her. She hadn't had sex in over six months and she was glad she waited for him. He placed his hands on the bed on either side of her in an inclined push up position. She reveled in the moment, knowing she had a man, a strong man, naked between her thighs and he was her man. Jonathan was making passionate love to her.

Lost in the moment, Shaine's heart raced trying to keep up with the passion and delight what was covering her body. She felt her stimulation levels rise as Jonathan thrusts began to intensify. He pushed himself all the way into Shaine in circular motions, ensuring he stimulated her clitoris as well as her vaginal walls. Her body responded by producing more lubricant which allowed him to slide in the depths of her abyss. Shaine knew what was coming next when she was no longer able to squeeze down on Jonathan. Her body took control of the situation as she exploded into waves of pleasurable elation. Her body shuddered as the pleasure flowed through her and out to her fingers and toes. She shook as her body was seized in orgasm. Her pussy pulsed stronger and stronger as he continued to thrust inside her. After what seemed like an eternity, Jonathan's body tensed up signaling he was close to his climax. He thrust himself deep in Shaine, as sweat dripped from his balled head. His sex swelled filling her even more than his already large manhood had.

His manhood pushed into her pelvis. Shaine felt him collide with her soul. They were one in this moment and she knew he was the one she waited for. As she gave into his passion, something happened to Shaine which she would never forget. His orgasm was strong as his abdominal muscles contracted. He continued to thrust in and out of her, moving quicker and harder. His chest rumbled as he moaned over and over. Struggling to catch his breath, he refused to stop. Shaine shivered as her second orgasm hit her. They both moaned and shook. Satisfaction traveled from his body through his engorged sex into her sex and throughout her body. She smiled inside as warm tears ran down her cheeks. Jonathan, though out of breath and spent, wiped the tears as he collapsed on the side of her. He kissed her softly as Shaine rolled onto his chest and soon fell asleep, satisfied, safe and serene.

CHAPTER TWENTY-FIVE-MONTI

"Good morning, Mr. Burroughs. How are you doing?"

"I'm doing well, Bruce. How are you?"

"I'm blessed and highly favored."

"That's great to hear. You have a good day."

"Thank you Mr. Burroughs. You do the same."

Monti enjoyed coming to work and enjoyed the respect he received. He was four months into his probation period at his new location and he was ready for it to be over. He was a hard worker and wanted to look for a promotion, but he had to wait until he had successfully completed this six months.

Once settled in his office, Monti decided to call Cameron again. It had been a couple weeks and Monti felt Cameron would have worked through some of his anger over what happened. He hoped he would be ready to give their relationship another chance. He picked up his phone and looked for *Pooquie* in his contacts. Finding Cameron's number, he called him. The phone rang…Monti's heart began to race with anticipation that Cameron would answer the phone. After six rings, Cameron's voicemail came on. Monti's face sunk as he listened to Cameron's deep voice instructing the caller to leave a name, a number and a brief message and he would return the call just as soon as he could. Beep.

"Hey Cameron. I hope you are doing well. You were on my mind and I wanted to give you a call to hear your voice. Give me a ring when you have a minute. I'll talk to you soon."

Monti knew Cameron wouldn't call him back; he knew he would have to work hard to bring him back into his arms. How he would do that, evaded Monti's thoughts. Monti read his hand-off report from his night shift counterpart and was prepared for another uneventful day. Monti's alarm sounded, alerting him it was time to make his rounds. Within a few minutes, he was in the hallways of Providence hospital. Monti liked the set-up of the new hospital.

Walking down the hallways, Monti spoke to hospital staff and visitors alike. He was a personable person and always allowed his personality to shine in the presence of an audience. He knew he would need to do some relationship building. He noticed how some of the contracted staff looked at him. He knew people talked and he was sure people at this new facility knew about what happened to him in the fall. He needed some advice and he knew just who to call.

Once he finished two of the eight floors he was responsible for, Monti returned to his office to make a call. He had to get his image back and figure out what to do to get the ball rolling.

"Harper & Associates, how may I help you?" The voice on the other end answered.

"Good morning, Is Mr. Williams available?"

"May I let him know who is calling?"

"Sure, this is Monti Burroughs. We met a few months ago when he was in Detroit."

"Just a moment, Mr. Burroughs."

Monti waited while the receptionist patched him to Harper. Monti didn't know what he wanted to talk about but he knew he needed some direction. It seemed like an eternity he was on hold and would have normally hung up the phone but his drive to get Cameron back made him find patience.

"This is Mr. Williams. How can I help you Mr. Burroughs?"

"Good morning. I'm not sure if you remember who…"

"Yes, I remember you from the hospital right?"

"Exactly." Monti replied.

"So what can I help you with Mr. Burroughs?"

"Well you gave me your card when you were at the hospital. I want to see if you can help me. I did some research about your company and you all help people rebuild their image as well as handle various scandalous situations."

"That's correct. We handle clients who are public images and celebrities."

"Well I'm neither of those but my integrity, image and even my swagger has been tarnished."

"What do you mean tarnished?"

"I was the target of a guy who took some photos of me."

"Mr. Burroughs, if you are wanting my assistance you have to be up front and honest with me about what happened. I will need to know exactly what happened. You are going to have to face your ugliness so I can ascertain if I can be of assistance to you."

"Okay but please call me Monti."

"Alright Monti…please go ahead."

"I was in Palmer Park here in Detroit and I met a guy. We ended up hooking up…well fucking in the park. Someone took photos of me while we were getting it in. Then I was blackmailed by this guy to tell my partner about what I had been doing and how I had been cheating on him or he was going to ruin my life."

"Well this sounds more like a personal vendetta rather than a scandal. Do you know what the motives were behind all this?" Harper asked.

"No, I never found out why."

"Did you notify the authorities when you were blackmailed?"

"No, I didn't."

"Why?"

"I didn't know what was going on initially. It wasn't until I saw the photos that I knew what he had on me."

"Why didn't you just tell your partner about your indiscretions?" Harper asked.

"I was already on my last chance with him. I didn't want to lose him."

"So you are both still together?"

"No, he left me. I'm trying to win him back. He is stubborn and hard-headed so it is taking more time than I anticipated getting him back." Monti said.

"So what is it you would like from me? I tried to holler at you when I was in Detroit but you blew me off. You didn't seem to be having these issues at that time. If you did, you sure hid it well."

"Well, I apologize for not taking you up on your offer. I wasn't having these issues then. In fact, all this happened after your visit."

"No problem. I'm sure we would have had a good time but that's neither here nor there. So now, what is it you think I can do to help you in this situation?" Harper said.

"I desperately need to get Cameron back. I feel we didn't get to work on this relationship and grow together as a couple. This situation came and interrupted our life together. I just want to have another chance to prove to Cameron I'm a good guy and I can make him happy."

"Honestly Monti, I can bring up your request to our image consultant team and see if they are willing to take on your case."

"I don't want your team. You are a handsome brother and you have your stuff together. I want you to help me personally."

"Monti, I don't come cheap. I'm here to make money. I'm the CEO of one of the most respected consulting firm in the country. I deal with A-list actors, sports figures and politicians."

"I know…I did my research about you and your company. I'm not saying I have deep pockets but I'm sure we can figure something out. Even if you just give me guidance on what I can do personally."

"Monti, I'm a busy man and I'm not sure I can effectively

address your issues. Generally, my company makes public scandals go away. We deal with elections and those types of things. You want me to make a person whom you don't deserve get back with you."

"I know it sounds bad. Harper…I'm desperate. He is all I think about. He is who I'm supposed to grow old with. Yes, I have dated and tried to move on but I just can't let go of him. I'm in love with this man."

"I will tell you what…I will take your case on pro bono to help you and guide you, but you are going to have to do the work."

"I can do that. Thanks…by the way, how much does one pay you to take on their case?"

"My retainer is $50,000 to start and depending on the complexity of the case it goes from there." Harper explained.

"Damn, you are big time."

"I'm the top of what I do. So the first thing that you are going to do is find out why this person or people did what they did to you? Did they do it because they wanted your partner or was it something deeper? You want to ensure that you don't anger them anymore than you have."

"Okay, I will do that. How often should we meet or talk."

"We can chat as needed. Once you have completed one task then we will regroup and go from there."

"That sounds good. Who knows maybe I can make it out to Chicago to make up for missing you while you were here in Detroit?"

"Mr. Burroughs…isn't that what got you into the situation you are in now?"

"You are right, but you can't fault a brother for trying."

"You are a piece of work Monti. I have to get off of here. I have another client coming in that I have to prepare for. Don't get yourself into any more trouble."

"I won't. Thanks again for your help. Have a nice day."

"You as well." Harper replied.

Monti hung up the phone feeling like he had taken the right step. He knew that Harper had a reputation for handling situations with great outcomes and Monti wanted a great outcome in his situation. He was contemplating how he was going to approach Calvin to get to the bottom of why he would set out to destroy him, when his phone rang.

"Monti Burroughs, EMS Supervisor, how can I help you?"

"Mr. Burroughs, this is Bruce. I'm up on the sixth floor by the waste disposal room. Britany was complaining about her chest hurting and she passed out. I called the nursing station and they are here working on her now. I think you should come up here right away."

"Okay Bruce. Stay calm. I'm on my way." Monti responded.

Monti hung up the phone and made his way to the elevator. Once he reached the elevators, he pushed the up button. It took what seemed like an eternity for the car to arrive. Once it did, he entered it and inserted his key to make the elevator express to the sixth floor. The elevator doors closed and he was on his way to do what he could do to help his staff member who was in cardiac arrest.

Once on the sixth floor, he walked over to the waste disposal room where ten other people had already gathered outside of the room. They were watching the trauma team work on his employee. They had the defibrillator connected to her and there was so much commotion all around her. Monti felt bad as he saw his employee lying lifeless on the floor with tubes and people working on her. He had seen people code at the hospital time and time again but this concerned him that this was time it was his own employee.

"Mr. Burroughs, I'm glad you made it. The other employees that are here are having a hard time seeing her that way." Bruce said.

"I will go talk to them in a minute." Monti noticed that the trauma team now had Britany on a stretcher and were headed to the elevator. "Excuse me, Bruce."

Monti walked back to the waste disposal room, where he saw the room in disarray with various disposable medical equipment strewn throughout the room. Monti decided that he needed to clean up the room. He put on a pair of gloves and bent down to gather some of the discarded items in his hands. Once his hands were full, he put the items in the disposable waste container. He returned back to the items on the floor. He gathered more of the items that were on the ground and took them to the container. When he bent over to throw the discarded items, his ID badge fell into the container. He heard the sound of it falling in and reached into the container after it. When he was removing his hand from the container, he felt a sharp pain in his hand.

"Damn." Monti yelled. "Fuck." He walked out of the room and to the nursing station as blood traveled down from the top of his index finger to the palm of his right hand.

"I have been stuck by a needle in the sharps container." Monti said.

CHAPTER TWENTY-SIX-CAMERON

"Is Cameron available?"

"Speaking. Who is this?"

"Calvin man...you don't recognize my voice anymore?" He said.

"Fool...what is up with you? Since when do you start calling from blocked numbers and all that?"

"I was just messing with this new phone. What you been up to?"

"I'm chillin at the moment. What you up to?"

"I'm doing the same thing. I wanted to see if you wanted to go see that movie with Will Smith and his son?"

"You mean *The Pursuit of Happyness*?" Cameron asked.

"Yeah, that's the one. I heard that it is a good flick."

"Interesting..."

"What is interesting?"

"I never thought that you were the type of guy that was into that kind of movie."

"I'm always good for a good movie. I do want to see this one but I want to spend some time with you. If you aren't too uncomfortable with that?" Calvin inquired.

"Do you remember our last conversation...I was cool with it. I think you are cool. Though it has been about a month since we last talked and we were supposed to go for drinks or something."

"You are right...my bad Cam. Let me make it up to you...we can do, drinks, a movie and allow what is to follow...follow."

"Are you trying to sleep with me, Calvin?" Cameron asked.

"Well it ain't no secret that I think you are sexy as fuck; I'm down with it if the night goes that way."

"Humm...you better be ready for me then." Cameron said playfully.

"Oh you got it like that?"

"If it goes down...I can handle whatever comes my way."

"We'll see, but anyway, I'm going to pick you up about seven o'clock. Is that good?" Calvin said.

"Oh so I get chauffeured as well?"

"Don't be grand, Cameron. I'm feeling you and I may like dick but I'm all guy here, too."

"Don't get all wrapped up in those titles. We can talk about this later. I got some things to do before my chariot arrives."

"I will see you later."

"Don't you need my address?" Cameron asked.

"Oh yes, I almost forgot. Text it to me and I will put it in the GPS." Calvin said forgetting that he hadn't officially been to Cameron's house.

"Okay. I will do that right now. See you tonight."

* * * *

"Calvin, are you sure you are okay to drive?" Cameron asked.

"Yeah man. I'm good. I had only a couple drinks."

"A couple, is that what you call six drinks? I think maybe you should let me drive. I had half of what you did. Plus you are slurring your words now."

"Okay Cameron…just don't wreck my shit." Calvin slurred.

Cameron took the keys from Calvin and got into the driver's seat. Calvin got in on the passenger's side. Within a few minutes, they were traveling westbound on Eureka road towards Cameron's house.

"Hey yo…that movie was good as hell. Will Smith is a good ass actor."

"Yes, I agree the movie was good. It is good to see African-American guys in a positive role. It gives me hope that I will find someone that's family oriented."

"Yeah. I mean he is sexy as hell."

"That's the only thing you got from the movie, that he is sexy as hell?" Cameron asked.

"No, I got more but a dude is horny as hell right now."

"Oh so your hormones are speaking for you tonight. I see how that is."

"Cam...you ain't gonna blow a muthafucka off. You know you got me feelin some kinda way." Calvin reached across and put his hand on Cameron's right thigh. "Man, I been wantin to be with you for a minute."

Cameron knew that Calvin liked him but he didn't know to what extent that like was. It had been a minute since Cameron had some too. Calvin was sexy as hell and Cameron wanted him as well.

"I won't blow you off Calvin. It's all good here. I'm down with you too."

"Straight up?"

"Yes, straight up."

Cameron continued to drive. They were about ten minutes from his house. He knew that there was no way he was letting Calvin drive home tonight. He didn't want something to happen to him...plus this was a good time to fulfill his desire to be with Calvin.

Calvin reached into the glove compartment and retrieved a container of tic-tacs. He put a couple in his mouth and handed the container to Cameron. He did the same thing. Cameron kept his eyes on the road, while Calvin kept his eyes on Cameron's crotch. Cameron's pants left very little secret. They weren't tight but sitting down and his arousal caused things to show more. As they got closer to Cameron's house, Calvin's hand went from Cameron's thigh to his crotch.

They pulled up to Cameron's townhouse and parked right in

front. The two exited Calvin's car and headed to the front door. Once inside, they took the stairs up to the living room.

"Damn Cam, your spot is nice."

"Thanks Calvin. I try…"

Calvin smiled and pulled his jacket open. His t-shirt embraced his muscles. His shirt had a distressed emblem of Superman which seemed to be stretched from the size of his muscles. Cameron's first thought of the shirt would normally have been 'damn that's a little childish' but at this moment, it was 'damn, that shit is hot'. Calvin stepped out of his tennis shoes "I'm glad to be spending time with you Cam."

"Likewise." Cameron said as he stood there watching Calvin get undressed. Something about Calvin's confidence made Cameron get excited. He had planned how he wanted the night to end but he saw that Calvin had ideas of his own.

Cameron watched as Calvin unbuttoned his jeans. "You are giving me a show?"

"Shh…just enjoy the moment Cameron."

Cameron dimmed the lighting and took a seat watching this live performance. Calvin slid his fingers into the waist band of his pants. The jean material clung to his muscular ass and thighs as long as it could before he pushed them down to the floor. Cameron smiled at the caramel complexion of Calvin's tattooed skin. Cameron was excited from the show that Calvin was giving him. Calvin turned around showing Cameron that he was wearing a black jock strap. His muscular ass flexed as he bent over to take off his socks.

Once his socks were off, he turned back around to face Cameron with just his Superman shirt and black jock on. "Are you gonna take off your clothes or what?"

"Yes…sure." Cameron said as he crouched down to untie his shoes. Once his shoes were loose, Cameron unbuttoned his shirt. As he was trying to take his shirt off, Calvin walked over to him and pulled it from his back. He reached his hand down to help Cameron up. Let me handle that part…referring to Cameron's pants.

Calvin reached down and unbuckled Cameron's pants. He ran his hands around Cameron's waistband and then got down on his knees taking Cameron's pants and boxer briefs with him. There was no hiding Cameron's arousal at this point. Standing there in the dimly lit living room with nothing but socks on, Calvin was eye to eye with Cameron's semi-erect manhood.

"Now that's better." Calvin said as he wrapped his hand around Cameron's sex. With Cameron, in his hands, Calvin pulled him closer as he inhaled Cameron's manicured pubic hair. Lust moved through Calvin. His mouth began to water as he stroked and caressed Cameron. He treated Cameron's sex like it was a lollipop, the kind you get after a doctor appointment. He wanted it like a drug addict wants another hit.

Cameron echoed Calvin's touch except he was rubbing Calvin's head anticipating the warmth that waited for him inside Calvin's dick sucking lips. "What are you waiting on? You know what you want." Cameron said surprising himself by his choice of words.

Instinctively, Calvin opened his mouth and in one swift move, he inhaled Cameron's manhood to the back of his throat. Cameron exhaled from the feeling of the warmth and wetness of Calvin's mouth. Calvin gagged on the girth and length of Cameron's sex, but desire made him go further ignoring his overwhelming urge to take a breath. Calvin knew what to do with his mouth, with his tongue, with his lips and with his hands. He was an expert head master.

Cameron spread his legs to stabilize himself from Calvin's oral assault. Calvin reached around grabbing Cameron's ass pulling him in deeper. Cameron groaned from lust and soon was meeting Calvin's head with thrusts of his own.

"Fuck you taste good, Cameron." Calvin said.

"You feel good as fuck."

Calvin grinned, pleased to be pleasing Cameron. Calvin's head moved as if it was dancing and Cameron's manhood was his partner. Soon Calvin knew why he had wanted to be with Cameron. As he continued to orally service Cameron, he received a surprise of his own with the appearance of Cameron's precum, sweet and silky. Calvin grabbed Cameron's stiffness from the base and moved his hand up the shaft bringing up more of his pre-cum. He licked the head of Cameron's dick to try to draw more up.

Calvin loved Cameron's scent. He loved the taste of Cameron. He loved Cameron's bowed legs. He continued to deep throat Cameron's manhood while grabbing his ball sack, trying to urge them to release more precum. With his eyes closed, Cameron stood there enjoying Calvin's skills. It has been a while since he had relations and he was going to make sure this was thoroughly enjoyed.

"Let's go upstairs. I have to put in some work to reward you for your good oral skills." Cameron needed a break because Calvin had him close to the point of no return.

"Anywhere you want me to go, I'm there." Calvin said getting up from his knees.

"After you." Cameron said as he motioned towards the stairs.

They hit the stairs ascending to Cameron's room. As Calvin got halfway up the stairwell, he sat on the stairs, without saying a word, and pulled Cameron to him and kissed him. Cameron kissed him back in the darkness. The heat that radiated from the two of them burned hotter as each minute passed.

"Damn, I want you!" Cameron said in between kisses.

"It's all yours."

"Are you down for some hardcore shit?" Cameron asked.

"Hell yeah. I'm down." Calvin replied.

Cameron looked at him with left on but Calvin's jock. Cameron could tell Calvin was ready. Calvin turned around and knelt down on a stair exposing his jock strap framed ass to Cameron's face. Cameron saw this as an opportunity to see just how far Calvin would let him go. He rubbed his open hand on Calvin's ass. Calvin responded by arching his back and pushing his ass into Cameron's hand.

Cameron smacked Calvin's bare ass cheek.

"Ahh...yes." He said.

"You like that don't you, boy?" Cameron asked.

"Hell yeah." Calvin replied.

Cameron smacked his ass again...this time with more force. "Hell yeah...what?" Cameron asked.

"Hell yeah...Sir." Calvin said.

Cameron began to spank Calvin with a rhythm only he knew. Calvin's body responded for more and more. Soon, Cameron was able to feel heat radiating from Calvin's ass. It had warmed up quickly. Cameron's attention was distracted when he noticed that his own manhood had stiffened and was dripping precum. Cameron surprised himself by his reaction to the spanking. He didn't know that he had a sadistic side. He remembered being in Amsterdam and how aroused he became in the bar. He knew that he wanted to explore this more and Calvin was the receptive vessel. Cameron was going to make the best of this night.

Cameron grabbed Calvin's ass cheeks and spread them to give him time to come down from the corporal punishment. He probed Calvin with his fingers and his tongue. He was turned on eating Calvin's ass. He wanted Calvin with an urgency unparalleled to anything he'd felt before. Coming up for a breath, Cameron smacked Calvin on his ass and said "I'm going to tear this ass up. Let's go!"

Once in Cameron's room, Calvin climbed face first into the bed. Cameron just took in the sight of his muscular frame spread eagle in his bed, with nothing on but his jock strap framing his now reddened ass.

"Stay there." Cameron ordered.

"Yes Sir." Calvin answered.

Cameron got condoms and lube out of the drawer on the side of his bed. He sat on the edge of the bed while he opened the wrapper. Once ready…Cameron rolled over in between Calvin's already spread legs, pressing his manhood against his waiting ass. He leaned into Calvin "I'm going to beat that ass up tonight." Cameron said.

Without waiting on a response, Cameron put his hand on Calvin's neck, holding him down, as he slid his manhood in his willing ass. Once he felt himself all the way in, Cameron wasted no time to allow him to adjust to his thickness, he started grinding into Calvin.

He knew Calvin was enjoying himself when he started to gyrate his hips with Cameron plunged all the way in. Cameron stroked him slowly, listening to him moaning softly. After a while, Cameron started to pick up the pace, fucking him harder and faster.

"Yes Sir, fuck me harder." Calvin said.

Cameron was happy to oblige this request as Calvin raised up on all fours. Cameron stepped one leg over Calvin, into a modified scissor, to reach the depths of Calvin, long-stroking him with everything he had. Calvin only responded back by asking for more. Calvin had an insatiable desire to be filled and Cameron was there to fuck him silly. Cameron moved him to the edge of his bed where he used the floor as leverage. Cameron smacked Calvin's ass with his large open palm.

"Oh shit…" Calvin responded.

"You like that boy?" Cameron said.

"Hell yeah…I like it."

"Hell yeah…what?" Cameron asked hitting him harder with both his hand and his sex.

"Hell yeah, Sir." He responded.

Cameron continued his sexual assault on a willing Calvin. When he was ready to see Calvin cum…Cameron grabbed the lube he left on the nightstand and poured some in his hand. He turned Calvin on his side, giving him access to his rock hard manhood. With Calvin's right leg on Cameron's left shoulder and Calvin's sex in Cameron's right lubed hand, Cameron stroked him while stroking his ass. Cameron knew Calvin was close to his climax when Calvin's muscular leg locked around him pulling him closer to him.

"Oh shit, Sir." He said

"You ready to come for me?"

"Yes…" Calvin responded.

"Yes, what?"

"Yes, Sir."

"Show me…" Cameron commanded. "Jack that dick for me."

Calvin took his sex into his hand and started stroking it. Cameron felt his manhood thicken at the same time he felt Calvin's ass start to pulsate. Cameron reached down and grabbed Calvin's throat.

"Show me how much you like this." Cameron said.

"Here it comes, Sir."

Cameron was pulled violently by Calvin's muscular legs that were now squeezing the life out of him. Calvin's body began to convulse from the stimulation. Cameron let up on Calvin's throat as creamy white sex juice shot out from Calvin's stiffness landing on his chest and stomach. The sight of Calvin climaxing sent Cameron off. While still deep inside of Calvin, Cameron's stomach seized sending cum out of his body and into the tip of the condom he was wearing. Cameron was exhausted, as he pulled himself out of Calvin and laid beside him. Calvin rolled over and laid his head on Cameron's chest and threw his arm around Cameron. They held each other. A few minutes later, Cameron heard Calvin snoring.

"Damn…he fell out!" Cameron said to himself.

CHAPTER TWENTY-SEVEN-YOLANDA

"Hey honey. We are about five minutes away."

"Okay. I'm here. I'm looking forward to this weekend with you and the boys here with me and my daughter. I think it is time they get to know each other." Roderick said.

"I'm looking forward to this as well. I will see you soon."

Yolanda was excited about what this weekend meant. This was Roderick's weekend with his daughter and he thought it would be good to introduce the kids to each other. She and Roderick had been dating for about three months. Things were going well. Her two boys liked Roderick, who became more like a father figure with them, since Monti wasn't spending time with them. She made attempts to call him to see if he was going to address his anger issues. Many of her calls went unanswered so she just continued to do what she needed to do in the best interest of the boys. She wasn't trying to replace Monti in their lives but wanted them to have a consistent male figure in their lives. She saw some of Monti's traits in Monti Jr.

As Monti Jr continued to grow up, she began to suspect her son was gay. He was an intelligent kid but he had begun to have a smart mouth. She overheard some of his conversations on the phone where he would 'read' some of his friends. Even his mannerisms became more and more feminine. He also began to be reclusive. His brother, on the other hand, wanted to play football and basketball. Monti Jr decided to go into band and student government. Yolanda tried to talk to him but lacked the experience and courage to tackle this conversation. She decided this weekend she would talk to Roderick about it and they could tackle this together.

They pulled up to Roderick's house and got their bags out of the car. Yolanda used the key Roderick gave her during Thanksgiving to let them in.

"Roderick, we are here." She called out.

"Hey baby, I will be there in a second."

"Don't rush. I'll let the boys get settled and I will be right there."

"Okay." He replied.

Yolanda took the boys to the guest room in Roderick's four-bedroom house. Though he didn't have full custody of his daughter, he had a bedroom for her.

"You guys get settled in and we will talk about what we are going to eat for dinner, okay?"

"Yes mom." Corey said.

Yolanda left the room and walked towards the master bedroom. When she got to the room she found Roderick sitting on the bed with a smile on his face. Sitting next to him was a bed tray which had two glasses of red wine in them.

"Were you expecting someone?" Yolanda asked.

"She just arrived. Now come here." Roderick responded.

"Oh…I like it when you take control." She smiled

"I know you do."

Yolanda started walking towards Roderick seductively. As she made it closer to him, he reached out and grabbed her. He pulled her close and started kissing her.

"I've missed you so much baby." Roderick said.

"I missed you as well, but I'm here now so you won't have to miss me, at least not for this weekend."

"Just this weekend…you plan on going somewhere else?" He said jokingly.

"Humm…I don't know it depends on how you act."

"Oh really…what if I do this?" Roderick said as he began to tickle Yolanda, who was extremely ticklish.

"Stop that…"

"Why does it depend on how I act?" Roderick said as he continued to tickle her.

"You…know…I…am…" Yolanda was trying to talk but couldn't get the sentence out.

"So are you going anywhere after this?"

The tickling was getting too much for Yolanda. She had to get him to stop. So she leaned into Roderick. He wasn't anticipating her moving closer to him and her momentum pushed him back in the bed. The motion of the two of them disturbed the two glasses of wine sitting next to him. They both fell over toward Yolanda and

Roderick. The wine quickly travelled towards them, finally spilling onto Roderick's light blue shirt and the top of his blue jean shorts. Yolanda got up giving Roderick room to do the same.

"Oh no…that was a good glass of wine too." Roderick said.

"I'm sorry honey. I didn't mean for that to happen."

"Don't worry about that. I have Scotch Gard on the mattress."

Roderick ran to the bathroom to get a cleaning towel to soak up the wine as Yolanda picked up the glass and removed the tray off the bed. She placed it on the dresser as he returned with the towel. Within a few moments, he had soaked up the majority of the wine and was removing the bedspread off the bed.

"You have some wine on your shirt and your shorts." Yolanda said.

"I know…I can feel it."

"You better go and take off those clothes. We have to soak them so the stain can't set. I'll go get some detergent."

"Okay…it is in the laundry room by the kitchen." He said.

"Okay…run some cool water and take those clothes off. I will be right back."

Roderick went to the bathroom and turned on the water. Yolanda walked out of the room and made her way towards the laundry room. When she made it to the kitchen, she heard a knock on the door.

"I'll get it." She said. She walked over to the front door and opened it. She saw a brown-skinned, medium sized woman standing about five foot tall with a naturally curly hair style. She wore earth toned bronzing makeup which was radiant. Next to her stood a young caramel skinned girl with long silky ponytails, Yolanda was reminded just how diverse and beautiful her black sisters were.

"Who are you?" The woman said with an attitude.

"Excuse me...I'm doing well thank you. What about you?" Yolanda responded.

"Oh...you are one of those sadity bitches, I see."

"I'm sorry...do we know each other?"

"You should know me...you're the bitch that took Roderick from me."

"I don't think we know each other. I also don't believe I took Roderick from anyone. Who are you?"

"I'm Stacy. Roderick's daughter's mother." Stacy said. "How does it feel to be the home wrecker?"

"Stacy...I don't know what you think this is, but I'm not a home wrecker. I'm not sure what to think about this or about you. Why do you have an attitude with me?" Yolanda questioned.

"Look bitch...don't think you are better than me. You deserve him, if you think you are going to be the only one..."

"Stacy...please don't do this in front of you daughter. Have some respect for yourself." Yolanda interrupted.

"Don't tell me what to do and where to do it. You don't know me."

"I'm just saying we should be better than this. I don't know you...not that I would want to, seeing how ghetto you are acting."

"You ain't gonna talk to me like that. I'll tell you what..."

The next thing Yolanda knew, Stacy had slapped her and she felt the sting of it on her face. Something in Yolanda snapped and she lunged at Stacy. The two women fell down with Yolanda on top of Stacy. She took advantage of the situation, pinning Stacy's arms to the ground with her knees. Yolanda saw red as her adrenaline flowed through her veins. She grabbed a handful of Stacy's curly natural hair and started punching her on the side of her head.

"Mommy..." Diana screamed.

Corey and Monti Jr. heard the commotion and were standing in the doorway taking on the scene.

"Mom...Stop!" Corey said.

Roderick came to the hallway when he heard the noise. When it finally registered what was happening, he came out the door and caught Yolanda's fist as it was preparing to connect with Stacy's head again.

"Wait...What is going on?" He asked, pulling Yolanda off Stacy.

"Ask this tramp. She had an attitude when I answered the door. Then she hit me."

"What the hell is wrong with you Stacy?" Roderick asked as he turned to a battered Stacy, who was just getting to her feet.

"She had an attitude with me when she opened the door. Why didn't you tell me your whore was going to be here when I came to drop off our daughter?"

"Whore…" Yolanda lunged and connected a fist to Stacy's jaw. "I got your whore."

"Stop acting like this in front of the kids…both of you." Roderick said pulling Yolanda back again.

"Daddy…" Diana sobbed.

"It's going to be okay honey. Go into the house to your room and I will be there in a minute. Boys you do the same." Roderick ordered.

The three kids went into the house. Roderick closed the front door. He turned around to see the mother of his daughter battered and the woman he fell in love with fuming. He could see Yolanda's face turned red where Stacy slapped her. "You both have to stop acting like little kids."

"I'm not going to let some strange crazy woman hit me for no reason." Yolanda said. "I had to make sure she knew not to fuck with me again. She better have gotten the lesson the first time, because next time she won't come out so lucky."

"You don't scare me." Stacy said.

"Damn…Stacy. Why can't you just act right for a change? It didn't work between the two of us. We have to get along because we share a beautiful child. You might as well get that understanding. Yolanda and I are together and that isn't going to change no time soon. Who knows…maybe she will accept me as her husband one day. But I'm not going to allow you to disrupt our lives."

"Husband? Whatever." Stacy asked.

"Yes…husband. Like it or not…she is going to be in my life and in the life of our daughter. She is a good woman and a great mother."

"Oh…it's like that?" She said.

"Yes…it is very much like that. I'm happy…I'm loved…and I'm in love."

Yolanda felt horrible she let Stacy push her buttons to get her to that point. Stacy's words stung like they did when her step mother told her she was an ungrateful, sadity girl. She had held the pain of her step mother in for a long time. She felt a release of the pain and the hurt she had. However, it was Stacy on the receiving end of that pain.

"It's time for you to leave…Stacy." Roderick said. "I will bring Diana home tomorrow night."

"This ain't over Roderick." She said as she turned to go back to her car.

Roderick turned around and looked at Yolanda. He shook his head as he walked over to her and put his arm around her. "Come on champ. We have to make sure the kids are okay." The two of them walked into the house to check on the kids. They had to make sure they knew this wasn't appropriate behavior.

CHAPTER TWENTY-EIGHT-SHAINE

"Good morning Shaine." Adrienne said.

"Hey sista girl. How was your weekend?"

"It was okay. I spent most of the weekend cramming for my exams. I have to finish up my designs for the end of this course, so I don't have time for a social life or just to have fun."

"I remember those days. You just have to keep pushing. You are very close to being done."

Adrienne sat there for a few seconds day dreaming. She thought about how successful Shaine was. She thought about how she lived a perfect life. She was successful in her career, had a great group of friends, and such a handsome, eligible man. Adrienne wanted this life for her.

"Can I ask you a question?" Adrienne asked.

"Sure what's up?" Shaine responded.

"How did you do it? I mean you have the life any woman would want. You have the best of the both worlds...a great career where you are respected and valued and guy who loves and supports you in your endeavors."

"Adrienne, it didn't happen overnight. There have been many days and nights where I was alone. I would want to give up my dreams and find something that would allow me to just get by, but I had to remember the situation I saw on a daily basis was my destiny. I had to understand I had to do my part and prepare myself so when it came, I would know it and would be ready for it."

"I want that for me…it is just so hard to see if from where I sit." Adrienne exhaled in defeat.

"Do you have a relationship with God?"

"No, I don't believe in that religion stuff."

"That's not what I asked you. Religion is a bunch of manmade rules created to oppress people. What I asked you was do you have a relationship with God? That makes a big difference in life."

"What do you mean?"

"Relationship opens doors for you that religion doesn't. Relationship comforts you when you are hurting. Relationship holds your hand when you are walking and lets you know all will be well. Religion hurts when you don't agree with them. Religion oppresses you when you aren't on the same sheet of music. Religion doesn't allow you to question when you don't understand. Religion isn't the same as relationship." Shaine explained.

"You are so deep…I guess I have to say I don't have one."

"Honey…that's what you should be looking for right now. If you look for a relationship with God, then you will find that walking on your path to destiny will be better. I didn't say easy, I said better. Right now you are walking blindly through this thing called life with ambition and aspirations but no guidance and direction."

"You are so knowledgeable Shaine. I want to be in your shoes."

"My shoes are already filled…you need to be in Adrienne's shoes."

Adrienne sat back down and thought about the things Shaine had shared with her. She was still unable to understand the concept of patience bringing satisfaction. She was young and wanted what she wanted. Adrienne was a part of the microwave generation but was living in a crock pot world. Success wasn't created overnight for most people. Sadly, Adrienne wanted it today.

"Hello?" Shaine said bringing Adrienne out of her moment of thought.

"Yes, Shaine. I'm sorry. I was just thinking about what you were saying."

"It's okay. I understand how heavy it can be sometimes. I'm about to head to an off-site meeting. I will be gone for most of the day. If you need me, I will be on my blackberry."

"Okay."

Shaine gathered her briefcase and her Prada purse and left to the parking structure. Adrienne sat in the stillness of the room. She couldn't focus on homework or the project Shaine had her working on for the spring fashion show. Something had to happen for her and it had to happen soon. She was determined to help destiny out. She sat there for another few minutes thinking about her past. She thought about her mother, whom she never got a chance to meet because she died in child birth. She thought about her father who was so hurt with grief he couldn't be a parent to her. She remembered when she woke up and saw her dad passed out with a rubber tube tied around his left arm. She remembered calling 911 when she was twelve years old because she came home from school and he was on the floor. She remembered being raped at the age of fifteen when she was coming home from the store after pan-handling money because there was no food in the house. She remembered leaving the clinic twelve weeks later because she was pregnant as a result of the rape. She remembered being classified as a whore because she was a pregnant teenager. She cried because she had her share of life's downs. Life wasn't good to Adrienne. She had decided she was taking her life in her hands and she was going to make it the best she could.

"Are you okay?" Adrienne heard.

Wiping her eyes…"Yes, I'm okay. Sorry." She replied, looking around.

"No need to apologize, Adrienne." Jonathan said. "I came here to surprise Shaine but I see she isn't here. I guess the surprise is on me."

"No she left to go to a meeting off-site. She said she will be gone for the majority of the day."

"Oh okay." Jonathan could see Adrienne wasn't in a good place. "Are you sure you are okay. Want to talk about it?" He offered.

"I was just thinking about some things that happened to me when I was younger."

"Oh you had a rough time?" Jonathan asked.

"Rough time…that isn't even the half of it." She responded.

"I'm sure I can tell you some stories of my upbringing as well. I'm here. I cleared my schedule." He said as he sat down across from Adrienne.

Adrienne started to talk about her upbringing. She was hesitant to tell about all the things she had gone through. She didn't share she had been in and out of foster homes while her dad went through rehab. She didn't tell Jonathan about her mom's parents turned their back on her because they blamed her for their only child's death. In some people's eyes, the sun never rose in Adrienne's life.

Jonathan was moved by hearing Adrienne's story. He couldn't watch her just sit there without trying to support her in her purging. He got up and walked over to her.

"I'm so sorry to hear you have been through so much." He pulled out his handkerchief and wiped the tears flowing from her eyes.

"Thanks. It means so much to hear that. My dad never even acknowledges anything bad happened."

Thinking about her last statement, Adrienne began crying again. Jonathan pulled her close to him and held her. "It's okay. Let it out." He said.

Adrienne sobbed as Jonathan held her in his arms. "I just wanted to be loved. All I wanted I wanted was someone to love me."

She looked up at Jonathan and decided in that moment Jonathan loved her. She pulled him close to her and kissed him.

Jonathan was in shock by what was transpiring and was paralyzed while he was trying to gather his thoughts. His mind said "This couldn't be happening." His body was saying "This is happening." Rational thinking finally hit him when he heard…

"What the hell is going on in here?" Shaine stood in the doorway with disgust, hurt and pain on her face.

"Shaine…" Jonathan and Adrienne said simultaneously.

"It's not what you think baby." Jonathan said as he let Adrienne go.

"No, it isn't what I think…it is what I saw." Shaine said.

"Shaine…I'm so sorry." Adrienne said.

"Adrienne…I need you to leave right now. I need to think about this. We will talk about this later. I just can't stand the sight of you right now."

"Okay…I'm sincerely sorry." She said as she picked up her purse and walked out of the door.

Shaine turned her attention to Jonathan.

"Can you explain why I walked in and found my fiancé locking lips with my intern?"

"Shaine…it isn't what you think. I came here to surprise you. I cleared my schedule to come see you. When I got here Adrienne was sitting here crying. She was upset…then she started telling me about her upbringing. She shared she was raped and her father was a drug addict. She was torn with emotion. I was just trying to give her a shoulder to cry on. When I went to hug her and let her know it was going to be alright…she grabbed me and kissed me. I guess that was when you walked in. I was in shock and didn't know what was going on…honey you have to believe me. I love you and want you to be in my life. I was just trying to be a friend…"

"A friend…she is an intern and not your friend. You barely know her…"

"I know baby. You should have seen her." Jonathan said.

"So you went to comfort her and she kissed you?"

"Yes honey, she kissed me. I was just trying to console her. She has had a rough life."

"You are going to have a rougher life if I ever catch you locking lips with someone again." Shaine said.

"Thank you for being understanding. You know you are my one and only. I'm in love with you Shaine Holloway and I want to be with you for the rest of our lives."

"You know I love you too. Unfortunately, I have to handle this situation with Adrienne though. I won't have a snake in my office on a daily basis."

"I think you should talk to her. She has no mother figure…she just needs help and guidance. I think you could turn this particularly disastrous situation into something that's good."

"I'm not a psychologist…I'm a woman who sees another woman is trying to replace me. I have to eliminate the threat."

"There is no threat, Shaine. I only want you…period…end of the story."

"We will see. Let's go to lunch. My meeting was cancelled. They called me when I was halfway there. They rescheduled it for next week."

"Okay my leading lady. Let's go."

CHAPTER TWENTY-NINE-MONTI

"Mr. Burroughs, hospital policy mandates that with an accidental needle stick, we test you for several different items. We tested you for HIV, Hepatitis B and C and took an alanine aminotransferase (ALT) test. These tests are taken to establish your pre-exposure health. Since we were unable to identify the patient connected to the needle, we also ran a full sexually transmitted disease battery to gain baseline data."

"Okay Doc. I understand that. So just tell me what is going on. Am I clean or what." Monti asked.

"Mr. Burroughs, your medical records show you have previously received your HBV vaccine. You are fully protected and need no further treatment for that. Your HCV or Hepatitis C test came back negative as well. We are going to do two follow-up tests for this one month and two months out to make sure you are clear of Hepatitis C. I have reviewed your ALT test which measures the amount of ALT enzyme in your blood. This test confirms you don't have any liver damage."

"Okay…that's all good. So I guess I'm alright then." Monti said.

"Almost done here Mr. Burroughs…how many sexual partners have you had in the past six months?"

"Excuse me?" Monti responded

"I'm sorry…how many sexual partners have you had in the past six months?"

"What does that have to do with me getting stuck with a needle?" Monti responded.

"Have you flu-like symptoms in the past month?" The doctor asked.

"Yes…I was sick about two or three weeks ago. Why?"

"We performed an HIV test and the results came back that you have HIV antibodies. This test was followed up with a Western Blot test to ensure that the first test was correct. This also came back positive, confirming that you are HIV positive."

"You mean to tell me that I got HIV from getting stuck by a needle last week?"

"No, Mr. Burroughs. That's why I'm asking you who your sexual partners have been in the six months. We did a viral load test on your blood sample to determine the potential length of time you have been infected. Your viral load is way off the chart at over one million copies. This would tell me your infection occurred six to eight weeks ago."

"You are playing with me right?" Monti said.

"Mr. Burroughs, this isn't anything to play with. I'm required to report your results to the Center for Disease Control. We also need to get the names and contact information for anyone you have had sexual contact with in the past 6 months."

"You are going to tell them I gave them AIDS?" Monti asked.

"Mr. Burroughs, we would have to test you more to determine if you have AIDS. We need to do an additional blood test which will check your CD4 count. This will help determine your course of treatment along with the other baseline information we have."

"So again Doc, you are going to tell them I gave them AIDS"

"No, we are prohibited to disclose that type of information. We will only notify them of a potential exposure to the HIV virus and try to get them to come in for testing. Your identity will be protected."

"How long do I have to live?" Monti asked.

"I wouldn't tell you to go out and spend all your money. You will need it when you retire. HIV isn't as complicated to treat as some other conditions. For instance, if you were diabetic your doctor may have a harder time treating the diabetes. Generally, HIV treatment includes one or more pills you would take once a day."

"I saw that movie *Philadelphia*, where Tom Hanks had it. He got skinny and sick then died."

"Medicine has come a long way since that time. People are living happy, healthy and meaningful lives now. As long as you follow your doctor's instructions and minimize damaging behaviors you should be okay."

"What is my family going to think about me? I'm never going to be able to have a relationship again."

"You will be able to lead a full life, Mr. Burroughs. I haven't given you a death sentence. I have given you the information you need to take the necessary actions to live."

"No one wants a guy that has this. I'm damaged goods." Monti said.

"I will tell you this, Mr. Burroughs; you are just gaining this information. Don't make any judgments or rash decisions. I'm going to give you a few resources to help you understand what is going with you now. These people are great at what they do and you will be treated with the utmost respect and dignity."

"Thank you Doc." Monti said.

"But I will also need to know the names and contact information for the people you have had sexual encounters with."

The doctor handed Monti a notepad and pen. He stood up and patted Monti on his shoulder. "Sit tight. I will be back in a moment. It is okay you will get through this. We will need all sexual partners male and female. When you are done, just stick your head out and I will come back."

"Alright."

The doctor walked out of the exam room closing the door behind him. Sitting in the cold exam room just him and a note pad, the weight of what Monti had been carrying finally broke him. Monti broke down in the doctor's office. He felt he was on the right track making moves to get his life back in order and now his life was over. As tear after tear escaped his eyes, as his sinus cavity filled up, he wept. He wept as he thought about the times in the park. He wept recalling his escapades in the book stores. He wept thinking about him cheating on Yolanda. He wept at the thought of getting Cameron back. Monti wanted to scream, he wanted to run away and hide. He felt numb, but he had to make a choice. He needed to take time and space to think about the situation.

Monti went through his phone and wrote down the names and numbers of a few people he could remember. When looking over his list, what was clear to him was there were no females on this list. He was able to identify six guys he had sexual encounters with. He knew there were more; Monti just didn't keep contact information with guys he met in the park or bookstores. That was the purpose of the anonymous sex hook-ups…to keep them anonymous.

Looking over this list, he tried to identify which ones he had unprotected sex with. This only frustrated him even more because he wasn't able to. Most of the people he had sex with, he didn't know. He knew it was going to be a rough road ahead of him. Monti also noticed the lack of female names on his list. Feeling like he had completed his task, Monti called the doctor back in.

"Here you are doc. These are all the people I can think of right now."

"Thanks Mr. Burroughs. I want you to stay strong through this. I see you have been crying, just know it is okay and natural to be hurt. Think about it and know we are here for you if you need. You will probably get a phone call in the next day or so from the Center for Disease Control. Just be cooperative with them or they will keep calling you."

"Okay." Monti responded quietly.

"Here is the number to an HIV/AIDS organization located on Jefferson Avenue. They do great work there and have many different resources available to you. I strongly suggest you call them today after you leave the lab and get to see someone in the next day or so."

"I will." Monti stood up and walked to the door. As he

walked out of the door the doctor said.

"It will be alright, Mr. Burroughs. Trust me it will be." The doctor replied.

CHAPTER THIRTY-CAMERON

Cameron was in awe as he pulled up to the Renaissance Center. After he parked, he walked towards the five-story glass structure which resembles a glass ornament sitting at the edge of the Detroit riverfront. The Wintergarden is a beautiful addition to one of Detroit's signature buildings. Along the insides of the Wintergarden, palm trees majestically grow from circular holes in the gardens granite flooring. Natural light flooded the edifice, as the Saturday sun reflected off of the frozen river, making the winter grays obsolete at this location.

"Hey man how are you doing? You must be Brian?" Cameron said as he approached the table where Brian was sitting.

"And you must be Cameron. Pleasure to meet you." Brian responded.

"Likewise."

Cameron shook Brian's hand as he took a seat across from Brian at the small round table.

"I'm glad to finally be able to meet you. Kim tells me so

many good things about you." Brian said.

"She has told me great things about you as well. Normally, I don't mix business with my personal life but Kim has been a listening ear for me over the past two months."

"Yes, she is a good person. I'm glad she suggested we meet. I like what I see before me."

"Aww Brian, you are too kind. I got a lot of work to do to get this body back in shape. I appreciate the compliment thought."

"You look fine from where I'm sitting. Your eyes are amazing." Brian said.

"You are sexy as well. Tell me more about you? What are some of your likes and dislikes and stuff like that."

"I'm a no nonsense type of guy who isn't into drama. I like to enjoy life. I have spent far too much time in senseless relationships with people who were not a good fit for me. I was in a circle of ill-chosen relationships. I found I was with the same type of guy over and over again. They didn't have the same look per se; they had the same personalities."

"Wow Brian, that's deep. I know that oh to well. I just got out of a relationship with a guy who wouldn't know the truth if it slapped him in the face."

"Sounds like you haven't gotten over that situation." Brian noted.

"I'm over it. Believe me I'm. I'm ready to move on with my life. I refuse to be in a situation with someone who can't be honest with me and also just being honest about whom they are."

"If that's the case, I will tell you that you should do your research about me and find out who I'm. I don't mind getting to know you better. You are a sexy guy and I like what I'm looking at."

"Thanks Brian. I will do that but can I just get to know you with a conversation for now, Mister Handsome?"

"I'm okay with that. Your bowed-legs are the business. You are the type of guy that catches my attention."

"I'm glad to hear that." Cameron said.

Brian and Cameron continued to chat. They both were interested in each other physically but they also found they had several other things in common.

"I had an experience a few months ago when I was in Amsterdam and it really opened my mind to exploring some things which may not be considered your typical type of stuff." Cameron said.

"Oh…you did." Brian responded.

"Yes…and I'm not sure how well it will be received but I'm sure there is some guy out there that's open to exploring sexual freedom."

"I'm at a place in life where I'm into exploring. You know I'm feeling you on that sexual tip so how about we cut all the bullshit and do what it is we know we want to do? I'm sure with that mindset, you and I will hit it off just fine."

"Aren't you the most forward guy I've met…interesting, I like it though. It is attractive to deal with someone who is up front, open and honest." Cameron said.

Cameron was taken aback at the forward nature of Brian, but he found that sexy about him. He felt this was a good start and a good lesson to learn. Speak his truth…that's what Cameron would do moving forward. The two continued to talk and agreed to get to know each other.

"I acknowledge I'm honest and a straight shooter, but let's both be honest. We both want to get it in so let's not bullshit and do what we do." Brian said.

"I'm not saying we should rush to get into a relationship or anything right now but let's see where this can take us. I've been talking to a few guys over the past few weeks and it feels good to be back in the saddle."

"Got back in the saddle huh? I know you said you are over your last relationship; however is he over it as well?" Brian asked.

"Well, honestly, he isn't. He has some preconceived notion we are going to get back together. I will tell you this though…I'm over it. I can't let his inability to let go hold me hostage. I can understand if you don't want to talk to me, but I'm done with that situation."

"Okay, I can handle that. I think you are a cool guy so far. I hope you will think the same about me as you get to know me more."

"Great…I look forward to getting to know you better."

"I have to take care of some business…so let's talk tonight if you don't mind."

"I'm down with that" Cameron replied.

Brian got up from the table and shook Cameron's hand. He had a strong grip. Cameron watched as Brian walked out of the Wintergarden.

* * * * *

"Hello?" Cameron said answering his phone.

"Good afternoon, my name is Mrs. Jones. I'm calling from the Michigan Department of Community Health. May I speak with Mr. Cameron McNeil?"

"Speaking...how can I help you?"

"I'm giving you a call because we were informed you may have come in contact with someone who has been infected with Human Immunodeficiency Virus (HIV). We are strongly suggesting you see your health care professional as soon as possible."

"Excuse me?" Cameron responded.

"I said...I'm giving you a call..."

"I know what you said. I guess I should have asked...who have I had contact with that has HIV?"

"Mr. McNeil, for privacy purposes, we can't identify who you may have come in contact but please go to your doctor and get tested."

"Gee, thanks for being the bearer of good news." Cameron said as he hung up the phone.

Several thoughts went through his head. He thought about whom he had sex with and there was only three, Calvin, Manny and Monti. He thought Manny was good, but he really didn't know. Someone once told Cameron to assume everyone was positive. He knew at this moment the advice was sound advice. He decided to start by calling Manny. He wanted to avoid contact with Monti.

"Hey Papi, how are you doing?"

"I'm doing well. I haven't heard from you in a minute. Is

everything okay?" Cameron asked.

"Hell yeah…I'm doing good Papi."

"Okay…what has been happening lately?"

"I just been flying, flying and more flying. We really miss having you around."

"I really miss flying also." Cameron said. "It would be so good to fly somewhere right now."

Cameron didn't know how to approach Manny with the conversation of the phone call he received, so he just went with the flow. He felt Manny was okay because he didn't hear any distress in his voice. After a few minutes, they ended the call. Calvin was next.

"Hey wassup, Cam? How you been?" Calvin answered.

"Hey Calvin. I'm okay. What have you been up to?"

"Man I have been alright. Just staying above water."

"So you called to talk to me about staying above the water?" Calvin asked.

"No…" Cameron got quiet.

"No…what?"

Cameron thought about how to say this but he figured it would be best to just come out and say it. "I know we used protection when we hooked up, but I just got a call from the Department of Community Health. They seemed to have gotten my name from someone I had been with. They say I may have been exposed to the HIV virus. I'm not sure who I was potentially exposed by but I wanted to tell you."

"Oh wow man. That's some shit. This is the first I have heard about that. If you are asking me if it is me…hell no that ain't me. I don't remember whether we used protection or not but I will go get myself checked."

"Okay man. Yeah you were drunk as hell but I enjoyed our night. I'm sorry to have brought this to you but you know we have to do what we have to. I need to make my appointment, too." Cameron said

"I'll let you know when I get the results, but Cam it isn't me who caused you to get the call." Calvin replied.

"Thanks Calvin. I don't care what they say about you…you are cool in my book. I will let you know my results as well."

Cameron knew the source of the community health call…Monti.

CHAPTER THIRTY-ONE-YOLANDA

"Good afternoon Mrs. Burroughs. What brings you in to see me today?" Dr. Carlyle asked.

"It's Ms. Burroughs. I'm divorced." Yolanda responded.

"My apologies. So what brings you here today? Your intake form says you are seeking therapy for childhood issues."

"Yes…I recently had an incident with my boyfriend's ex. This brought me to a place where I feel I need to deal with things from my childhood. I snapped and ended up getting into a fight with her in front of my children and her daughter."

"Okay…I have looked over your information. You said you were referred here from Roderick. He is a good guy. I have known him for some time." Dr. Carlyle said.

"Yes he is. I want to be able to have a healthy relationship with him and I also want to deal with things from my past so they don't impact my present and my future."

"That's understandable. I would like to start with some historical information about your childhood."

Yolanda told Dr. Carlyle about her drug-addicted mother, her adopted parents and her adopted siblings.

"So tell me more about what happened to you. Are we talking about something that happened to you from your siblings, a parent, a family member or another person you don't know as well?"

"I think the personal relationship I need to focus on right now is my adopted mother."

"What about that relationship are you concerned about?"

"I just don't feel I was loved. She never had kind words for me. I didn't live up to any of her expectations."

"So let's talk about it some more."

"Well, I thought when I came to live with my adopted parents they wanted me. Sitting in foster homes, all I thought about was someday someone would want me. Someone would love me. It was hard for me when couples would come to the home and look at us. I tried my best to be good and hoped they would want me. For a year, no one wanted me." Yolanda began to cry as she remembered those days.

"How did you feel when your adopted parents came?" He asked.

"I thought someone finally wanted me. I felt they would love me and we would be a family."

"What changed that?"

"My adopted father loved me like I was his biological child. I remember he would bring me candy home when he got off work. He would listen to me and tell me stories. I really appreciated the stories he told me about him in the military. I looked forward to him getting off of work. My adopted mother, on the other hand, she was always mean. She would hit me for no reason. I didn't speak loud enough…I spoke to loud. I didn't clean up right. I got a grass stain on my dress. Nothing was ever good enough for her."

"Have you heard about irrational thoughts?"

"No, I haven't. I'm sure I can understand it though, if you explain it to me."

"According to certain beliefs in psychology, a thought is irrational if it distorts reality, is illogical, prevents you from reaching goals, leads to unhealthy emotions and leads to self-defeating behavior."

"Okay. That makes sense."

"Here are a few examples of irrational ideas. Firstly, the idea that it's necessary for an adult human being to be loved by every significant person in their community. It isn't possible for one to be loved by everyone. You can be the most popular person in the world and still find someone that doesn't like you. No matter what you do, some people will admire you and others won't. The time you spent paying attention to how much love and approval you weren't receiving from your adopted mother meant you didn't pay enough attention to the love and attention your adopted father had given you. Does that make sense to you?"

"Yes, Dr. Carlyle. I never thought about it that way. I was just expecting my adopted parents would give me the love parents are supposed to give their children."

"In a perfect world this would be the case. However, not everyone is given this. In some cases, even biological parents don't necessarily give their children the things you were wanting. You have to also understand human beings aren't perfect. We all mistakes from time to time and we treat others badly because we don't know any better, we can't do better or we are disturbed as well. You can't keep blaming or punishing her for this when one of these reasons describe her. This won't stop her from making these mistakes in the future."

"I know that makes sense but it doesn't make me feel better."

"I understand that as well. Let's re-evaluate and re-frame these thoughts. We have identified they are the cause of your psychological distress. Would you agree?"

"Yes. I think that would be true in this instance." Yolanda said.

"This is important because if you were to hold these beliefs, it would be impossible to respond to this situation in a psychologically healthy manner. This type of belief leads to disappointment, regret and anxiety. Too often, these irrational thoughts tend to be our easy way out. We can think that things in my life should go my way. This just doesn't pan out most of the time."

"I'm just realizing that. I didn't want to be abandoned by my own mother and then when I got an adopted mother, I didn't' expect her to abandon me as well." Yolanda said.

"See, you understand this process. The presence of a mother doesn't assure a child gets the nurturing of a mother. Some women are unable to mother. They don't have maternal instincts."

"You are so right. I had that in my life." Yolanda said. Even though this was her first therapy session with Dr. Carlyle, she was truly getting great insights to things that are really common sense but thinking about the situation through an irrational childlike experience had her stuck on being the victim. She was able to free herself from being the victim of a gay, lying husband and move on to find love with Roderick; however, she was paralyzed because she was a motherless daughter.

"The next thing we have to do is challenge these irrational beliefs."

"How do I do that?" Yolanda asked.

"Yolanda, you can't have everything you want." Dr. Carlyle said sternly.

"Excuse me?"

"You heard me…you can't have everything you want."

"I know that." She responded.

"No, you don't. You have been harboring this I can have what I want mentality for a long time."

"Dr. Carlyle, with all due respect, you don't know what you are talking about."

"Oh really…isn't it you that said you are mad at your adopted mother because you didn't feel love?" He said.

"Yes, but what does that have to do with me getting what I wanted."

"You wanted a mother. Am I right?"

"Yes." Yolanda answered.

"You didn't get a mother. You got a woman who wasn't a mother."

Yolanda sat there speechless. She knew Dr. Carlyle was right. She didn't get what she wanted in a mother. Dr. Carlyle let her sit in that truth. He didn't interrupt the work of his psychological challenge. She needed to marinate in this…she needed to breathe this…she needed to embrace this. Yolanda cried. The tears flowed from her eyes. Emotional scars and scabs had been torn opened. This was the only way to heal properly by reopening the wounds and applying the rational truth to them.

"Yolanda, you are going to have to face these unhealthy beliefs and accept them as unhealthy beliefs. It isn't going to be easy. But that's why I'm here to help you. I'm here to walk with you through them and to help you formulate healthy beliefs where unhealthy ones once resided."

Yolanda just cried.

"I want you to say this with me…I don't always get what I want." Dr. Carlyle said.

"I don't…" She said.

"Always get what I want." He coached.

"Always get what I want."

"Do you hear what you are saying? Breathe this statement Yolanda. Repeat it again."

"I don't always get what I want." She said.

"This time say it like you mean it."

"I don't always get what I want." She said with more conviction.

"That's right. I know it sounds scary but it is truth."

"I know it is." She said wiping her tears.

"Now say this…I may not have had a mother…" He

coached.

"I may not have had a mother…"

"But I have a loving father."

Yolanda broke down again.

"Come on…you can say it." Dr. Carlyle reassured her.

"But I have a loving father." She managed to repeat.

"All this time, you were holding the pain of a mother when you had the love of a father. You were diminishing the value your father brought to the table because you wanted a loving mother. That isn't a bad thing to have. Many people in the African-American community grow up without a father figure in the home. You had one and one who gave you love. He showed you how a man is supposed to love his daughter. He showed you this is the love you should expect from your husband. You have spent these years mad at her but it only punished you because you didn't hold your husband up to the standards your father set."

"Oh my goodness. I never realized that." Yolanda said.

Yolanda felt warm. She felt love…not the love Roderick gave her but she felt a parental love. She remembered all the times spent with her adopted father growing up, and realized he was giving her the love she didn't get from her mother. Yolanda had reached a turning point and realized she had to focus on the good she had in her life and readjust the ill feelings she had towards others who had taken her to hurtful places.

"Our time is up for today. Will we be meeting at this time moving forward?"

"Yes, Dr. Carlyle. This works well for me."

Dr. Carlyle got up and shook Yolanda's hand. He opened his office door and motioned for her to lead. As Yolanda walked out of the door, she stopped and turned back to Dr. Carlyle.

"Thank you." She said.

CHAPTER THIRTY-TWO-SHAINE

"Shaine…again I can't tell you how sorry I'm. I didn't mean to let that happen."

"Let that happen, Adrienne? Please tell me in your own words what happened."

"I was working on the project you assigned me when Jonathan came by. I was surprised he came because you weren't going to be in the office. He startled me when he showed up. He told me he came by to see me because he knew you were going to be out of the office."

"Oh really. What else happened?" Shaine asked.

"Well I asked him what he needed from me. Shaine, I thought he was trying to give you a surprise or something. So he came in and sat down. We started talking about some things and then he put his hand on my leg. I didn't know what to think…I froze. He kept talking telling me he thought I looked sexy and he saw me flirting with him. I told him I wasn't flirting with him but he didn't stop. He moved his hands up my legs further."

"Did you tell him to stop? Did you scream?" Shaine asked.

"No. He told me not to say anything. He said if I did, he would tell them I tried to hit on him and when he turned me down I screamed." Adrienne replied.

"What else happened?"

"He told me he wanted to sleep with me. He said I had nice breasts and kissable lips. I stood up to walk away and I started to cry because I knew you had been so good to me. He was so aggressive. Then he walked over to me, reached out and pulled me closer to him. I couldn't get away from him. He held me by the shoulders and then he kissed me. Shaine, you don't need this kind of arrogant creep in your life. You are too good for him."

"You didn't initiate this at all?" Shaine questioned

"No, not at all. He just came on to me."

"Adrienne, you aren't even describing the man I know. You mean to tell me you are willing to ruin a man's good name because you want something that isn't yours?" Shaine asked.

"What do you mean Shaine? I don't want Jonathan. He is nice and all but he is a cheater and a manipulator."

"There is one thing I can't stand is a liar. I can smell a lie a mile away and Adrienne...you stink."

"Shaine, I promise you I'm not lying. I didn't invite him here and I didn't come on to him. He isn't a good man...I tell you. He got you twisted into thinking he is one thing but he is another." Adrienne said trying to convince Shaine.

"Don't lie to me Adrienne. Jonathan is a good man. He loves people and will help anyone who needs it. You are a manipulative piece of work. Here I'm doing you a favor by letting you work with me. I have given you access to things many students dream of and this is how you repay me." Shaine said.

"I'm sorry Shaine. I never wanted to hurt you."

"Jonathan didn't know I had a meeting today. I never told him about it." Shaine said. "I can't believe how much you would give up trying to take something from someone. You have the potential to be great in this business but your personality is disgusting and you will have a hard time getting doors to open for you. Especially when you can't be trusted."

Adrienne began to cry.

Normally Shaine is a level-headed, compassionate woman. Today wasn't a compassionate day. "Save those damn tears because that bullshit isn't working on me today. You have exactly ten minutes to get your belongings and get off of these premises. Security will be here in five minutes."

"What do you mean?"

"Adrienne, your services are no longer needed." Shaine said coldly.

"You are letting me go?" Adrienne asked in disbelief.

"You thought you would have the opportunity to work for me after this stunt you pulled?"

"But he…"

"Nine minutes left." Shaine said as she walked over to her desk.

"You are a fake bitch you know that. All this talk about empowering people and helping them get on their feet. I said I was sorry and never meant for this to happen."

"And I said…get the fuck out of here. If I ever see you again in life." Shaine was becoming emotional. She didn't know where the emotions were coming from. She and Jonathan had a long talk after yesterday's incident. She knew he wasn't the type to try something like this and jeopardize his relationship. She just couldn't put her finger as to where these tears were coming from. She turned away from Adrienne.

There was a knock on the office door.

"Come in." Shaine said wiping her eyes.

"Ms. Holloway. We are here as you asked. Is everything okay?" Said a security guard.

"I'm okay. Please escort this woman out of my office and off the premises." Shaine said.

Adrienne got angry because the realization of her dismissal became true. The security guard took her by her arm and was headed to the door. She jerked her arm saying, "Don't touch me or I will have your job when I file a sexual harassment lawsuit against you, bastards. Don't think this is over Shaine."

"That will be enough ma'am!" The guard said as they walked her out of the office.

Shaine just sat at her desk as the tears started to flow again. She picked up her office phone and dialed Jonathan.

"Hey Sweetheart. How are you feeling today?" Jonathan answered.

"Jonathan, I don't know what is going on. I have been so emotional these past few days."

"Well, you have been through a trying period yesterday. What happened with Adrienne?"

"She said you came here and told her you wanted to be with her. She said you made a pass at her. Then, when I called her a liar, she told me I was a bitch and a fake. You try to help someone and show them success can be had, and they turn on you and try to take your place. I'm so tired of women who can't uplift each other but want to steal the very essence of the bonds of womanhood."

"Honey, I'm so sorry you had to experience that today. She is a disturbed person who needs more than just someone seeing her potential. You are a wonderful person…don't let this get you. I'm here in your corner one hundred percent. Don't let this change you. There are still so many other deserving people you can help. Don't let one spoil it for everyone else."

"Thank you honey. I'm glad I'm your fiancé. You are truly a blessing…but next time you decide to listen to a disturbed female, make sure I'm there with you so I can punch her when she goes left." Shaine said.

"You are too much Shaine Holloway, but that's why I love you. You keep it real with me."

"You got some hood in you…let me find out you're hiding some ghetto in you." Shaine joked.

"I learned it from the guys on the block. What you don't like it?"

"I love you Jonathan. This is all that I need."

"And you, Shaine Holloway are all I need. I love you."

"I love you as well, Mr. Blanchard."

CHAPTER THIRTY-THREE-MONTI

"Hello?" Monti said.

"You fucked up piece of shit."

"Who is this?"

"You know who the fuck this is, you sick bastard. Or do I have to put your business on blast again?"

"Calvin?"

"That's right. It's me." Calvin said.

"So why are you calling me? You have already caused Cameron and me to break-up, you outed me at church and you showed pictures of me fucking you to my mother. What more can you do to me? For the life of me, I don't know why you did what you did. I didn't do anything to you. I didn't even know who you were. You stalked me and God only knows what else you did."

"I called to tell you to leave Cameron alone."

"Cameron…what does he have to do with you? And what Cameron and I do in our relationship is none of your business."

"Oh you and Cameron are in a relationship?" Calvin questioned.

"Yes…we are working on our relationship. What you realize is that sick fuckers like you can't destroy true love. No matter what crazy set up's you do. We will always bounce back." Monti said.

"You are a delusional crazy fuck. You think that you are working on a relationship? What kind of relationship is this? An open one where Cameron can do what he wants?"

"What are you talking about?"

"You are such a liar. I see why Yolanda left you. You wouldn't know the truth if it slapped you in your monkey-assed face." Calvin said.

"Leave my wife out of this."

"You mean ex-wife?"

"Whatever…I don't have time to deal with your bullshit Calvin."

"Make sure you tell your son about you being sick."

Monti was silent. Once again Calvin was one step ahead of Monti. He had resources that Monti didn't and he didn't know how Calvin was able to get the information he did. Monti's silence told Calvin what he said was the truth.

"You don't know what you are talking about." Monti said.

"Aww…poor wannabe down low Monti. You think people don't know you got the package?"

"What are you talking about?"

"You can be in denial if you want Mr. Sick Dick. I know your dirty little secret. I have a little secret of my own...you ready for it?"

Monti wanted to hang up the phone on Calvin, but something wouldn't let him. He needed to know what this secret was.

"Yeah what is it." Monti was waiting with baited breath but responded dryly.

"Cameron has mad skills in bed; you could take a lesson or two from him. Make sure you strap up...you wouldn't want to infect anyone." Calvin said as he hung up the phone.

Calvin's words stung Monti. He was still working through his new diagnosis. Again Calvin had succeeded at putting Monti in his place.

Monti got dressed and headed out to his vehicle. He had to talk to Cameron, but Cameron wasn't taking Monti's calls any longer.

"How could he fuck Calvin?" Monti said out loud. Many thoughts ran through Monti's head as he was driving the forty minutes to Cameron's house. He had to figure out what he was going to say when he got there.

After about ten minutes of driving, Monti's phone rang.

"Hello?" He answered.

"What's up with you, Monti?"

"Allen?"

"Yes, it is Allen. You finally remembered me. What you up to?"

"Allen look. You want something more from me than I can

give you. Yeah, we fucked a few times and, to be honest, you are a lousy fuck. I'm not feeling you and we won't be doing this again. I suggest you get some hygiene lessons and learn how to clean yourself out if you plan on being a bottom. No one wants your shitty ass. How about you start now and leave me the hell alone."

"It's like that?"

"Hell yeah it is like that. I'm not feeling you. Oh yeah, brush your damn teeth too, your breath is fucked up too."

"Fuck you Monti. You are just a damn park queen. That's why ole boy outed you. I'm able to improve my hygiene but your nasty attitude and fucked up face can't be improved on." Allen said.

Monti looked down at his phone seeing the call was disconnected. He wasn't in the mood to deal with Allen and he didn't mind leaving his nasty ass in his past. Monti knew somehow Calvin knew about his diagnosis, but he didn't know how he knew. Did he tell Cameron he was infected? From Calvin's conversation, Monti knew Calvin and Cameron have been spending time together but he didn't know how much and for how long. He wanted Cameron to answer his questions.

"Calvin is the reason Cameron doesn't want to be with me. That's why he won't give 'us' another chance because he been kicking it with Calvin." Monti thought about a plethora of things as he made his way to Cameron's. He got off the freeway at Telegraph and knew he was about five minutes from Cameron's house.

"What if he isn't there?" Monti thought. "What if Calvin was there?" He still had to press his way to nip this in the bud.

Monti pulled into Cameron's complex and parked right in front where he used to when they were together. He sat in the truck for a minute to get his thoughts together. He had come all this way and knew there was no turning back now. He took a deep breath and got out the truck. He walked up to Cameron's door and remembered the night when the horn got stuck. A flood of emotions came over him. Here he was facing the loss of his relationship again. A few months ago, he had free access to Cameron's home and had his heart. A string of bad choices came to destroy that which, to Monti, was good. Monti rang the doorbell.

"Who is it?" Cameron's voice said through the door after a few minutes.

"It's me…Monti."

There was silence on the other side of the door. The silence was deafening to Monti. He didn't know what to do. He decided to knock on the door again.

"What are you doing here?" Cameron said.

"Open the door. I just want to talk to you."

Cameron opened the door and Monti smiled. He remembered the chemistry he and Cameron shared.

"What are you doing all the way out here?" Cameron asked.

"It's good to see you again."

"Can we skip this mushy moment?"

"I wanted to talk to you." Monti said.

"Well here I'm…but you aren't talking."

"So are you dating anyone now?"

"Monti, who I'm seeing isn't any of your business. If this is what you came for, you wasted your time and your gas." Cameron stepped back into the door and began to close the door.

"Okay. I get it. Can you tell your boyfriend Calvin to leave me alone?"

"Calvin isn't my boyfriend."

"Well tell your fuck buddy to leave me alone. He already did enough damage. Cameron…why did you have to sleep with him? Were you in on hurting me? Did you want to add salt to my already open wound?"

"You did the damage. All you had to do was to be honest about who you are. You were the one who was out at Palmer Park fucking God knows how many people. But even now you can't even accept responsibility for that. You come over here trying to check me about something…haven't you gotten enough of that? You haven't changed. I was the one hurt through your actions. Did I fuck Calvin? Yes, I did and it was good too. If he was good enough for you to do it…I figured it was good enough for me. But since we aren't together, I'm free to do what I want to do. You, on the other hand, didn't mind keeping tabs on me at the same time sleeping with guy after guy."

"It wasn't like that…" Monti said.

"Did you come by to tell me you are HIV positive? Too late, I already know."

"I'm just dealing with this myself. I was going to tell you. I know you won't want me now because of this."

"Again you are wrong. I'm not shallow like that. I don't want you because you are a liar and you can't be trusted."

"I'm sorry Babe." Monti said.

"Don't Babe me. So you were willing to put my life and my health in jeopardy because I wasn't enough for you? You aren't relationship material. You should maybe keep your dick in your pants for a while. Maybe you can give sex a break."

"Damn, can't a brother get some sympathy from you?"

"Humm…no. Monti I don't have any good feelings for you. I want you to leave me alone. I don't want you going to get therapy in hopes of reconciliation. That isn't going to happen. Not now…not ever. You have a track record of failed relationships and I'm already a part of that statistic.

"Can I just have one last hug and kiss?" Monti asked.

"No. You should be leaving."

"Well at least can you tell me how you found out I was infected?"

"Unlike you, Monti, I have only had two sexual partners since you and I split. One was protected and the other not. Process of elimination, plus your track record, puts you as the reason behind my call from the Department of Community Health. For your record, my test came back negative today. However, I have a couple months worth of testing in my near future. Cameron said."

"That's good you don't have it."

"I don't need your relief. I'm sure you can explain yourself to Taylor's finest."

"What?"

Monti turned around to see two police officers getting out of their squad car.

"You called the police on me?"

"I told you I was over you and didn't want to talk. You showed up unannounced and unwanted, I believe that's called trespassing."

"Which one of you is Mr. McNeil?" The officer asked.

"I'm." Cameron responded.

"And you are?"

"Monti."

"Monti what?" The officer asked.

"Monti Burroughs." Monti responded.

"Please step over there and speak with my partner." He ordered.

Monti walked over to the other police officer.

"Let me see some ID please." The office stated.

Monti handed over his license. He was pissed Cameron pulled this stunt. He looked over at Cameron and the other officer. He didn't know what they were talking about. "What was he asking him?" Monti thought.

"Mr. Burroughs, why are you here?" The officer asked.

"I came over to talk to my ex. Cameron and I were lovers and I had some questions I needed him to answer."

"Did you realize Mr. McNeil doesn't want to talk to you?"

"We just had a small disagreement. Many couples go through ups and downs, but they work through them." Monti explained.

"It is okay to work through them but from where we stand, it looks like you are the only one working on this situation. Mr. McNeil called us here and reported you as a trespasser."

Monti shook his head.

"Stay here for a moment." The officer said. He walked over to where Cameron and his partner stood. After a few moments, Cameron went back into his house and the officers both walked back to Monti.

"Mr. McNeil doesn't want communication with you any longer Mr. Burroughs. You are going to just get a warning tonight. If we have to come back here again because you choose not to heed this warning, we will have no other choice but to arrest you. Do you understand everything I have just said?"

"Yes, officer. I understand." Monti said.

"Here is your license back…please return to your vehicle and leave immediately."

Monti complied with the officer's instructions and left.

CHAPTER THIRTY-FOUR-CAMERON

It had been two days since Monti showed up unannounced. The officer said the police report would be ready for pick up today. Cameron felt he needed to make a stronger statement to Monti. The officer told him what he needed to do when they talked to him. He did his research and made a few phone calls yesterday ensuring he had all the information needed. Cameron got dressed and was headed to the Taylor Police Station. He could have walked to the station, which was only three blocks from his house, but he also planned to do some other errands while he was out.

Obtaining the police report was a simple process. Cameron was optimistic he was doing the right thing. He didn't want go to the 36th District court. He wanted to be left alone to live his life but it was obvious Monti wouldn't allow that. Monti had a way of showing up in places Cameron was. With a police report in hand, Cameron headed to downtown Detroit to the courthouse on Jefferson, across from Hart Plaza. Once at the courthouse, he made his way through security and up to the eighteenth floor. He had never dealt with such a situation before. He checked in at the Personal Protection Order office and showed the clerk his paperwork.

They processed his paperwork and sent him to the

courtroom. In the courtroom, he waited three hours before his name was called.

"Mr. McNeil?" The clerk called.

"Right here." Cameron replied.

"The judge has granted your Personal Protection Order. It is your responsibility to have the defendant Mr. Burroughs served. Though this order is in effect immediately, Mr. Burroughs must still be served. Once you get that done, please have the person serving the order sign the back and return it to the court. Do you have any questions?"

"No. I think it is straight forward."

"Good luck Mr. McNeil. Please be safe." She said.

"Thank you. I will."

* * * * *

Two weeks had passed since Monti was served. It was two weeks before Christmas and so far it had been quiet. Cameron was bringing in groceries when a gust of wind took his copy of the personal protection order from his car. He tried to chase after it but it was moving faster than Cameron could move to get to it. He decided to go back to court to get an additional copy. The next day, Cameron showed up at the courthouse and went back to the PPO office. Explaining what happened to his copy, the lady said, "Mr. McNeil, you will have to go to the records office to get a copy of your paperwork. Give me a second."

She went to a stack of forms and pulled out a green colored form and began to write some information on the form. She returned to Cameron and said, "Mr. McNeil, here is the form you will need to take down to the records office in the basement. They will make you a copy of the documentation you will need. Don't worry about paying for anything because I made it free of charge for you. Do you have any other questions or have I addressed all of them?"

"No, you have answered them all. Thank you Ma'am. I really appreciate all your help over the past few weeks."

"No problem Sir, I wish you the best. I'm proud you stood up for yourself…. Most people, men and women, do not report and subsequently don't follow through with stopping the people who harass them. Staying in an abusive relationship isn't what you should do. I'm glad you made that decision to get out of it." She said.

"Thanks a lot. That really means a lot to me. You take care." Cameron responded.

Cameron left the office and went to the elevators that went down to the basement to get a copy of his paperwork. There were hardly any people in the records office. As he walked into the room, a tall heavyset lady asked, "How can I help you?"

"I was sent down here from the PPO office to get a copy of my personal protection order."

"May I see your paper?" She asked.

"Sure." Cameron gave her the paper and she said, "Just one moment." She typed something in her computer and then said, "You can have a seat. I will get this ready for you."

After a few minutes she was back. "Mr. McNeil?"

"Yes, Ma'am." Cameron replied.

"Here are the documents you requested."

Cameron took the paperwork and thanked the lady. He walked by a row of computers as he walked out the exit side of the room. Once out of the records room, something made him stop right where he was. He turned around and walked back into the records room. "Excuse me ma'am. Can you look up old cases on the computers here with just one person's name or does it have to be both parties of the case?" Cameron asked.

"It depends on how they put it in the system." She replied.

"May I do a quick search?"

"Sure you can. There are signs above the computers with instructions how to long in."

"Thank you." Cameron walked over to one of the computers and followed the instructions to log in. Once he was logged in, he went to the search tool and typed '*Montague Burroughs*' and hit the search key. The computer began its search. A few moments later Cameron didn't believe what he saw. He wrote the information down and proceeded back to the counter.

"Excuse me ma'am. I would like to get copies of the following items." Cameron said as he handed the lady an additional piece of paper.

"Sure, let me see if there are still located in this location." She typed something into the computer and then said. "Mr. McNeil, just take a seat outside and someone will call your name shortly."

Cameron went out into the hallway and waited for what seemed like forever.

"McNeil?" A lady said from a different doorway.

"Right here." Cameron said as he walked towards where the

lady called.

"That will be ten dollars and fifteen cents."

Cameron reached into his pocket and pulled out fifteen dollars. He handed the money to the lady.

"Just one moment." She said.

In a few moments, the lady returned with Cameron's change and his documents. He thanked her and proceeded back to his vehicle.

* * * * *

Cameron took the day off for a good purpose. Once he got home, he logged into his laptop. He put in a google search for David Knight. There were about forty hits that came up. Cameron scrolled through several of them. He didn't know which one to look at. Once he clicked on the third page, he found some hits on a job posting site.

He clicked on the link to take him to it. He read a resume of one David Knight. This guy wasn't the one he was looking for. Then he got to the next one. He looked at the work history and found out this David Knight at one point worked in Detroit, Michigan. Cameron knew this was the one he needed to reach out to.

He drafted an email to David.

Hello Mr. Knight,

My name is Cameron McNeil. I'm writing you because I found your information on the job search. I would like to discuss an opportunity with you if you would. Please call me as soon as possible.

Cameron McNeil

Cameron left his phone number and proceeded to read the documents he got from the court. It turned out Monti had quite an extensive history with the legal system. There were three previous protection orders against him by three different guys. As Cameron was reading the first court document his phone rang. Cameron didn't recognize the phone number. He did know it was a New York City area code.

"Hello?" Cameron answered.

"Hello Mr. McNeil. This is David. I received your email."

"Hey David. Thanks for giving me a call back."

"No problem. Were you calling me for a potential job opening?"

"Well actually I was calling to ask you if you knew a guy here in Detroit by the name of Montague Burroughs."

The phone went silent.

"Mr. Knight, are you there?" Cameron asked.

"Yes, I'm here. I'm sorry. I just haven't heard that name in a long time."

"Well let me explain something to you. I didn't ask you to call to offer you a position. What I reached out for is to see what happened with you and Monti. I'm one of his exes. I had to file for a PPO against him. It seems like we have a lot in common. He has been stalking me. He has showed up at my home unannounced. He has come by my place of employment."

"I can tell you this. He won't stop until he is deeply involved with someone else. I had to move out of the country to get away from him. I changed my phone number and he still found me. I don't know how he found me but he did. I took a job overseas and then he stopped communicating with me. I have only been back here for about six months. I heard from my cousin that he was involved with someone else but he was going to get him back for me."

"What do you mean get him back?" Cameron asked.

"Monti stalked me and harassed me until I had no choice but to move. He showed up at my job and outed me at work; he tried to get my supervisor to make me talk to him. My cousin saw all the drama and stress Monti caused me after I broke up with him. So, he told me he was going to get him back for me."

"Okay that must be Calvin?" Cameron said.

"Yes, my cousin's name is Calvin. We have been close since we were kids." David responded.

"Have you talked to Calvin lately?"

"No, I haven't. Do you know him?

"Yes, actually I do know him. I think you should call him. He can tell you how he got revenge for you."

"I will call him today. Listen I'm glad you contacted me. I'm sorry you had to go through this stuff with him. If you need something from me, feel free to let me know. You can lock my number into your phone."

"Thanks David. I appreciate the information you shared and the insight you gave me." Cameron said.

"No problem man."

"I will talk to you soon. Bye."

"Ok…Bye."

Cameron had one more call to make. He had a voice message from Calvin. He needed to return it because Calvin's voice didn't sound too good. He dialed Calvin's number.

"Hello?" Calvin answered.

"Hey Calvin. How are you? Man, you will never guess what happened to me today. I went to the courthouse and did a search…"

"Cameron…" Calvin interrupted. "I got my test results this morning."

Cameron noticed Calvin didn't sound his usual, normal self.

"What test results Calvin." Cameron responded.

"You know what test results I'm talking about."

"Oh no…Calvin tell me something good."

All Cameron heard on the other end of the phone was Calvin sobbing. He immediately knew what this meant.

CHAPTER THIRTY-FIVE YOLANDA

"Monti, this is Yolanda. I have been calling you repeatedly because I need to talk to you about our son. This is important. Please call me back when you have a moment."

Yolanda had been thinking about how she would talk to Monti about their son. She was giving him one last opportunity to answer her call or she was going to leave it alone and just deal with it on her own. She thought Monti should be involved in this issue because he would be able to support her and most importantly, support Monti Jr.

Yolanda was at her place getting ready to go to Roderick's. They had planned to have a night together. The kids wanted to go to their Uncle's house so she was free for the weekend. She was almost done packing when her phone rang. She picked it up and saw it was Monti calling her back.

"Hello?" Yolanda said.

"Yeah…what is up?" Monti said.

"I'm doing fine. Thanks for asking."

"Yolanda, cut the bullshit. What do you have to talk about that's so important? I haven't seen the kids in over a month." Monti said.

"I wanted to talk to you about our son, Monti Jr."

"What about him? Is he okay?" Monti asked.

"Yes, he is fine."

"Okay, so what is it?

"Monti, I think our son may be gay." Yolanda said.

"What the hell you telling me that for? You think I made him gay? Ain't this some bullshit." Monti said.

"Monti, I'm not saying anything like that. Why are you being so paranoid? I'm just coming to you because we are his parents and we have to be on the same page with this. I'm not sure what to do or how to handle this situation. I figured you were gay and would have some kind of input about what is the best way for us to handle this."

"Oh you think I'm some gay expert and all that. You never quit trying to tear me down I see. What does he do that makes you so confident he is gay?"

"Can't we have a conversation about our son without you getting an attitude? I didn't ask you to pay for anything. I didn't ask you to spend any more of your precious time visiting or picking them up. I'm simply asking what the best way to handle this is. You know I'm tired of you jumping to conclusions. I talked to Roderick about this and he suggested I have the conversation with you. Now I'm trying to do that, you jump off the deep end."

"So now you are talking to your new boyfriend about our son?" Monti asked.

"Yes, I talk to him about things. You aren't consistent in their lives. You have been missing in action for a couple weeks. I don't know what is going on with you most time. I don't keep tabs with you. So when I have something to ask a man about, I will ask my man first. If you have a problem with that, you should have thought about that before you decided to become attracted to muscles and dick."

"Now that you've gotten that dig off your chest, I will talk to him."

"That isn't what I'm talking about. I'm talking about what we do as a parental unit to address this in our child. He is getting older and soon he may be interested in dating. Plus we have to be his support system so he can be a successful well-adjusted grown-up."

"Well, I don't know what you are going to do but I'm going to be his father. He will have to man up and be a man." Monti said.

"I was thinking more about you teaching him how to be a respectful gay man. I thought you would teach him to be who he is without having to lie and mess up someone else's life. You know I thought you would teach him to do the opposite of what you did."

"See there it is again. What else do you want from me, Yolanda? I made some mistakes in life."

"Yeah, I know you did. I made mine as well. I just want to move from the mistakes. I have a good man and trust me you are the furthest thing from my mind."

"I have someone in my life as well. So I'm not looking for another situation like I had with you, Yolanda."

"Trust me; we will never be there again. I have heard you told people if you wanted me you could get me back. Monti…that won't happen. Don't think you are all that and a bag of chips. If you were a bag of chips, you would be a stale bag. If you don't want to work with me to help our son, I will do it by myself, like I did all the other stuff. I just thought you would want to help your son."

"What is he doing?" He asked.

"He has a smart mouth. He has been rolling his eyes and his neck. He has started to pull away from the rougher sports and gravitate to more social stuff. He prefers student government and he likes more feminine things. I did some research on this and the research was saying this is more gender nonconformity. I know he is getting to the age where he will start to show some interest in a relationship and all. I feel we need to let him know if he is gay, we accept him for who he is. I don't want him to be afraid of telling us anything that happens with him."

"Okay…I don't know what my mother will think about this but we can talk to him."

"This has nothing to do with your mother, Monti. I just don't want him to be miserable. I want him to lead a happy life and I think if we are supportive of him then he will be able to deal with the discrimination he may face growing up. I know I have to work on how I speak about gay people. Since that stuff with you, I have a hard time dealing with it. I know that isn't your issue but I'm just sharing. I think you should spend more time talking with him."

"Fine, I will call him more."

"I think he would appreciate that as well. He took our separation very hard, Monti."

"I said I will spend more time with him. I don't have to rehash our divorce."

"It seems like you are going through something and are irritable. I'm going to get off of this phone and head out to do what I have planned for the weekend. You take care."

"Later." Monti said as he disconnected the phone.

Yolanda sat down and rehashed the conversation trying to see if she had done or said anything to Monti that would cause him to be upset. She realized she had done what any mother in her shoes would have done. Whatever Monti was going through she would make sure she wasn't in the cross fires of that. She didn't want to go back to her old self. She was enjoying her sessions with Dr. Carlyle and didn't want any setbacks. She decided she would leave it alone with Monti and deal with Monti Jr. on her own.

CHAPTER THIRTY-SIX-SHAINE

Jonathan knew Shaine wasn't angry with him regarding the Adrienne incident but he felt he had some making up to do with Shaine. He decided he was going to go out and give her a gift and give her some good Blanchard loving. He knew just where to go.

"Sandra?" Jonathan said.

"Yes, Mr. Blanchard. How can I assist you?" She said.

"What does my schedule look like this afternoon?"

"You have a couple of in-house meetings with management."

"Do I need to be present for those meetings?" Jonathan asked.

"No, you aren't presenting at any of them."

"Okay great. I have to run a few errands. You know how to reach me if something is an emergency."

"Okay Sir."

"Thank you very much. I will see you in the morning."

"You are welcome Sir. Have a good evening."

"I plan on making it a great evening. You have a good one as well."

Jonathan headed out of the office and into the elevator. Within a few minutes he was out of the elevator and in the parking structure. As he was driving, he called ahead to made sure his people were in and they knew what he was looking for. Tonight was going to be a special night.

"Hey handsome, how are you?" Shaine said as she answered the phone.

"I'm doing well. How is my only lady doing?" Jonathan asked.

"She is ok. I have been feeling a little nauseous lately. I'm okay though."

"Can I steal you for the evening?"

"Of course. What do you have up your sleeve?"

"That's my surprise for you."

"Okay."

"I will send a car for you at 7:00 pm sharp."

"I will be ready."

"Okay see you then…and Shaine…I love you very much." Jonathan said.

Shaine knew from the sounds of Jonathan's voice he was excited about whatever he was planning. She needed something to take her mind off the event that happened with Adrienne. Shaine made sure she would finish Adrienne's projects on time but knew she could leave a few hours early so she could be ready for Jonathan's car when it got to her house. She went back to working on her project when her phone rang again.

"Hey did you forget to tell me something?" Shaine said answering the phone without looking at the caller ID.

"I'm sorry Shaine. This isn't who you think it is." A familiar voice on the other end responded.

"Adrienne…how can I help you?" Shaine said dryly.

"I know I can't finish this internship but I wanted to apologize to you again. I have been thinking about this whole situation and I feel so bad because I allowed my impatience and immaturity get in the way of this internship. Most importantly, I allowed some stupidity to come between our friendship. I wanted to call you again and give you my sincere apology for what I did. I hope you will see the change me over time."

"Adrienne, it takes a big woman to do what you just did. I accept your apology and I do wish you the best in your career endeavors."

"Thanks Shaine. You don't know how much that means to me. Good luck with you and Jonathan."

"You have a good day Adrienne."

"You too."

Shaine was surprised she was so calm towards the woman who just tried to take her fiancé from her and then lied about it. "I guess all those sermons on love must have sunk in." She said as she let out a slight chuckle. Shaine looked at her watch and found out it was just after one in the afternoon. She knew if she left now she could get home and take a nap. She found a good place, in her work, where she could take a breather. She gathered her things and headed to her SUV.

Once at home, Shaine went into her closet and found a burnt orange pullover sweater dress and her knee high black leather high-heeled boots. She took off her clothes and got in the bed. Within a few minutes, she was knocked out. Shaine slept deeply for about three hours when she stirred in her sleep. She looked at the clock on the nightstand and saw it was 5:45 pm. She knew she had to get up and shower.

She got out of the bed and dizziness forced her to sit back down. She rubbed her temples in an effort to be able to see straight. After about five minutes, she was able to get up and get to the bathroom. She turned on the shower, allowing the water to heat up to her liking. Once it was at temp, she entered her natural stone tiled walk-in shower and allowed the warmth of the water to cascade over her womanly curves. She inhaled the steam and was soon invigorated.

Once out of the shower, she quickly got ready for her surprise evening with Jonathan. At 7:00 pm sharp, her phone rang and she knew it was the driver there to pick her up. She walked out of her home and down towards the awaiting limo. The driver stood at the ready as she approached the limo.

"Good evening Ms. Holloway." He said.

"Good evening." She replied.

He opened the door to let her in…to her surprise; sitting in the back of the limo was Jonathan with his beaming perfect smile.

"Wow…look at you. You are radiant this evening." Jonathan said.

"And you are handsome as ever."

Shaine got into the limo and gave Jonathan a kiss. Soon they were on their way to a mystery dinner Jonathan had planned.

"Shaine, I know the past few days haven't been the best, with the Adrienne situation and all, so I hope this evening helps change that around."

"You didn't have to do that." Shaine replied.

"I know but I wanted to." He said with a smile. "Can you do me a favor?"

"Sure what's up?"

"Can you reach over there and get me a napkin?"

"Sure."

Shaine reached over to the bar area and went to get a napkin. She didn't find any over there…what she did find was a professionally wrapped gift box. The wrapping paper was metallic gold and it had black ribboning around it.

"What is this?" Shaine asked.

"My gift to you. Open it." Jonathan said.

Shaine carefully removed the wrapping paper and ribbon to find a set of two carat teardrop diamond earrings set in platinum. Shaine screamed and then cried.

"Are you okay back there?" The driver said as he lowered the partition.

"We are just fine." Jonathan replied raising the partition back up.

"Oh my goodness. These are beautiful Jonathan." Shaine said.

"I was expecting you to be surprised but not moved to tears." Jonathan said.

"I have been emotional lately. I don't know why but thank you." Shaine took off her diamond studs she was wearing and replaced them with the new earrings she had just received. Within a few minutes, they were pulling up to the Whitney for dinner.

* * * * *

After dinner they went back to Jonathan's place. They walked into the foyer and Jonathan stopped and asked Shaine, "Are you tired?"

"No. I'm not tired. What do you want?"

"You." He responded. "What do you want?"

Without saying another word, he bent towards Shaine and she met his lips. Jonathan's lips engulfed Shaine's. He placed his hands on Shaine's hips as they kissed in the foyer, Jonathan's tongue slid effortlessly into Shaine's mouth. His hands floated up and down Shaine's spine with a caress so soft and gentle it sent shivers across her whole body. Shaine ran her hands up his arms, feeling how hard his biceps and triceps were under her palms. Jonathan's hands relented their gentle assault on Shaine's back and found the hem of his shirt, pulling it over his head.

The heat inside of Shaine pulsed deep inside her abdomen, warming it like a shot of Wild Turkey. She breathed as Jonathan got on his knees and lifted her dress, kissing her thighs, hips, navel and abdomen. She raised her arms above her head as he got back on his feet, carrying the dress over her head and off of her arms. Letting her dress fall to the floor, his lips found the rise of Shaine's breast still bound by her black laced bra. She instinctively wrapped her arms around his neck as he kissed and licked her breast.

"You still taste sweet. I crave the taste of your body." He said.

He found her neck and ears, kissing around the new earrings she was wearing. He stopped and stepped back to admire her. Standing in his foyer was a nearly naked Shaine with knee-high black leather boots, black lace panties and a bra to match. The sight of Shaine only served to make Jonathan desire her more.

She looked at Jonathan wearing just his black slacks and Kenneth Cole loafers and a belt. His chocolate skin glowed in the dim lighting of the foyer. He walked back over to Shaine, picked her up and carried her up the staircase and to his bedroom. Once in the bedroom, his kisses continued, rougher and deeper, with more passion than before. His hands unclasped her bra releasing her full breast. His touch was sweet torture as her body wanted sexual attention. Shaine blindly unbuckled his belt and loosened his pants. He eagerly obliged removing his shoes. He knelt on one knee and took the zipper of her boot in his teeth. Unzipping it while cupping her round ass, he never released contact with her skin. Shaine braced herself on his shoulder as he removed on boot. Then he repeated the motion with the other one.

With her boots removed and her bra, his hand grabbed her panties, sliding them aside allowing his free hand to meet her moist flesh. His fingers stroked just around the outside of her vaginal opening, teasing her. She lay back in the bed. She pulled him closer and harder, spreading her legs apart. His fingers slid into her easily as the moistness of arousal lubricated his fingers. His tender kisses and finger strokes caused Shaine to arch her back.

This told Jonathan to go there with her.

"Yes Jonathan…" She said.

His tongue pressed into her, tunneled her and scooped any juice that was in its path. Her arousal burned inside like an incinerator. His mouth was the accelerant. She yearned and pleaded for more. Jonathan rose above her and kissed her deeply. She could taste the sweet, saltiness of her juices. With her legs still spread, Jonathan entered her and made her gasp as she felt his stiffness stretch her. Shaine moved with him as he pushed deeper in. She was more sensitive to him than in previous times they had sex. Their bodies met each other with equal force as Shaine received Jonathan. He continued to thrust his manhood into to her to his balls while he kissed her passionately. He massaged her breast, attempting to ensure all her pleasure receptors were stimulated.

Jonathan let her legs down as he rolled over onto his back. Shaine followed his lead and was soon straddling above him. She rode him with such roughness. She arched her back to allow him to hit her spot. She dug her hands into his chest as she gyrated and worked her hips. Jonathan watch as Shaine's breast bounced with each gyration.

"Oh Shaine…you are going to make me nut, baby." He said.

"Oh yeah, I'm close too."

She didn't let up on her stride. She felt his hips thrusting into her as his legs began to shake.

"Shaine…baby."

His face twisted as his stomach tightened.

"I'm…ahhh."

He exploded and convulsed as she tightened her knees around his hips and braced herself as her climax radiated from her clitoris throughout her body. They both came so much it began to ooze out of her as she lay on him, feeling his damp body under her trying to catch its breath. He was still inside her and she didn't want him out.

"Ready for round two?" Shaine asked.

He smiled at her and pulled her closer to him and began to kiss her again.

CHAPTER THIRTY-SEVEN-MONTI

"Welcome back Mr. Burroughs." Dr. Carlyle said.

"Thanks Doc."

"Let's take a moment to talk about accountability and responsibility. You have missed several appointments. You are responsible for making your scheduled appointments. You can't work through your presenting issues when you don't come to your therapy and therefore you can't begin to manage borderline personality disorder. It is also proven that you aren't accountable to therapy when you don't come to your appointments and this leads to poor success rates among patients."

"I know…I'm sorry. I will make a better effort to be here when I'm supposed to be." Monti said.

"Mr. Burroughs, I'm going to hold you to this accountability. Now that's out of the way, how are you feeling today?"

"I have been better." Monti said.

"Care to elaborate on that statement?"

"I just had a major setback. I'm not sure what to do."

"Okay what was this setback?"

"I received a call from someone who told me they were with Cameron."

"Cameron is the gentleman you were in a relationship a few months ago, correct?"

"Yes. That's correct." Monti replied.

"Okay, please proceed. What happened with this call?"

"The guy who broke us up called me. He still knew way too much about what is going on in my life. I think he just called to get under my skin." Monti said. "His tactics actually worked."

"What do you mean his tactics worked?"

"Well after the call, I couldn't shake his words out of my mind. I had to find out, so I went to Cameron's house to talk to him about it. I wanted to know why he would sleep with this guy after what he did to break us up."

"Do you know if Cameron actually knows Calvin was involved with the demise of your relationship?" Dr. Carlyle asked.

"No, I'm not really sure if he knows." Monti said after pondering the question.

"I want to ask you another question regarding this situation. Why do you blame Calvin for the demise of your relationship?"

"Because he sent those photos to Cameron, my mother and the people at the church." Monti said.

"Let's look at this closer. You are looking at one of the series of events that happened. What about us addressing the root cause of the situation."

"Okay…let's talk about it." Monti said.

"I believe the root cause of your break up is you…Monti Burroughs."

"What are you talking about Dr. Carlyle?"

"You are focused on pointing fingers at this Calvin as the reason your relationship failed. This is the pattern you have chosen to follow, because it is easier for you to point blame at these others. You decided your marriage failed because your wife cheated on you, when in fact you were cheating on your wife before she cheated on you. You also married a woman, giving her the impression you are a heterosexual man, when you are at best bisexual."

"What does that have to do with Cameron and me?"

"You blame Calvin for you break-up which is putting blame in the wrong place. Calvin wasn't the reason for it…Monti…you were the reason for your break-up. You went to the park and you chose to have anonymous public sex. The unfortunate thing was you were caught and exposed."

Dr. Carlyle could see his confrontation angered Monti.

"Say this after me…I'm the reason for my relationships failing."

Monti refused to talk.

"Mr. Burroughs…I'm waiting for you to become engaged in this session."

Monti still sat quietly.

"Mr. Burroughs, please tell me why you don't want to take responsibility for your relationship's ending?"

"It isn't that I don't want to take responsibility for them…I just feel they did it to me."

"They did what Mr. Burroughs."

"They pushed me to it." Monti said.

"So they pushed you to be unfaithful?" Dr. Carlyle countered.

"Yes, they did."

"What did Cameron do to make you unfaithful to him?"

"He was gone all the time."

"So was he dishonest to you about his occupation?"

"No."

"So you chose to get involved with someone who traveled for a living, and now you are choosing to blame him for your actions. Mr. Burroughs…therapy can't be effective if you choose to not take responsibility for your actions and their subsequent reactions."

"Dr. Carlyle, maybe therapy isn't what I need right now. I'm not ready for this. You are trying to make me be the bad guy here. I'm not the bad guy, they did things to hurt me and you can't tell me it is my fault. You don't know what is going on with me. You have no clue…you really have no clue."

"Therapy is what you need right now, Mr. Burroughs. You have to be committed to the process. You have to want to be better and you have to want to do better."

"Why should I try to get better…I don't have much to live

for anymore. Cameron doesn't want me. I just got served with a protection order and I just got told I'm HIV positive."

Dr. Carlyle sat there with Monti as he finally released emotions about his recent diagnosis. Monti had tried to be strong through this process but he felt alone and lonely. He didn't have people to talk to about this. He didn't intend to even bring this up with Dr. Carlyle but he couldn't keep this secret anymore because it was eating him up within.

"Have you considered going to a support group?"

"They gave me some contact information for that at the doctor's office but I'm not sure I want to go that route. I don't want people to know my business."

"You aren't doing it for people to know your business but you are doing this because you need to talk about it. You have to be able to ask your questions and get some understanding about what is going on within your body. It is important for you to talk to someone."

"I'm talking to you, aren't I?" Monti asked.

"Yes, you are, however, I'm not extensively trained in that type of therapy. We can discuss things related to that but I'm not equipped in that area."

"Okay, isn't our time up now?" Monti asked.

"We are running close to it being up, how about you calling the people you were referred to and checking that out?"

"I will think about it." Monti said.

"That's a start. So next week when we meet, I would like to discuss how your first meeting went with these people. Is that a plan?"

"I will think about it."

"Okay…I will see you next week. Just stop off at the front desk and Tracy, my secretary will take care of you."

Monti walked out of the doctor's office and checked out from his appointment. He got in the truck and sat there to get his thoughts together. Monti needed to talk to someone about the incident at Cameron's house, not Dr. Carlyle, but his secrecy limited his options. His only options were either Dee or Stephanie; he knew either way he was going to get lectured. He decided to call Stephanie. He didn't know how honest he was going to be but he just wanted the comfort of a friend. He pulled out of the parking structure and was headed towards her house.

"Hello?" Stephanie said.

"Hey Steph. What are you doing?"

"I'm just here cooking dinner what you doing? You coming over for dinner?"

"Well…I'm coming over right now. I need to talk to you."

"Is everything okay?" She asked.

"I don't know…but I will be there in about twenty minutes."

"You know I don't like surprises but I will be here."

"Okay, later."

* * * * *

"Come on in here. What the hell is going on with you, Monti?" Stephanie said.

"I don't even know how to tell you this."

"Monti, just tell me. There isn't anything you can tell me to be acting all crazy about it."

"I went over to Cameron's house a couple weeks ago."

"Why the hell would you go there, Monti? I told you to leave that man alone."

"Calvin called me and told me he had slept with Cameron. I wanted to know why Cameron would do something like that. I wanted to ask him why he wanted to hurt me like that."

"Monti, Cameron isn't in a relationship with you anymore. He is free to be with who he wants to be with. You can't go around trippin' out on him and you can't check him."

"I know…but that isn't the only thing I wanted to tell you."

"What else happened?" Stephanie said raising her eyebrows.

"The conversation got heated and the police showed up."

"The pigs came?"

"Yeah…he had called them."

"I told you to leave his ass alone."

"That's not it…"

"The fuck…there is more?" She said.

"Yes, they told me he didn't want me there. Three days later, I was served with a PPO."

"Monti…you can't keep bothering Cameron. Why do you even want to have anything to do with him? You said he told you he didn't want to be with you and he was moving on with his life."

"I just wanted him to know Calvin wasn't good for him. I wanted him to know I'm still trying to get him back."

"Monti listen to me and listen to me real good. You have to leave him alone. Don't go by there starting no shit with him."

"I know…I'm going to stop. I don't know why that fucker called the cops on me. I'm pissed off. Now I got this damn PPO on me for a year. I just can't let go. Stephanie, I love this man. It is just fucked up."

"I know how that feels Monti…but you have to leave Cameron's ass alone. This isn't going to pan out well."

"Okay enough about that…what is for dinner." Monti said changing the subject.

CHAPTER THIRTY-EIGHT-CAMERON

Cameron was in his kitchen making ceviche. He had been craving it for a while and he gave into his cravings. He heard a pounding on his front door. Cameron walked down the stairs and made it to the front door. "Who is it?" He asked.

"Open the door. I want to talk to you." Monti demanded.

"What do you want?" Cameron asked sarcastically.

"I told you, I want to talk to you."

Cameron opened the door and saw Monti standing outside in the dark on a cold December night.

"Can I come in?"

"No, you aren't welcome here." Cameron said as he began to close his front door. Monti put his hand on the door to stop Cameron from closing the door.

"Look Cameron, I wanted to tell you to keep your mouth off of me, or else."

"I don't know what you are talking about Monti and for the

record; I can talk about whomever I want."

"I have been hearing all the stuff you have been saying about me and if you want to keep up with this faggot shit then you are going to be the one that's hurt with it."

"Don't come to my house threatening me about something you 'think' I'm doing or have done. I have moved on with my life and you should do the same thing." Cameron snapped.

"So are you still talking to Calvin? You didn't waste any time did you? I knew you were a whore."

"I'm the whore? I find that to be interesting. You are the one who had the multiple affairs in our six-month relationship. Now that I have moved on with my life and am not taking your bullshit anymore you are just going to get gutter with me? For what reason Monti? To make me feel bad?"

"Look, I didn't come here to argue with you. I just wanted to talk to you." Monti said changing his tone.

"Well you could have fooled me." Cameron retorted.

"Look, I know I messed up and I know who I didn't treat you right. I know who when you needed me I dogged you out. I'm not proud of what I did and I don't know what I can do to make it up to you. Are you really done with the relationship?"

"You haven't treated me right in the time we were together, Monti. I gave you time to show me who you were, put up with your insecurities and your cheating. I tried to make a life with you. Nothing has changed from our last conversation. I'm beyond done with this. I'm actually tired of this same conversation over and over again."

"Can you give me another chance? Can you give us another chance? You know we have chemistry together and we work together."

"You must think I'm stupid. We fit together like oil and water. There are no more chances of reconciliation with you and me."

"You didn't answer my question. Are you still seeing Calvin?"

"Again, I don't see how that's any of your business."

Monti was angry. He understood he had made some bad choices in the course of their relationship. He knew they had bounced back each time. He didn't realize that every time they bounced back the bond they had was becoming weaker and weaker. He had crossed the line and was now seeing the results of his insecurities and bad behavior. "So you just gonna to throw us away?"

"You threw us away a long time ago. Monti, I'm not going to re-hash this with you over and over again. The love we had has expired and you have to accept that reality. I know you refuse to live in the real world but your fantasy world with me has ended."

Their conversation began to escalate and their voices began to elevate. Soon even the neighbors heard the argument that began to ensue at Cameron's townhouse.

"You are the one who had inappropriate conversations with guys around the country." Monti said.

"Monti, a text message isn't an inappropriate conversation. I can't control what people say to me. I can't make them stop complimenting me. Hell, I couldn't even make you treat me right. You just continued to treat me poorly, and now you really think I'm going to entertain your insolence?"

"Don't justify your poor choices on receiving compliments and all that. You were just caught and you don't want to admit to it."

"You are wasting your time here. You aren't welcome here. We aren't going to get back together…ever. You have fucked over me for the last time. You should go get help for your sick self."

Cameron's phone rang. He took the phone out of his pocket and looked at the caller ID and saw it was Brian calling.

"Hey babe, how are you doing?" Cameron said.

"I'm good honey. I was laying here and had an urge to call you. Is everything ok?" Brian asked.

"Oh, so you are talking to Calvin?" Monti screamed. "How are you going to disrespect me by talking to Calvin in front of me?" Monti's anger increased and before he knew what he was doing he had his hands around Cameron's neck as he pushed him into the foyer, up against the wall. Cameron dropped the phone as he instinctively grabbed on Monti's hands.

Struggling for life, Cameron thought, "this can't be happening, not now and not tonight". He remembered his military and martial arts training and raised his knee with so much power when he connected to Monti's groin, Monti immediately released his grip on Cameron's neck. As Monti's body collapsed from the blow to his groin, Cameron swiftly put him in a standing guillotine Jiu Jitsu choke and began to choke him with all the force he had. As Monti reached the floor, Cameron refused to let his grip go.

"You gonna come to my house and attack me? Fuck you bastard. I have had enough of your shit."

After what seemed like an eternity, the Taylor Police department arrived. They walked up to door, with guns drawn and said, "Freeze, and put both of your hands up."

Cameron released his chokehold on Monti, who couldn't raise his hands because he was still holding his throat.

"Mr. Burroughs, move this way." The officer ordered. Monti struggled to get to his feet, still trying to catch his breath. "Put your hands up, right now." The officer ordered.

Monti put his hands over his head, as he walked through Cameron's door and into the cold darkness of the evening.

"Turn around Mr. Burroughs." The officer ordered.

Monti complied.

"Get on your knees and keep your hands where I can see them."

Monti complied. As he got on his knees he looked up at Cameron with tears in his eyes and mouthed the words "I love you, Cameron." Cameron dropped his head as he exhaled. The officer came up to Monti, who had been forced to submit by a badge and a .357 Magnum, and put handcuffs on him. The officer read Monti his Miranda Rights then told him, "Mr. Burroughs we told you two weeks ago you aren't to return to Mr. McNeil's place of residence. We also told you the next time you came here uninvited we would view it as trespassing and stalking." The officer had Monti sit on the curb as the other officer came to speak with Cameron.

"Mr. McNeil, are you ok, Sir?"

"Yes, Officer I'm ok. How did you know to come?"

"We got a call from Brian via 911 and your neighbor also called."

"Can you tell me what happened?"

Cameron told the officers what happened from his vantage point. He pulled his copy of the PPO out and showed it to the officer.

"Hold on here for a moment, Mr. McNeil."

The officer walked over to Monti. He asked him what happened.

"I came over here to talk to him. We were in a sexual relationship and I wanted to work things out with Mr. McNeil. Our argument started to get heated and then he got a phone call and I just snapped Officer. I don't really know what happened next, except he was choking me before you all got here."

"Mr. Burroughs, were you aware there is a standing Personal Protection Order from the 36th District court?"

"Yes, I did know that."

"Stay here again, Mr. Burroughs." The officer stated he walked back over to Cameron. "Mr. McNeil, please look up."

Cameron complied with what the officer asked him to do. The officer turned on his flashlight and looked at the marks on Cameron's neck. He asked his partner to bring the camera and the crime scene kit from out their squad car. Once he got the camera, he took photos of Cameron's neck from different angles with the tape measure to demonstrate the length of the marks that Monti had inflicted upon Cameron. The officer radioed to the police station to get a police report number. He wrote the number on the business card and handed it to Cameron.

"You will need this information at court when this goes to

trial. We are going to take Mr. Burroughs into custody and charging him with trespassing, assault and violating a personal protection order. He will probably be arraigned tomorrow."

"Hey Officer, what about his assault on me?" Monti interjected.

The officer walked over to Monti. "What assault are you speaking about, Mr. Burroughs?"

"He choked me. You walked up to his house and he was choking me."

The officer took the flashlight and looked at Monti's dark skin and said, "I don't see any choke marks on you Mr. Burroughs which would substantiate your claim. Plus, you are at his home and you are prohibited from being here."

"You have got to be kidding me, right? He was assaulting me." Monti said in disbelief.

"Mr. Burroughs, we only have your word against two 911 calls from two separate people. We came up and saw Mr. McNeil defending himself, as well as evidence to collaborate the statements of the neighbor and the recorded emergency calls and Mr. McNeil. We warned you before to stay away."

They placed Monti in the back of the squad car and took him to the police station for processing and booking.

CHAPTER THIRTY-NINE-YOLANDA

"I think something is going on with Monti." Yolanda said.

"Where did that come from, Babe." Roderick responded.

"I called him the other day to talk about Monti Jr. When I told him I thought he was going to be gay, he flew off the handle."

"What do you mean he flew off the handle?"

"He started yelling at me. He said I was trying to get back at him by bringing the gay stuff up. He said I was telling him to make him responsible for Monti being gay."

"How did you tell him?" Roderick asked.

"I told him like we talked about. I suggested he spend some more time talking with him. I asked him to see if Monti would open up to him about any feelings he was having."

"And he said you were trying to pin this on him?"

"Yes. Then he started talking something about the police and a warning or something. He mentioned something about a Calvin."

"What does that mean?" Roderick asked.

Yolanda sat there thinking for a minute; then it dawned on her. "Calvin is the guy Monti thought I had known. A couple months ago he called me asking me to tell my friend Calvin to leave him alone. He thought I was setting him up or was trying to get him back."

"Did you know who Calvin was?"

"I don't know any Calvin. I remember I told him his sneaky ways were probably catching up with him. Humm...I wonder if this has something to do with those photos spread all over the church parking lot."

"Hold up...what are you talking about?"

"I never told you this but in August or September, Monti crossed someone wrong and they got him back by putting pictures of him, in revealing positions, on the church members cars at church one day."

"Are you serious?"

"Yes. I remember being at his mother's house hearing her tell someone the photos were given to her but they were also distributed to the church Monti attends."

"Wow, that's crazy. See that's why I'm honest because I don't want something coming back to bite me later on. Are you sure he is alright?"

"Roderick, I couldn't even tell you. He must be under a lot of stress. He was going off on the phone that day, but this last time he seemed to be ready to snap."

"Honey, I see it every day. When I go to work, other officers have that look in their eyes. If you heard some of the confessions some of the criminals I have arrested, you would cringe. Stress is a powerful vice that has brought many people to their breaking point. When you live a double life, it is hard for your brain to keep things together."

"I don't know…but I'm concerned he may do something crazy."

Roderick started laughing.

"I know what you are thinking. I know he has done a lot of crazy things before but you know what I mean. He is going to do something that's going to hurt himself." Yolanda added.

Roderick stopped laughing enough to ask, "Do you think he is suicidal?"

"I don't know. It just worries me. He was talking incoherently. The stuff he was saying didn't make sense."

They continued to talk about the different things, when Yolanda asked "What do I do with my son?"

"What do you mean…what do you do with him?"

"I don't know many gay guys. For the longest time, I blamed them for what I went through with Monti."

"First, you don't do anything with Monti Jr. except love him. He is your son regardless who he chooses to love. Remember love sees no color or gender. You just have to make sure he can trust you enough to talk with when the time comes. You may even have to let him know it is okay to be who he is."

"It isn't that…"

"Secondly, you don't need a gay friend to do anything with him. He is a bright kid and I'm sure we can help him get through this situation."

"We…that sounds so good. Thank you for leading the way on this with me." Yolanda said.

"You are welcome. We are going to get through as many things as we need in order to be a couple. I want you to know you aren't alone in this. I know your boys are yours and sometimes you won't want my input. I vow I will talk to you and step in when you want and tell me you want me to. I'm not their dad but I hope one day I can be their stepdad."

Yolanda leaned into Roderick and gave him a kiss. He instinctively pulled her into an embrace. He loved her and made sure to show her the love each opportunity he had. Whether it was holding her through the night, when they stayed with each other, or grabbing her hand at the movie theater. He wanted her to be safe and secure knowing they were in this situation together. They were enjoying their grown up time when Yolanda's phone rang.

"Are you expecting a call?" Roderick asked.

"No, the boys are at their grandmother's house."

Yolanda got up off the couch and got her phone from her purse. She looked at the display and *Mrs. Burroughs* displayed on the phone.

"Something must have happened to the kids." Yolanda said as a slight panic came over her.

Roderick saw the panic on her face and he got up and stood beside her and held her free hand.

"Hello?" Yolanda asked.

"Yolanda. I know you are busy, but I have to talk to you."

Mrs. Burroughs encouraged Yolanda to find a relationship. She was aware deep inside her son was gay and not going to try to reconcile with his estranged wife. It was never an imposition for her grandkids to come over for a weekend.

"Yes, what is going on? How are the boys?"

"My grandkids are doing well. They went to the store with their uncle."

"Okay, I thought something happened to them. What is up?" Yolanda asked.

"I need to borrow some money from you. I'm not sure how much yet and I'm not sure when I will be able to pay you back." Mr. Burroughs said.

"What happened?"

"Montague got arrested last night. He needs money for bail."

"Arrested? What did he do?"

"He didn't tell me for sure but I do know the funny guy he was messing with has something to do with this. He told me the truck is over at funny guy's house. He said he left the keys in there before they arrested him."

"Can you come with me to get my truck from over there? I can't drive both vehicles back."

"I don't have any money to help with his bail. He hasn't been paying me child support so I don't have any extra money. I can help you drive one of them back. I will see if Roderick can come with me so you don't have to drive me back home as well."

"Okay…Thank you very much. What time will you be able to meet me there?"

"Hold on a moment." Yolanda covered the phone to ask Roderick about driving out to Taylor.

"We can leave here in about five minutes." Roderick responded.

"We will leave here in a few minutes. We will probably beat you there so we will wait on you."

"Okay, thank you. I will see you soon."

They got in Roderick's car and headed to Taylor to meet Mrs. Burroughs. Yolanda got the address while they were driving.

* * * * *

Yolanda and Roderick pulled up to the address Mrs. Burroughs gave to them. Yolanda saw Mrs. Burroughs' truck and knew this was the right place. Roderick pulled up in the spot next to her truck.

Yolanda's phone rang again.

"Yolanda?" Mrs. Burroughs said.

"Yes, Mrs. Burroughs. We are here."

"Can you get the keys…they are inside the truck. He said the doors are open."

"Hold on, let me check."

Yolanda got out of Roderick's car and looked into the window. She saw the door was unlocked. She opened the door and check in the arm rest for the keys. She found them.

"Yes, I have the keys." Yolanda said.

"Okay that's good. Now can you drive the truck back to my house? Montague said he could have visitors today. I'm going to go to the jail, to talk to him and see what is going on. I will call you when I'm on my way back home."

"Okay not a problem." Yolanda replied.

"That fool boy of mine is going to worry me to death."

"Don't worry about that. I'm sure it will all work out."

"Yes, I'm a praying woman and the good Lord will answer my prayers."

"Okay, I will put the keys in the mail slot when I leave it." Yolanda said.

"Thanks again." Mrs. Burroughs said as she hung up phone.

Yolanda got out of the truck. She leaned in to tell Roderick the new plan. He agreed and put his car in reverse to back out of the parking space. As Yolanda turned to get in the truck, she noticed a light skinned guy looking at her from the third floor of the townhouse. They locked eyes for a moment before the guy left the window. She started up the truck and backed out of the parking space. As she drove past the townhouse, she saw the front door open. She wanted to go back to see who this was that was watching her but Roderick had already left the complex and she couldn't stop. As she made the turn onto the street, she glanced back but the man was gone and the door was closed.

CHAPTER FORTY-SHAINE

Shaine took some time off because she wasn't feeling well. Last week, she worked through the sickness, but this week she decided she may be overworking herself. Since she let Adrienne go, she took on the projects Adrienne was working on. Shaine didn't know if she had picked up a virus or something else. She was fatigued and found herself sleeping a lot but her sleep was so intense. She went into the kitchen to make herself a cup of coffee. She opened the refrigerator door to get her hazelnut cream. As she poured the cream into her coffee, her stomach turned.

She stirred the coffee and brought it up to her nose to smell the scent of hazelnut. When she did that she felt nauseas. Setting the coffee mug down, she went to the garbage can to avoid having to clean up vomit from the floors. After a few minutes her stomach settled without expelling anything. She decided it would be best to just drink some water. She poured her coffee in the sink and ran some water behind it to flush it all down.

She went back to her bedroom and got into the bed. She didn't know what was wrong with her. Sleep is what her body craved at this time. As she lay there, she thought about Adrienne and how she tried to manipulate her way into Shaine's shoes. She cried because she saw a lot of herself in Adrienne. She was a go getter who didn't mind going the extra mile. It was these extra miles that landed Shaine this new position. She knew Adrienne would go places but she didn't know one of the places she would try to go was with her man. A few minutes after her Adrienne moment, Shaine had fallen asleep.

After about an hour of deep sleep, Shaine was startled by her phone ringing. She reached over to the night stand and picked up the phone. Looking at the caller ID, she saw it was Cameron calling. She answered the phone, "Hello?"

"Hey Shaine…you sound like you were sleep. I thought I would catch you at work."

"I didn't go. I haven't been feeling well for a couple days so I took some time off to give my body some rest."

"Oh do I need to come over and bring you some soup?"

"That sounds so good. Will you do that for me?" She asked

"Really Shaine?" Cameron said. "You think I wouldn't take care of you?"

"I know you would. I don't know what got into me."

"I will be over there in an hour."

"I will be here."

"Okay honey. Bye."

Shaine rolled back over and curled into the fetal position and was soon fast asleep again. She slept so hard she didn't hear when Cameron came. He went straight into the kitchen and started to warm up some soup. He also bought a chicken and some vegetables.

He was going to give her some canned soup first to help settle her stomach and then give her the double whammy of his homemade chicken noodle soup with the extra love in it. He filled a stock pot with water and put some salt in it to get it started boiling. Once the canned soup was ready, he looked in the cupboard and got some saltine crackers. He put the soup in a bowl and crackers on the side.

"Hey gorgeous!" Cameron said as he walked down the hallway towards her room.

He walked into her bedroom as she stirred slightly.

"Hey honey. Can you sit up for me?" He asked.

"Thanks for coming by." Shaine said. Sleep wasn't trying to let her go, but she managed to sit up in the bed.

Cameron brought the soup over to her and sat on the other side of the bed.

"We haven't done this in a long time." Cameron said.

"I know…it brings back good memories. Remember when we were flight attendants and we would get our trips together. Staying in the same hotel room sometimes we were inseparable."

"Yes, those were the days." He said.

"So what are you doing?"

"Right now I'm making you some homemade chicken soup in the kitchen and taking care of my friend."

"Oh really…wow, I could have waited for yours to be done."

"Enough said. Eat that up right now." Cameron said.

Shaine took a moment to smell the soup. She was prepared to

get nauseous but it didn't come. "What's new in your life Cameron?"

"Are you sure you are ready for this?"

"Yes…I'm as ready as I'm going to get."

Cameron told Shaine about everything that had happened between him and Monti. He told her about his call from Wayne County, he told her of the results of his test. He told her about the court case coming up and Monti was sitting in jail because he couldn't make bail. He told Shaine about Calvin and his involvement with outing Monti.

Shaine couldn't believe her ears, hearing all the things Cameron shared with her. She knew his involvement with Monti would bring drama but she didn't know it would be this much drama.

"I'm surprised you are still so optimistic after all this." She said.

"I just know the end is in sight. He has charges for trespassing, assault and violating a PPO. The District Attorney says he can get a maximum of 216 days in jail for the charges. She thinks the judge will sentence him for at least 180 days. The trespassing charge may not stick because I opened the door for him. So we will see."

"When is court?"

"The Friday before Christmas." Cameron answered.

"Right before Christmas?"

"Yes…right before Christmas. So I hope I get a good Christmas present from the legal gods."

"You know that ain't right, but I feel you. He put you

through too much stuff, Honey."

"This has been a long nine months and I can't wait for this baby to be done." Cameron joked.

"You are at the end of your time just a few more days."

"I agree. So what do you have planned for the rest of the day?"

"I made a doctor's appointment so I can get something to knock whatever this is in me out so I can feel like me again."

"Okay. You need me to go with you or are you okay?"

"I think I will be fine. I'm feeling a lot better since my best friend brought me this soup. I can't wait to get some of that homemade stuff that smells so good."

"Okay. Well I'm going to go put these veggies in the pot and turn it down slightly. After about thirty more minutes, just turn it off."

"That gives me enough time to get up, shower and get dressed." She said.

"Sounds like a plan. You better call me when you are done with the doctor's appointment."

"Yes sir. I will." Shaine joked.

Cameron went back to the kitchen and put the final touches on the soup. He yelled good-bye as he went out the door.

Shaine got out of her bed and went to her closet to get something to wear. All she felt like wearing was some sweats but she decided to put on some jeans and a sweater. She opted out of wearing heels. She jumped into the shower and let the hot water help soothe her. She noticed her equilibrium was off but she braced herself against the granite-tiled wall as the warm water cascaded down her body. The heat from the water felt good as she said a silent prayer that all would be well at the doctor's office.

CHAPTER FORTY-ONE-MONTI

Monti sat in his six by six jail cell remembering not too long ago when he was in the same place as a result of him following David to the hotel. It was the first time he got a felony. He remembered jail wasn't what he saw on television or in film. It wasn't as photogenic as they show on television. It was dirtier and more cramped than her remembered. It was more primitive and more institutional looking.

The cellblock he was on comprised of a long hallway with two person cells on one side. Directly across from the cells was the common area, with dual doors leading into it. The common area had a section with three indestructible black phones, with short cords providing lousy sound quality even when the inmates were being quiet. There was an unlimited amount of calls the inmates could make, however, the calls were collect calls with a nice introductory message telling the receiver the call is from an inmate at the Wayne County jail.

A second area could be seen which had a television visible. The walls were painted a dirty beige color that reminded Monti of baby food. The common area lacked any external lighting and there were no clocks. In the center of this area was institutional grey picnic-like tables setup and bolted to the floor.

The two person cells are just long enough to fit two long metal shelves, which they guards call beds, extending out from the walls. Each bed had a foam mattress covered in an institutional thick plastic that held the musty dank stench of the jail permanently imprinted into the pores. The plastic has a way of sticking to skin and causing it to sweat. The 'bed' lacks pillows. The bed is wide enough for one person to sleep on, limiting the room for tossing and turning. Each inmate was given a blanket during In-Processing. They are made thick from the grey scratchy material resembling burlap. It was impossible to tell how clean the blankets were but if the smell was any indication, Monti thought the blankets hadn't been cleaned in the past five to ten years.

The room is wide enough for the bunks and a toilet, with just enough room so the bunks aren't butt up against each other. The toilet is also made of indestructible cold hard steel having no toilet seat and no privacy. The cold steel meets ones ass as they sit down. The sink is built right into the toilet where the tank would typically be, making you lean over the toilet to use the sink. The smell of aged urine permeated the room. Toilet paper was on the top of the sink and no soap was present. The floor was a concrete like material also grey in color with no identifying markings.

The three walls were made of the same cinder blocks as those in the common area and painted the same baby food beige. The bars across the front of the cell were a dark dull metal grey set less than six inches apart with horizontal cross pieces in three places. The door to the cell is directly in front of the toilet and wired to move on a noisy, unsettled track.

The whole set-up was designed to be claustrophobic and emasculating. It was created to reduce a human being into submission. Everything in the cell from the walls to the clothing was institutional, giving the impression it was dirty, even if it wasn't. The color palate of the jail was made to be depressing in order to keep the inmates aggression at a minimum. The heavy thick air in the facility is recycled warm air. There is no way for the inmates to be able to tell time…they don't know if it is light or dark outside except to ask the officers patrolling through the jail. Inmates eat when told to do so, sleep with told to, all rights are stripped of the inmate the moment they are in-processed. Lockdown is used at the discretion of the officers. It may be impossible for the guards to physically see you from their station in the cell block, but the video cameras in each cell showed them everything they needed to see. There is no privacy in this jail and it is downright impossible for an inmate to forget they are in jail.

Monti was here in his own personal hell. He was only able to do what the guards allowed him to do which wasn't much. He had called Mrs. Burroughs to help with bail money but she was unable to come up with the funds. He originally started in the Taylor jail until he was arraigned, then he was taken to Wayne County jail while he waited for his trial.

"Burroughs." The guard called.

Monti looked up at the guard on the other side of the bars.

"You have a visitor." He said.

Monti left his claustrophobic cell and was instructed to walked on the right side of the hall way. The guard followed closely behind him. At every check point, the guard had to call out to another guard in an isolated room to open the door. After what seemed like ten various checkpoints, Monti entered an open room. He scanned the room to see who was coming to visit him. He found his mother sitting patiently at a table facing the inmate entryway. He walked over to where she was. She stood up and gave him a hug. She held him in her arms as a tear fell from her eye.

"Break it up, Burroughs." A guard said.

The two of them released their embrace and sat down across from each other.

"Montague, what happened? What did you do?"

"Mom, I really don't want to talk about this right now."

"Son, I need to know what is happening with you. These funny people have you acting so different then how you were brought up." She contended.

"Really Mom?"

"Just tell me what happened."

Monti began to explain the events which occurred between him and Cameron. He didn't tell her about Calvin's involvement.

"So you mean to tell me you were arrested because this Cameron person had some marks on his neck?"

"Well yes and no." Monti replied.

"What is it then…yes or no?

"Mom, we were talking and we got into an altercation."

"Was he arrested also?"

"Mom, I don't know. I know they put me in the car and took me to the police station." Monti lied because he didn't want the third degree from his mother, though it was a possibility she would find out at the trial. He just wanted to have a nice visit. So he began to try to change the subject. "How are the boys?

"They are doing fine, Son."

"Okay good."

The two of them talked for a while and Monti made sure to keep the conversation light. He didn't want to deal with anything heavy. He would be meeting with his attorney in the next day or so. After what seemed like only a few minutes, they were interrupted by a guard telling them it was time to say goodbye. They stood up and gave each other a hug.

"This is going to work out, Son. You need to take time while you are waiting here and talk to the Lord. You are going to have to change your ways."

"Okay Mother. Okay." Monti said.

The guard walked Monti back to the common area. It was recreation time so he would be able to make phone calls. He figured he needed to call Harper. He was sure he had some resources to help him get through this situation. He dialed Harper's number.

"This is a collect call from an inmate in the Wayne County jail…do you accept the charge?"

"Yes." Harper said.

"Hey Harper, this is Monti. How are you?"

"What did you do to land yourself in Wayne County jail?" He asked.

"Man, I got a call from that fucker who blackmailed me and sent the photos out. He was fucking with my dude, Cameron. I want to get his ass back."

"Aren't you in enough trouble already?"

"Hell no! I need you to come up with a way to get his ass

back. He did this and caused me to be here. When I saw Cameron, man I snapped and next thing I know, I was choking his ass against the walls. So can you help a brother out?"

"Monti, I don't have anything for you. You are where you belong." Harper stated.

"What the hell does that mean?" Monti asked.

"Monti, you have been screwing over people for years. You mess up a woman because you allow her to develop feelings for you even though you know you aren't into women. You destroyed a guy because you couldn't give him what you promised him. You stalk him until he is forced to leave the country. You then cheat on this last guy. You did everything in your power to keep him under your suspicious eyes. That's why you deserve what you get."

"Ain't this some bullshit...You took on my case knowing all that."

"Just as you did your research, I did my research on you long before you thought to call me. I have a good group of people who do a great job fixing scandals and often times they have to also do a good job creating drama. We are very thorough with what we do. Surprise...I was the one who forced you out of your darkness. I took the photos of you in the darkness with Calvin. You were so stupid to let a lens catch you with your pants down. You can only guess how you looked that Sunday at church when your cover was blown."

"What the fuck? You were involved with this too?" Monti said in disbelief.

"You twisted fuck, you need to get a grip on your life. You are spiraling out of the control."

"I came to you for help." Monti said.

"Only a psychiatrist can help you Monti. You have to know people can see through your games. You aren't the victim you try to get people to see. You fuck over people for no reason at all. I'm sure Cameron is doing a lot better now that you are out of his life."

"I can't believe this."

"A word of advice for you…when you are in jail, be careful what you say on the jail phone they do record your calls. Bye for now. I'll see you in court." Harper said.

Monti hung up the phone. "How could I be so stupid?" He asked himself. He sat there in the common area and thought about what was happening. He wanted to see how he could have avoided this and how he could adjust the outcome. He wasn't allowed to call Cameron from jail. Wayne County wouldn't allow him to further violate his PPO. He needed to find a way to see if Cameron would drop the charges or if he could talk to the District Attorney and get them to recommend probation. He had heard sometimes victims could request a lenient sentence or probation in lieu of jail time. He was desperate and had to find a way out of this.

"Inmate Burroughs." Monti heard.

He looked in the direction he heard his name. When he finally found out the person who was calling him was his boy Dee.

He got up from the table he was sitting and went over to greet his friend.

"Hey man…how did you know I was here?" Monti asked.

"Man, word travels fast. They said you got picked up in Taylor at a guy's house. Please tell me it ain't the guy I think it is."

"Yes, I was at Cameron's."

"Monti, what were you thinking? You have a PPO against you and so you just willy-nilly just waltz over there and think he is going to welcome you with open arms? You can't be that stupid."

"Man, I don't know what to even say. I just don't know what to do. Can you do me a huge favor?"

"It depends." Dee responded.

"Can you talk to Cameron for me? I need…"

"Hell no. Are you crazy? I can't tamper with a witness. I'm an officer of the court and I can't put my job in jeopardy."

"I don't know what to do man. I'm losing my mind in here. The food sucks, the smell is horrible and my back is killing me sleeping on that mattress."

"I can't do anything now that you are here. You are going to have to tough it out man and hope your attorney can get you probation. You are facing some felonies and with the PPO they don't tolerate you violating a court order. You basically told the court to go fuck themselves." Dee said. He looked at his friend behind bars and just shook his head.

"If you can think of anything Dee…I mean anything. Please let me know."

"Monti, it is not about me trying to think of anything for you this time. Can't you see the pattern you have. Last time, you ended up here because of some crazy stuff. You have not learned the lesson you are supposed to learn. You can't keep tripping out on these guys you get wrapped up with. If you don't get it together, you will be in this very place for a long time. Don't let this place make you crazy. This place has a tendency to have that effect on people."

"Aiight man. Thanks Dee." Monti said pondering the lecture he got from his friend.

CHAPTER FORTY-TWO-CAMERON

"The court is calling the parties for The State of Michigan vs Burroughs." The court clerk stated.

Cameron walked up to the petitioner's side of the podium. Monti was brought out to the courtroom from the back. Once he got to the respondent's side, the court officer took the handcuffs off of him.

"Raise your right hands...Do you promise to tell the truth and nothing but the truth so help you God?"

"I do." Cameron said.

"I will." Monti stated.

"Your Honor, this case is a motion brought by the People against Mr. Montague Burroughs, on behalf of Mr. Cameron McNeil for allegedly trespassing on Mr. McNeil's property, alleged assault and battery on Mr. McNeil and violating a personal protection order. I would like to present States evidence taken from the scene of the incident by the law enforcement officers." The District Attorney presented.

"Counselor, do you have any objection to the evidence presented by the People?" The judge asked Monti's attorney.

"No, Your Honor we don't have any objections." He responded.

"Mr. McNeil, please tell the court what happened on the night in question." The Judge asked Cameron.

Cameron told them about the night Monti showed up at his house and started arguing and ultimately choked him. He told the judge he feared for his safety once Monti started choking him. He explained he had to use his martial arts training to protect his life.

"Mr. McNeil, are these the marks that were left on your body from the alleged incident?"

"Yes, Your Honor." Cameron affirmed.

"Can you tell me who caused you to have these marks on your body on that night?" The Judge asked.

"It was Mr. Burroughs, Your Honor."

"Was Mr. Burroughs, properly served the personal protection order?"

"Yes, Your honor. The proof of service is included in the complaint." The district attorney answered.

"Mr. Counselor, please state your case for the respondent."

"Mr. McNeil, did you in fact open the door and invite Mr. Burroughs into your home on the night in question?"

"No, I didn't invite him into my home. I did answer the door."

"So you didn't open the door for my client to come in?"

"No, I opened the door so I could see who it was. When I saw it was Monti, we began to talk. He asked me to get back with him and I refused. When my phone rang, Mr. Burroughs went into a rage."

"Your Honor, will you please instruct the witness to answer the question and refrain from adding additional narrative?" Monti's attorney said.

"Mr. McNeil, please answer the question the attorney asks you." The Judge ordered.

"No problem Your Honor." Cameron replied.

"Was it your testimony that my client assaulted you?" The attorney asked.

"Yes it was Monti who assaulted me."

"Did you at any point attack Mr. Burroughs?" He asked.

"No, I never attacked Mr. Burroughs. I just defended myself and saved my life." Cameron responded.

"Your Honor, my client insists he was, in fact, the one who was assaulted by Mr. McNeil. My client doesn't have a history of this type of behavior. Mr. Burroughs has been an upstanding member of society. He is employed by one of the local hospitals and gives back to the community through mentoring. Mr. Burroughs wasn't trespassing on Mr. McNeil's property. He was invited to Mr. McNeil's place of residence on the day Mr. McNeil is allegedly claiming he was assaulted. We make a motion that this case be dismissed and my client be allowed to go free without prejudice."

"Any objections by the people?" The judge asked.

"Yes, Your Honor, we object to both motions. Counsel has painted a portrait of Mr. Burroughs being the victim and that there is no history of this behavior. We would like to introduce the following evidence to the court."

The prosecutor handed the documents Cameron received from the records office. She studied the documents for a moment.

"Mr. Burroughs?" The Judge asked. "Your attorney stated you have never had a history of this type of behavior. Is this true?"

"Yes, Your Honor. That's true." Monti replied.

"Have you not learned your lesson yet Mr. Burroughs?" The Judge asked.

"Excuse me, Your Honor?" Monti responded.

"Mr. Burroughs, are you familiar with what perjury is?" The Judge asked.

"Yes, Your Honor, I'm."

"What is your definition of perjury?" The Judge asked

"It is when a person doesn't tell the truth under oath."

"Your Honor," Monti's attorney interjected. "May I ask what this is about?"

"Just one moment, Counselor. So, Mr. Burroughs, you are telling me you have never done anything like this in the past?" The Judge asked.

"No, Your Honor. I was simply trying to work out my relationship with Mr. McNeil. I didn't assault him and I wasn't trespassing." Monti stated.

"In my hands, I have three court documents presented in which you had three previous charges of domestic violence where a protection order was issued. These documents show you have a history of showing up to places you aren't wanted, such as homes and places of employment, which equates to trespassing. It also shows two of the three cases you actually assaulted the petitioners. The court records also show that you are currently have a felonious conviction for this same type of behavior. This, Mr. Burroughs, is what any reasonable person would call a pattern or history. Mr. Burroughs I find you to be in contempt of court."

"Your Honor?" Monti's attorney said.

"I'm not finished Counselor. I will assume the Prosecutors office will be pressing charges against you on the grounds of perjury." The Judge asked.

"You are correct, Your Honor. The people would like to amend the complaint to add perjury."

"Now, counselor what were you adding?"

"I would like to add that Mr. Burroughs has been attending therapy for a mental health condition."

"From where I stand, it seems that Mr. Burroughs is a pathological criminal. It may serve him better to continue with his mental health professional. Are invoking an insanity defense?" The Judge asked.

Monti's attorney looked at him and asked him a question. "No Judge. We won't be invoking an insanity defense."

"Do you have anything else, Madame Prosecutor?"

"The People have a witness, David Knight, which we would

like to present to refute Mr. Burroughs assessment of him not engaged in this type of behavior, and was also the initiator of previous legal proceedings with Mr. Burroughs." The Prosecutor said.

"I don't think that would be necessary; the documents presented, demonstrates this is a pattern of behavior and that he was tried previously for a similar offense."

"Okay, Your Honor." She responded.

"Counselor, do you have anything else to add?" The Judge asked to Monti's attorney.

"No, Your Honor. The defense rests."

"In that case, I'm ready to issue my verdict. Mr. Burroughs, our country is a country of laws. We have laws to protect our citizens. Citizens are required to follow the rules, when people do not follow the rules, anarchy exists. In the count of trespassing, I find you did in fact trespass on Mr. McNeil's property. On the count of assault and battery, I find you guilty of assault and battery. For the charge of violating a personal protection order, I also find you guilty. Sentencing of these violations is as follows…"

The court officer moved and stood behind Monti.

"The penalty for trespassing is a maximum of 30 days. I find you egregiously violated this law with full knowledge you were in violation of a personal protection order. For that reason, I sentence you to the maximum of 30 days. In the matter of the personal protection order violation, it is appalling you would willfully violate a court order barring you from any contact with Mr. McNeil. I don't care if you were trying to work on a relationship or if you just wanted to play patty cake. You have to understand you have a court order against you contacting Mr. McNeil for *any* reason. If you can't restrain yourself with that knowledge, maybe incarceration will ensure your compliance. Another aggravating factor is this isn't your first PPO someone had to get. This makes it number four, which shows me you haven't learned your lesson. In addition, the felony conviction you have has not deterred your behavior. The maximum penalty for this charge is 93 days in jail and up to $500.00 fine or both. It is a felony as well. In this instance I'm inclined to sentence you to the maximum 93 days in jail and the maximum of $500.00 fine."

Monti stood there emotionless.

"On the third charge of felony assault and battery, I find the evidence presented by the police department and Mr. McNeil's testimony to be sufficient to prove without a reasonable doubt you did assault Mr. McNeil. When your hands made contact with Mr. McNeil's throat, to which he didn't consent, you committed battery. The sentencing guideline for this offense is up to 10 years in jail and/or $5000.00 fine or both. I will be lenient in this sentence however; I hereby sentence you to three years in jail and a $500.00 fine. The perjury charges will be reviewed at a later court date."

"Oh no!" Mrs. Burroughs cried.

"The sentences for trespassing and violating a PPO will be served concurrently and the sentence for felony assault and battery will be served consecutively. Mr. Burroughs, you need to get your life together. You can't keep violating other people's lives."

With the sound of the gavel, the Court officers instructed Monti to place his hands behind his back. They put the shackles back on his wrists and took him out of the courtroom.

CHAPTER FOURTY-THREE-YOLANDA

Roderick sat in the court room with a stunned Yolanda sitting next to him. The sound of the gavel still rang in her ears. Had she heard the judge correctly? Monti got a sentence of three years and three months with $1000.00 fine. She could have given him the max for each count. The lecture he received from the judge about lying in court was given like a mother would give to her child. Monti should have gotten this lecture when he was a child but lying and deceit was what he did. He lied to cover up his bad actions. Yolanda was sad yet happy at the same time. She felt there was closure to her life with Monti. People wouldn't understand what she meant about this but seeing him pay for hurting Cameron, was like he was paying for hurting her as well. It was justice for all those who had come into contact with Monti who were left in the ruins of his lies.

"Honey…" Roderick asked.

"Yes."

"Do you want to go out in the hall?"

"I think that will be a good thing." Yolanda responded.

The two of them got up from their seat and quietly walked to the courtroom door. The judge was presiding over the next matter on the docket. Once outside, Yolanda held Roderick's hand tightly.

"Are you okay?" He asked.

"I'm alright. I don't know if the feelings I have are the right ones."

"Whatever feelings you have, are what you should be having right now. Don't second guess what you have been through."

"It is just I never thought I would see the day where he would pay for the things he did. As much as I don't like him going to jail, I feel he needs to be there now."

"He probably does. If he did those things Cameron said he did, and the things highlighted from his previous brushes with the law, I would say he is getting the punishment he deserves. He may have ended up getting a break. He still has the perjury charges to answer as well."

"I can't help but to wonder how many people he has messed over and cheated. All this time, I was thinking I was the only one. I thought the gay guys were trying to break us up. I was mad at them for all these years. I knew Monti did his share of shit but I thought he was somehow manipulated into all this. But after hearing the testimony in there, I see he was the puppet master. He did all the things he did without being coaxed from someone. He really is an abuser."

"I have to say I agree with you. I have never really had the chance to truly meet him but I've heard these stories time and time again from other domestic violence victims. Their attacker uses scare tactics and bullying to get the people to do what they want them to do. Cameron is really a strong man to endure all that. Most of the times, a domestic abuse victim doesn't press charges because they fear retribution from the abuser. Look at the David guy…he just ran. He left the country to get away. It was good to see him ready to stand with Cameron to tell his truth. This is a good day on so many accounts."

Yolanda exhaled. As she stood in the hallway, Cameron, Brian, Shaine and David left the courtroom and walked past Yolanda and Roderick.

"Excuse me, Cameron?" Yolanda asked.

"Yes ma'am. Do we know each other?" Cameron asked glancing at Shaine to see if Shaine knew who the woman was.

"No, we don't. I want to thank you for what you did. You didn't have to stick to your guns and fight Monti."

"Thank me? Why?"

"I'm Yolanda…Monti's ex-wife."

"Oh Yolanda…" Cameron smiled at her and reached out to give her a hug.

Yolanda was thrown off at his freedom and openness to embrace her. He didn't know her.

"I've heard so much about you. I'm so sorry you had to deal with a man like that in your life. I never got the opportunity to meet you when Monti and I were together. I did have the pleasure to meet Corey and Monti Jr. They are wonderful boys and I have to say you have done an exceptional job of rearing them. They are the sweetest guys."

"Thank you so much. It has been a struggle but they are my reason to keep fighting. I think I saw you last week when I came to get the truck for Mrs. Burroughs. You live in that townhouse right?"

"You are correct. I saw you that day but didn't know who you were. When I got down to the first floor, you had already left."

"Well, I'm glad we got a chance to meet today." Yolanda said.

"I bought the boys something for Christmas and I hope you would allow them to have the gifts." Cameron said.

"Oh you didn't have to do that. Yes, they can have your gifts. Thank you for thinking about them."

The two of them decided to exchange phone numbers. Cameron said he would bring the gifts by on Saturday.

"Yolanda this is my boyfriend Brian, my best friend in the world Shaine Holloway, and another Monti survivor David Knight." Cameron said as he pointed each of them out.

"It is a pleasure to meet you all. This is my boyfriend Roderick." Yolanda said as she shook Brian's and David's hand. Shaine opened her arms as Yolanda came her way.

"I have to give my sista a sista-hug. If you been through anything remotely close to what my best friend has, you are one strong sista." Shaine said.

"Thank you, Shaine. I did the best I could." Yolanda responded.

Yolanda didn't know why but she was taken aback at these total strangers and their outpouring of support for what she had been through.

"David, how are you doing after this?" Yolanda asked.

"I'm doing well. I'm glad this chapter in my life is finally over. You may not know this, but the reason I ended my relationship with

Monti is because I saw him in the mall with you and your children a couple years ago after the fourth of July. He never told me he was married and didn't tell me he had any children. When I saw you all and especially the younger boy, I knew they were his children and you all were a family. I never wanted to be in the middle of a family and definitely didn't want to share the guy I was seeing. Just so you know…I left him the following weekend."

"Oh so that's what happened that weekend."

"What do you mean?" David asked.

"I had to pick him up from the Southfield police station when they released him. We had broken up by then but we still saved face in the public. He said he had a warrant out for an unpaid parking ticket. I guess he lied to us all."

"It seems that was the case. Well I'm glad he is finally paying for his behaviors." David said. "Maybe he will get the psychiatric help he needs in jail."

"Who knows David? I guess we are going to be paying for that as well." Cameron said. "We are all about to go get something to eat. It has been a long stressful day. It is a pleasure to meet you. I will give you a…"

"Yolanda, why are you here talking to these funny people?" Mrs. Burroughs said interrupting Cameron mid-sentence.

"Funny people?" David asked.

"You know what I'm talking about. You all have no business living the life you are living. Do you see what a mess it ends up making?" Mrs. Burroughs said.

"Mess…" Cameron said. "The only mess is you not being a

real mother and raising your crazy ass son the right way. He is screwed up in the head. How can you sit here and talk to three people who your son messed over? You are the root of this problem. Instead of turning a blind eye and a deaf ear to his craziness, you should have taken him to a doctor and given him his medicines."

"Boy...don't you speak..." Mrs. Burroughs started to say.

"No, I have had enough of you Burroughs bullying people. This stops with me today. You will not berate me because you failed as a mother. You will not speak to me with such disrespect and venom. You claim to be a Christian but you act like everything opposite of what Christ stands for. You may want to re-evaluate your standing with God. You aren't leading people to him...you are pushing them away from him. If you don't have anything nice or positive to say to me, then you can keep on walking. I have been through enough at the hands of you son. I will not deal with anything else, especially from you."

The people stood around speechless. Cameron found his strength and his voice. He was done with being treated any kind of way. Mrs. Burroughs decided this wasn't a battle she was going to try to win. She looked at Yolanda, "I hope you will still allow the boys to come over this weekend."

"Sure, they will be there." Yolanda responded.

Mrs. Burroughs looked at the group of people and knew what Cameron said was true. "I'm sorry for what you all have been through." She said as she turned and walked down the hallway to the elevator.

CHAPTER FOURTY-FOUR-SHAINE

Shaine stood listening to the conversation with Cameron and Mrs. Burroughs in the courtroom. She knew this was a victory for all the parties concerned. For some reason, she wanted to celebrate this victory but at the same time she saw the look of failure on Mrs. Burroughs face. She didn't have any children but tried to understand what a mother would feel like to know her child was a convicted felon twice over. They started walking to the elevator.

"Cameron?" Shaine asked.

"Yes, honey. What's up?" Cameron responded.

"I'm so proud of you. You did what you should have done. I didn't doubt this would have been in vain."

"Thanks, I couldn't have done it without you by my side. You have been more than a friend to me. I'm honored to have you in my life." Cameron said.

"Aww." Shaine said as she felt emotional again. "What is this salty substance trying to come out from my eyes?"

"You are so dramatic. That salty substance is called tears. It means you are human. What is going on with you? You have been really emotional lately."

"I don't know. I was thinking the same thing. This past few weeks have been crazy. I guess it is the Adrienne situation."

"She isn't still hanging around, is she?" Cameron asked.

"Oh, now you think I'm a sucker." Shaine said. "Maya Angelou said *When a person shows you who they are, believe them.* I believe Adrienne is what she says she is. I don't have time for that in my life and definitely don't want that in my relationship."

Shaine and Cameron gave each other a high five. They knew they were destined to be best friends. They were strength for each other in the others weakness. "You know something?" Cameron asked.

"What's that?" Shaine responded.

"I guess now that you are all engaged and stuff…we aren't going to get married. You had to go and mess up my plan." Cameron joked. "I'm very happy you are happy. I can see the happiness in your eyes as well. I better be your best man in the wedding."

"Yes, I guess I did mess that plan up. You know you will have some prominent place in the wedding party."

Shaine's phone began to ring. She looked at the caller ID and saw it was Jonathan. "Hold on a second honey. It is my other man." She said.

"Hello?" She asked.

"Hey honey. How are you doing?" Jonathan asked.

"I'm doing well."

"How did the court case go?"

"Oh my goodness, you would have enjoyed the case. It was a simple case, but that judge ripped into Monti like I had never seen a judge do before. It was like we were watching Judge Judy in Detroit."

"Wow, sounds like it was interesting." He said.

"That's the understatement of the year." Shaine said.

"Please tell him congratulations for me. Wait…is it appropriate to congratulate a person for winning this type of lawsuit?"

"No, it isn't. We are about to go and celebrate…trust me we are. I need a good drink right about now anyway." Shaine said.

"Well tell Cameron I said congratulations."

"I will." Shaine said.

"Did I tell you our last night together was powerfully orgasmic? I can't believe what an insatiable sexual woman you have become." Jonathan said.

"You are just saying that. You were the one who surprised me. You really have some oral skills, and I'm not mad at you. I'm so glad we are together. I look forward to our future together."

"I do too. With an amazing woman I'm sure my future is going to be bright."

"You say the sweetest things, Mr. Blanchard."

"Hey I have to keep the future Mrs. Holloway-Blanchard happy."

"You already do." Shaine was in a comfortable space.

"Look, I'm about to run into a meeting. I just wanted to make sure things went the way they were supposed to for Cameron. I hope to see you later this evening."

"Okay. Go ahead to the meeting. I always hope to see you. Muah." Shaine said.

"Love you baby."

"Love you more!" Shaine replied as she hung up the phone.

"Y'all are truly in love. I like that. I know I don't have to worry about you. He has very capable hands." Cameron said.

"You don't even know the half of how capable his hands are." Shaine replied.

"Err umm…no hetero sex talk with me. You will make me gag."

They both laughed as the elevator pinged, announcing its arrival. The doors opened up and the people in the elevator exited. Shaine and the crew were about to get on the elevator when her phone rang again. She looked at the caller ID thinking Jonathan was calling her back. She saw it was the doctor's office calling. She was waiting for the results of the tests. She hoped nothing serious was going on with her. She didn't tell Cameron about the doctor visit because she didn't know the results yet and he was stressing about the case.

"Hey guys. Let me take this call. We can get the next elevator." Shaine said.

"Alright." They said in unison.

"Hello. This is Shaine. How can I help you?" Shaine said.

"Good afternoon Ms. Holloway. This is Dr. Winters."

"Hi Dr. Winters. How can I help you?"

"I was calling you with the results of your tests."

"Okay. Please don't tell me bad news." She said.

"Oh, Ms. Holloway your blood work came back fine. I'm happy to understand why you have been feeling sick lately."

"You are pleased? Please explain that to me."

"Well, Ms. Holloway. Your test results show you are pregnant. Congratulations."

"Pregnant..." Shaine said in disbelief.

"Yes Ma'am, pregnant. We will need you to come back in a week or so for an ultrasound and we will be able to tell you how far along you are."

"That's great news, Dr. Winters. Thank you very much. I will call tomorrow to make that appointment." Shaine said.

"Great. I will see you soon." Dr. Winters said.

"Shaine...Did I hear what I think I heard?" Cameron said.

"Yes. This is great. I have to call Jonathan."

"Okay...what are you waiting on? Call him."

Shaine called Jonathan's number back. It rang...and rang...and rang. Then his voicemail picked up. She hung up and called right back.

"Hello?" Jonathan said in a whisper.

"Honey, the doctor called." Shaine said excited.

"Just a moment, let me go to the hallway." He said. "Please excuse me for a moment." Shaine heard as he made his way out of the briefing room.

"Okay Shaine. Is everything okay?" Jonathan asked.

"Everything is beyond okay honey. You are going to be a Daddy."

"What?" Jonathan asked.

"The doctor told me I'm pregnant."

All Shaine heard was a loud "Woo Hoo...Yes...I'm going to be a dad!" She knew he was excited.

"Honey...where are you right now?" Jonathan said.

"I'm still at the court house. We were just leaving." Shaine said.

"Meet me at J. Alexander's...you and all your friends. Lunch and drinks are on me. Let's celebrate."

"Okay...Honey. I love you. I will see you soon."

"I love you too, Mommy!" He hung up the phone.

"Hey guys, we are going to J. Alexander's for lunch, Jonathan's treat." Shaine said to the guys.

"I'm down." David said. "Congratulations Shaine."

"We are so happy for you." Brian said. "Let's get out of here."

"I can't believe I'm going to be an uncle. What a perfect end to this day." Cameron said.

The four of them got on the next elevator and were on to celebrate the beginning of new chapters in their lives and to celebrate life itself.

ABOUT THE AUTHOR

G. Wayne Jackson is a freelance writer and author. He is a Gulf War Veteran of the United States Army and a graduate of the University of Michigan-Dearborn. He has earned two Master degrees in Finance and Psychology respectively, and is close to finishing his Doctorate degree. He decided, at the urging of his partner in life, to write what was inside. After a year of indecision, he began the process of putting on paper what was in his heart. *Forced Out of the Darkness* was the result of this effort and was released in the spring of 2014.

As a spiritual man, G. Wayne wants to share his life experiences to help others. He believes everything happens for a reason and it is for us to find the lesson and the reason in the experiences.

G. Wayne is a family man and loves being with family. Family isn't necessarily those who share the same blood but those who know who you are and love you anyway. G. Wayne is currently working on his next project. He resides in Chicago, Illinois with his partner Walter and their two dogs, Isis and NeeNee.